# On/Off

**Also by Mike Attebery**
Billionaires, Bullets, Exploding Monkeys
Seattle On Ice
Bloody Pulp

# On/Off

by Mike Attebery

Cryptic Bindings
Seattle, Washington

On/Off - A Jekyll and Hyde Story

Cryptic Bindings
Visit our website at www.crypticbindings.com
Read Mike Attebery's Blog: www.mikeattebery.com

Second Edition: March 2013

ISBN 978-0-615-59142-1

Publisher's Note:
This is a work of fiction. Names, characters, places, and incidents are either the product of the author's imagination or are used fictitiously, any resemblance to actual persons (living or dead), business establishments, events, or locales is coincidental.

Printed in the United States of America.

For my girls...

# FALL

There was a sliver of metal in his brain. He could feel it scraping against the tissue, biting into the swollen gray pulp. It hurt like hell. Every movement, every breath, sent a wave of pain rushing through his head.

The pain flipped a switch. His mind kept wandering back to the car accident with his father all those years ago. They'd been on their way to the movies when the truck broadsided them. Splintered glass had sprayed into his terror-stricken eyes. He was eight at the time. It was the same then, trying not to move, inevitably blinking; knowing what would happen, but unable to keep his head still. Until now, that had been the worst pain of his life. The glass was lodged deep in his eyes, and his inability to keep still had taken its toll. Eventually, they'd reached the hospital, where a patient surgeon with steady hands had removed the shards. The wounds healed, and Jamie recovered the majority of his vision, but he still saw floaters and shadows. Ten years later, anyone studying his face could still sense a distant trauma in the delicate tissues peering out through frozen eyelids. Even now, he rarely blinked, forever fearing the return of that stabbing pain. His doctor was always chiding him, "Your eyes are too dry. Blink! Blink!" But Jamie ignored him.  He used drops.

Yet, the accident had been different -- it was traumatic and unexpected; there was no anticipation, no time to bite his lip and dread the inevitable explosion of pain. In this case, the goal was not freedom of movement, but the ability to sit still, to think clearly for the first time in almost a year. The glass in Jamie's bloody eyes had been extracted by a lone doctor. This time, a team of surgeons had worked together,  meticulously slicing back a flap of scalp, cutting away a portion of his skull, and pulling back layer upon layer of mealy brain matter, testing each with an electrical pulse, before massaging a wafer-thin disc of polished metal into the soft, gray tissues beneath. The team had then tethered the implant in place with a series of microscopic barbs, before reconfiguring the displaced portions of his central nervous system, and closing his head back up. Now, sixteen hours later, Jamie ran a tentative finger over the crusty, tender sutures on his shaved head, hoping they hadn't left anything out. He lowered his hand, holding the fingertips in front of his face. There was no movement. He could actually hold still. He set his hands in his lap, listened to his own breathing, and stared into space.

# TWO WEEKS EARLIER

At the height of Jamie's condition, Dr. Price entered his office at the university and sized up his young patient's situation. He removed his glasses, wiped them with a handkerchief, and placed them back on the bridge of his nose. The horn-rimmed frames accentuated his owlish appearance, which he knew his patients found oddly reassuring. Yet, as he forced his best poker face, he knew his expression betrayed him. They'd exhausted the traditional options. All of them. The seventeen-year-old who had entered his office one year ago showing symptoms of early onset Parkinson's, now sat before him, a gyrating, head bobbing display of misfiring synapses. His legs were a constant blur of twisting, jarring movements. One arm was pulled up to his chest, the other cradled the elbow.

Until recently, these "on/off" episodes of tensed muscles and uncontrollable tremors had come and gone with the shifts in medication throughout the day, but now they were nearly continuous. Jamie twitched incessantly, nearly obscuring the wince of sweaty exhaustion he expressed with each wild corkscrew movement of his body. This display was all the more bizarre considering the patient's apparently peak physical condition. In an effort to control the symptoms, Jamie was adhering to the strictest of diets, and had been following a grueling exercise regimen during the now vanished "on" periods.

The medications, levodopa among many others, had become almost completely ineffective, and the degree and duration of Jamie's episodes had continually increased. Price had repeatedly gone over the treatment options with Jamie and his mother; they could attempt surgery and lesioning of the brain to slow or prevent what he described as the "electrical storms" in Jamie's head, but chances were poor that such an attack would hold any lasting benefits. Over time, the return of the episodes was certain, and chances were good that any relief would be short-lived. They could continue exploring emerging medications, but all current avenues had led to dead ends. Price felt it was time to take a bold, experimental approach, albeit one with questionable motives.

The severity of Jamie's PD symptoms, at his age, was unheard of. Even for a much older patient after decades of progression, the type of spine-shredding spasms he displayed would have been unnerving. Price had earmarked Jamie's case with his team from the start. The inherent possibilities in a case involving a relatively healthy young patient displaying such extreme symptoms had been an easy sell, the very subject they'd been looking for, and they leapt at the opportunity. As for the Peppers, desperation has a way of sweeping aside the obvious questions, like "what do you stand to gain from this?" They were only interested in helping Jamie regain control of his life, it never occurred to them that Price's own motivations might be less than transparent. Either way, the surgery would have gone through, the implant would have been tested, but this was perfect. If successful, a young "miracle patient" would be a boon for the program. Price was confident the boy would be interested. At this point there was nothing left to lose.

Within a week, he was again sitting with Jamie in his office, showing him the device that could change his life forever.

"It looks like a big metal tick," the young man muttered.

Price smiled ever so slightly as he rotated the prototype in his hands, "Yeah, I suppose it does, actually."

Jamie's muscles tensed as he strained to sit still. Even then, his head bobbed rapidly from side to side as he studied the implant from the corner of his eye. The overheard lights sparkled along the edges of the thin metal disc in the palm of Price's hand.

"What are those barbs on the side?"

"Those are the key. They're the filaments that will conduct the directional signals in your brain. They'll also act as tethers to hold the probe in place after surgery."

Jamie raised an eyebrow. "How much is this gonna hurt, doc?"

"It may be extremely painful at first." Price paused for a moment. "We'll give you medication for the pain and to prevent swelling, but our hope is that your body will attenuate itself to the implant after the first week, even forget that it's there."

"Sounds like a ball," Jamie muttered flatly. "Does this mean I can shitcan the meds?"

Price's mouth pulled tight. "You'll still be taking low levels of medication to manage the more minor symptoms, but they'll be minimal." He leaned forward, forcing sincerity as he looked Jamie in the eyes. "I have a great deal of faith that this will work. If it does, trust me, it will be worth it."

Jamie reached over and took the shiny metal object from Price's hands, turning it in his fingers. It was the size of a quarter with virtually identical dimensions. He ran his fingers over the edge, feeling the filaments scraping and catching ever so slightly on his skin like tiny Velcro fasteners.

"And this will let me paint again, doc?"

"Jamie, if this works, it will let you *live* again."

# THE PREVIOUS SUMMER

The Pepper home echoed with ghosts. Unborn children. Forgotten promises. The whisper of secrets behind the reflections on rippled glass windows. It was a big old house, hidden away at the end of a long, shadowy drive on the edge of Pittsford, one of the more upscale suburbs of Rochester, New York. Jamie had enjoyed a happy childhood there, for the most part. In the summers he liked to crawl under the bushes that hugged the bottom of the house, and play for hours in the cool darkness below. Then he'd run out into the bleaching midday sun, blinded by the light as he rolled down the grassy hill, losing momentum and tumbling to a stop, eyes closed, to stretch out under the broiling sun. In winters he'd gone sledding down the same hill, and wandered the snowy woods that surrounded the property. He knew the area by heart. Lynn Pepper had done many of these things with him, sharing the bond of a mother and her only child. Mostly, it had been a happy home, but it still held reminders of a life that had not gone as planned. During certain times of year, holidays especially, the air in the home grew heavy, clinging to their lungs like pollen in a humid northeast summer. That wasn't to say things weren't maintained. If anything, the place was spotless. Lynn had an obsessive determination to maintain order, the type of single-minded outlook often found in successful professionals and single parents. Lynn was both, producing a steady output of pieces for publication, maintaining a household, and supervising her son's upbringing with a head down, straight ahead sense of focus.

Large families have a sense of community that comes, in part, from minimal parental attention. Lots of kids, parents balancing family with work and their own relationships -- all this gives the children breathing room, space to grow and find their footing. The single-parent household is much different. Day-to-day pressures are easily ratcheted up. The importance of each decision is skewed by reliance on only one perspective, and even if the end result is successful, there's always the perceived burden that something, or someone, is missing. Jamie grew up in just such a home, and though he was relatively content, as time went on he found himself searching the brooding rooms of the house, looking for answers to the question of what was missing. An innocent curiosity compels children to search through their parents' bureaus, smelling perfumes and opening pocketknives, handling and examining trinkets once their owners have long since failed to notice them anymore. Pondering the belongings of relatives is not seen as dangerous or inappropriate for young children; after all, they're simply curious about the world of adults. Things change however, when the person you wish to understand has been missing or dead for more than half your lifetime.

Alone during the sweltering days after he graduated, Jamie again found himself searching the rooms of his mother's house like he did as a boy. He sat for hours at his father's desk, again digging through drawers of the man's letters and keepsakes. Jamie had rummaged through these things off and on for years, but this summer he felt a compulsion to go back. Ultimately, he'd come out of his trance, close the drawers, and go back to his room to read, or down to the living room to watch television, but increasingly that summer, with too much time on his hands, Jamie's mind wandered back to the past, and questions about what had happened.

By the fourth of July, life had become unbearable. His days were a series of extremes. He was either stranded on the couch, nervously flipping channels as he waited for the latest tremors to stop, or racing the clock to use every normal moment; exercising and running during the ever-so-brief "on" periods when the meds were still somewhat effective. For the better part of the summer, he hadn't known which way was up. Some days he woke early, feeling fine, but dreading the moment his body would begin to stiffen and shake. Other times, his eyes would open and he was paralyzed, his arms and legs drawn up tight, leaving him helpless until the next moment of relief. At this point, he couldn't tell the tail from the dog. Either his mind was a jumble from the medications, or his head was working overtime, sabotaging itself and the rest of his body. His brain had become the enemy, an enemy he tried to assuage with medicine and exercise, but which rejected both.

Almost worse than the PD symptoms, were the hallucinations. When he hit adolescence, Jamie thought the surge of hormones would drive him mad. The sight of a cute girl, or even the briefest suggestion of sex, would drive him over the edge. He was a cauldron of tension and excitement. Like any teenager, his brain was wired for just one thing, but this, this was indescribably worse. Dr. Price had mentioned the possibility of hypersexuality with the current levodopa dosages, but Jamie had no idea how extreme it could become. His dreams had become ever more erotic and bizarre, and his waking moments were a dizzying array of fantasies and frustration. He was embarrassed at how much time he spent beating off, trying to clear his head, but no sooner did the images and urges slip away, then his body was once again working overtime, his eyes dilated, a mist of sweat on the back of his neck.

Last year, things had been so different. None of the medications. None of the problems. He'd been working at the music store downtown, dating Jenny Conners, getting laid every night. Funny how she'd dumped him for that guy on the football team, Jamie knew it was because of the guy's looks. Now, a year later, he was the one with the better body, at least, the more muscular one. How well he could *use* it was another matter, entirely dependent upon when you caught him. Maybe Jenny would want to make an appointment. Before seven or after four, right around then he seemed to be in peak condition, ready for a good roll in the hay, and not quite exhibiting the movements of a latter day Richard Pryor. Poor guy. Jamie knew how he must have felt when his MS kicked in. At the peak of your career, the world in front of you, drug problems fading away, then – BAM! Some jokester sticks out his foot as you're completing your victory lap. It was just last fall, right around the time he'd realized where Jenny was spending her nights, that he'd had the first inkling that something in his head was shorting out.

He was sitting in the art studio, working on Mrs. Van Dyke's insufferable underpainting assignment, when he felt something in his head pop, and the feeling of hot liquid coursed beneath his scalp. Looking back on it, he knew he'd blown a fuse. He hated doing those goddamned underpaintings, with all the raw umber and black shadows. He hated this assignment: painting a couple of flower pots in front of a window, but first, painting the entire picture in black and white, and countless shades of brown. He didn't need a guide to help him feel his way through a painting. At that moment, there were two things he knew for a fact: the first was that he was once more a free agent in the high school dating world, the second was that he was one hell of a painter. He had the arrogant "modesty" of the true artist, knowing your work is good, but always downplaying your ability. But he knew. Just as he knew he could tie his shoes with his eyes closed, he had every confidence in his abilities with a brush. He already had his application in with the fine arts program at the Rochester Institute of Technology, and he knew with his gut that he was getting in. Sure, screwing around with Jenny was great, she was hot, and more than a bit crazy, but for him, a loose, quickly painted canvas was just as exciting.

As he sat in the empty studio, feeling just a bit too cocky for his own good, everything changed. He dipped the brush into the raw umber, swirled it with the black, and pulled the bristles back over the pallet in one smooth, confident stroke, then he turned and lifted his hand to the canvas, only funny thing – his hand wouldn't move. It just lagged behind, wavering in place. He raised an eyebrow and tried again. Nothing. His eyes narrowed as he looked out at the suddenly alien limb that hung in midair, quivering before him. And then his heart sank, 'cause he knew this had been coming. Somehow, he knew. And that was what scared him the most.

That was last October. By the spring he was a wreck, and his mother and Dr. Price were having weekly meetings to plan a strategy, first for management of the disease, and later for a counterattack. Now, though no one said so, it was clear they were losing ground. He'd barely made it through the final semester of high school, graduating by the skin of his teeth. Truth be told, he knew the school board had taken pity on him. His RIT scholarship was still official for the fall quarter, but he'd been incapable of painting for the last six months. The most creative pursuit he could handle was snapping some pictures with a digital camera. In the back of his mind, he was saving the images for a time he might adapt them for a canvas, but for now, he was enjoying manipulating them with a computer, and at least having some sort of creative outlet. It wasn't the same, but it was filling a void, and at the same time, he was discovering a surprising intensity for the medium.

Jamie was sitting on the couch now, sun streaming in through the windows, singeing the dust in the air around him. His eyes burned from the light, another side effect of the meds. Better not forget his shades later. He was between episodes now, his limbs relaxing, the signals from his brain easily connecting with each extremity. He focused on his breathing. Slowly. In and out. He had at least two good hours before the messages would become garbled again; he'd better make the most of them. Maybe later he could watch a couple episodes of *Friends* while his body battled its demons, but before that, he needed to jerk off and go for a run. He pushed himself up from the couch, his body exhausted from its own spastic movements.

"How long is this gonna last?" he muttered to himself as he staggered to his feet.

Maybe it was time to talk alternatives with the doc. They'd decided surgical treatment wasn't the right choice, but his days were getting shorter by the week; that is, the *worthwhile* portions of his days. He was ready to pursue desperate measures. What he didn't know was that Price was already laying the groundwork to help him do so.

# SHADOWS

Growing up, Jamie Pepper had always been unusually aware of his parents' careers. Then again, it's not the typical experience for someone's parents to be recognized by complete strangers whenever they went out in public. Until the age of ten, Jamie and his father were all but incapable of going to the movies without their plans being interrupted by a passer by who recognized Jeff Pepper and stopped him to discuss one of his plays or films, or inevitably, *the book*. Though a lifelong resident of upstate New York, Jeff Pepper had developed an enormous following for his body of work, which had begun with a single cult novel and had progressed over the years into a series of one-man plays and countless film adaptations. That Jeff Pepper was neither an actor, nor a director made his notoriety all the more remarkable, for the people accosting him on the street, or coughing softly to attract his attention in ticket lines, only knew his face through sheer, wholehearted fanaticism. That they liked his father's writing told Jamie all he needed to know about these individuals, as Jeff Pepper's greater obsessions were not happy ones. His stories were a mix of brooding tragedies and vaguely disturbing black comedies, which in later years Jamie would come to view as comedies that simply did not work. Jeff Pepper had also written one novel in his college days, one which had somehow cemented his reputation at the age of twenty-one. The book, *Dub Taylor,* was an altogether bizarre affair, in which the main character, a college slacker, spent the majority of his days reading Hemingway, smoking pot in his dorm room, and alternately masturbating and sleeping with any number of all too willing young co-eds, both male and female. The summer after his freshman year, Jamie had tried to read his father's book in an attempt to understand the man's huge following, but when he finished it, he'd only found the confounding nature of his father's celebrity all the more bewildering.

Jamie's mother was not without notability. Though less grandiose in her works, Lynn Pepper was at one time considered a mild mannered, female member of the school of gonzo journalism. She'd made her first mark with a series of *Rolling Stone* pieces published in the sixties and seventies, yet by the time Jamie was aware of her work, Lynn's reporting and other writing had taken on a more conventional form, focused less on the style of the text, and more on the whistle-blowing content of the stories, most of which she submitted to *The New York Times* and *Vanity Fair*. She had published two novels of her own, but found the inevitable comparisons and forced parallels to her husband's works too frustrating to make further attempts in the world of fiction. Content to produce a series of well regarded investigative pieces on any number of topics, from corporate kidnappings in South America to political scandals involving tobacco companies, Lynn had resigned herself to life as a well respected byline in highly regarded newspapers and magazines, always with the helpful footnote (\*) linking her to her late husband.

Undeniably, Jeff Pepper loomed largest over Jamie's childhood. The cult of tragedy, the romance of the tormented writer, both drew crowds with a morbid intensity. Even now, years after the man's disappearance, Jamie and his mother still felt Jeff's shadow in their day-to-day lives. Wherever they went, people wanted to know what he was like -- what had happened? Yet even if they'd wanted to respond, neither of them knew what to say.

**I**

# CHAPTER ONE
# **WINTER**

Damn it got cold fast. Just last week he'd been jogging in sweats and a T-shirt, pretty nice for the end of November. Now, a week later, it was bitter cold. The wind cut through his clothes. Even his wool hat did little good, the air slicing through it like icy needles, hitting his scars and making them tingle. He hated the feeling, but found it somehow exhilarating. Jamie pulled the hood from his sweatshirt up over the hat and pulled another box out of the back of his mother's car. They were parked in the traffic circle in front of his dorm tower. He'd been to the imposing brick-ensconced campus many times over the years, tagging along with both Jeff and Lynn for their respective readings, attending events through the Rochester school district, and of course, wandering the grounds when he'd been considering applying to the fine arts program. He'd only been on the residential side of campus once before, while taking a perfunctory tour for prospective students. On all of those occasions, the campus had been swarming with people. RIT ran on a quarter system, with the first ten week block of classes stretching from late August to Thanksgiving. The second quarter began in late November and ran for several weeks before Christmas horned in on the academic party wagon. This was the last day of the Thanksgiving break, and the first time Jamie had seen the place almost empty. It felt stark. The quad was all but deserted, the students either still returning from Thanksgiving break, or holed up in their rooms, screwing around before classes started the next day.

"I still feel nervous leaving you here," Lynn called from the drivers seat as she rummaged for some paperwork. "But I know it's for the best."

Jamie heaved a box out of the car, dropping it on the ground. "What did you say, Mom?"

"I said, I think this is a good idea. It's time."

Jamie nodded his head, wiping his nose with a gloved hand.

"How are you feeling?"

"Fine."

"No symptoms? No headaches?" She turned to him with that concerned, yet aggravating, expression that all mothers have.

"Nothing. I feel great," he said. "Just nervous."

"That's normal." She looked away for a moment, taking a deep breath, then blinked with a finality that told Jamie she had made up her mind. No more doubts. "I'm excited for you. Let me park the car and I'll carry up your last bag."

Jamie closed the trunk, picked up the box, and hustled towards his dorm. A thin layer of ice coated the steps near the door, and his feet started to slide out from under him. He grabbed a railing. The last thing he needed was to hit his head. He balanced the box on his hip, unlocked the door, and headed up the stairs to the third floor. The halls were quiet. Now and then he passed an open room with one or two kids inside, hunched at computers or watching TV, happy zombies in the soothing blue glow. The wind whistled outside. The school had given him a single since he'd missed the first quarter of classes. As Jamie opened the door to his room he noted that it was just two doors down from the resident advisor. No doubt his condition had played a part in getting him that location.

He walked inside and stood in the middle of the room, scratching under his cap. The wool was itchy on his shaved head. His hair was growing back slowly after the operation. He was still on a plethora of medications, but each at mercifully lower dosages. Most importantly, the implant seemed to be working. There'd been no complications. No infection. None of the laundry list of concerns Dr. Price had rattled off for months before Jamie went under the knife. Aside from an itchy scalp and a now-familiar feeling of dread, he was doing great. He still ran, still ate like a health nut, and was still a bit uncertain on his feet, but he almost felt like himself again. He walked across the room, peered out the window, then absentmindedly rapped his knuckles on the top of the desk. The itching was driving him nuts. He pulled off the hat and scratched gently along the raised incision scars. There was a knock on the door behind him and he turned suddenly, pulling his cap down at the sight of a tall, thin guy with glasses, dressed in a bathrobe, and carrying a wire shower basket in one hand.

"How ya doing man?" he said as he wiped water from his face. His shaggy hair was wet from the shower. "I'm Fritz, the RA on the floor."

"Hey, how's it going?" Jamie stepped forward and shook his hand.

"I saw your door open and wanted to welcome you. See how things were going."

"Oh, well it's good so far."

Fritz ran his fingers through his damp hair. "You need any help bringing stuff in?

"Nope, just about done. My mother's getting the last bag now."

"I guess you haven't had a chance to meet anyone yet then." Fritz pulled a beat-up watch out of his robe pocket. "Most folks won't be getting back from break until tonight, but, if you're interested we could run over to the Commons and get a bite to eat later."

"Sure, that'd be great."

Fritz started down the hall. "I'll come down in an hour and get you. That should give your mom enough time to make the bed and check your schedule for tomorrow."

Jamie gave him a questioning look.

Fritz laughed. "Trust me man, everyone's mom does that. Just watch." He disappeared into his room two doors down.

Jamie picked up his duffel bag and rummaged

through it for several prescription bottles. He took a pill from each, placing the canisters on the dresser as he headed back out to the hall. He tossed the handful of meds into his mouth, threw back his head, and took a drink from the fountain, and was just gulping down a mouthful of water when his mother rounded the corner.

Lynn's gaze immediately settled on the medicine bottles as she walked into the room. She blinked again and pulled a sheet of paper from her back pocket.

"Now, I know I'm a nag, but I can't help it. You should have it already, but I've written up a list with Dr. Price's phone numbers, a contact at the hospital, and a few other places you might need to reach people, if anything should happen."

Jamie nodded his head, smiling.

"Don't make fun of me."

He nodded faster.

"I'm your mother. I have a right to worry. Don't be an asshole." She laughed and turned to the bed. "I'm just gonna make your bed and get out of here."

Jamie nodded and started putting his clothes in the dresser. He pulled a bottle of eye drops from his pocket and placed it next to the row of medicine bottles.

"Have you looked over the list of classes for tomorrow?"

"Not yet, but I will before I go to sleep." He pulled off his cap and threw it on the corner of his desk chair.

"Are you getting excited?"

"Yeah, of course I am."

"Good."

Lynn pulled the comforter up over the sheets, shook the pillow into its case, and sat down on the bed, patting the spot next to her. "Come here."

Jamie sat down beside her. She turned to him, putting her hand on his cheek.

"I really am excited for you. This is a big deal." Her hand wandered up to the scars on his head, which still rose prominently from the surrounding skin. "You're gonna do great."

Jamie nodded his head, smiling slightly.

"Remember, I'm thirty minutes away if you need anything." Her hand slipped down to his cheek. She leaned forward and gave him a kiss on the forehead. "And now… I'm leaving you alone." She stood up suddenly, heading for the door.

Jamie followed her. She turned as if to say something more, but once again blinked. *No more doubts.* She leaned forward, gave him a tight hug, and strode off down the hallway.

\* \* \*

"I told ya, they *all* do that! When my parents dropped me off my freshman year, first thing my mother did was set the bed." Fritz laughed. "I had a 40 year-old exchange student from Sweden on my floor last year, the guy was married *and* divorced, his mom came up to see the campus, first thing she did was wash the sheets and make the bed. I swear to you!"

Jamie laughed. He took a sip of his drink and looked around. According to Fritz, the Commons was the dining area on the residential side of campus that had the least "institutional food."

"At least you won't feel like you're eating prison rations if you can grab a meal over here. No food loaf. Unfortunately, you're a freshman, so you'll have to take most of your meals over at Gracie's." He feigned an expression of severe remorse. "My condolences."

"Is it that bad?"

"Yes. It is." Fritz said. "Actually, it's not that it's *bad*, it's just that it gets exhausting. Same food every meal. Soggy grilled cheeses and half frozen French fries. And the lights in there make everything look green." Fritz paused to check out a girl walking up to the cash register. She looked at him and he arched his eyebrow. He looked back at Jamie.

Jamie nodded his head. "What about - ?" He bobbed towards the girl, watching her choose a chair a few tables away.

"Girls?"

"Yeah."

"They can be a little hard to come by, but… not impossible. The ratio's not great, but some of us do okay."

Jamie looked over at the girl again. She had a Courtney Cox look about her, but a Cameron Diaz smirk. She took her coat off and turned around. She was gorgeous.

"You like her?" Fritz asked.

"She's not bad." Jamie said with a slight laugh.

"I'll keep that in mind."

Jamie looked at him curiously.

The dining area was getting busy. Everyone wore heavy winter coats and stamped snow from their feet as they walked up the brick stairs by the trays. Everything, absolutely everything on campus was brick. Jamie noticed a girl in pink sweatpants and a small white tank top walking up to the deli line, scuffling along in fluffy blue slippers.

"That girl must be crazy."

Fritz turned to looked at her. "Oh, she probably took the tunnels. We can walk back that way. They connect all the dorms and buildings on this side of campus." He indicated the folks in the heavy coats. "Most of those guys are freshmen. It's usually around April that the newbies start to learn their way around down there. Most of them just stick with the parkas." He motioned towards the windows. Snow was starting to swirl under the lights. "Trust me, it's worth it to learn the tunnels."

They ate silently for a few minutes. Jamie continued to look around the room. Most of the students had their own small cliques. It certainly wasn't a campus of fashion plates. Blue jeans and sweatshirts were the norm. Now and then a programmer walked by in a Linux shirt, or something with an anti-Microsoft message emblazoned across the front. It was pretty clear which clique was which. The artists wore torn jeans and open flannels over paint-spattered t-shirts. The photographers were all in form fitting sweaters, or dark Gap ensembles. He had a feeling the business majors were the girls in the Reebok exercise outfits, hoisting the designer water bottles, or the guys in the corduroys with the v-neck pullovers. The software engineers were another crowd all together. Those not wearing t-shirts with little penguins stood around in small clusters, clad in too tight, too short khakis and enormous flannel shirts, buttoned all the way to the top. They all looked like upstate Martin Scorceses, motioning with their hands, turning their heads and bodies at once, as though they had no necks, and they all spoke with the same high-pitched air of irritation.

Fritz followed his gaze. "Those are the guys who don't get laid, and believe me, they need to."

"They'll be getting laid once they're making the big bucks though."

Fritz rolled his eyes. "Yeah, and I'm sure Bill Gates is an animal in the sack."

Jamie laughed, but as they ate, he could feel Fritz studying him from the corner of his eye. The resident advisor no doubt knew some sort of medical situation had delayed Jamie's arrival on campus. Now he was watching closely for the telltale signs.

"Can I ask you something?"

Jamie knew what was coming. "Shoot."

He was looking at the top of Jamie's head.

"What's with the hat? Is that like, your trademark or something?"

"Not exactly." Jamie picked his words carefully. "Did the school tell you the reason I missed the first quarter?"

Fritz nodded. "They said there was a health issue."

"That's a nice way of putting it, I suppose. I had brain surgery two months ago."

Fritz took a drink of water, narrowing his eyes.

"What was it? Were they taking out a tumor or something?"

"Nah, actually, they were putting something in."

"You fucking with me?"

"No, I'm not, actually."

Fritz looked puzzled. "Putting *what* in? Like a brain to stomach drain tube?"

"No, more like a pacemaker, to kind of keep my brain firing on all pistons."

"That's pretty far out." Fritz eyed another girl walking up to the register. "You're gonna have to use that one. Chicks will love that."

* * *

They took the tunnels back to the dorm. The conversation had stayed pretty normal. Jamie was slightly on guard after telling Fritz about the operation, but his new acquaintance didn't seem the least bit fazed. Apparently, he was in his third year in the school's biotechnology program, and he saw the implant as just one more example of the "cool shit" that was taking place everyday. He did, however, ask if he could bring Jamie in for show and tell, but Jamie just laughed off the question and moved on to another topic.

Fritz seemed like a pretty cool guy. Every so often they passed a crowd of older students, and more often than not, Fritz knew someone in the group. Several of the folks Fritz stopped to talk to were wearing Greek letters.

"Are you in a frat, man?" Jamie asked as they left another group behind.

"First of all. Don't let them hear you calling it that. They only say that to each other. It's the old do as I say, not as I do bit." Fritz seemed suddenly more serious, almost defensive. "Second. Yeah, I am. Phi Kappa Psi."

"That's cool." Jamie answered.

"You interested in checking any of the fraternities out?"

"I don't know. I hadn't really been thinking of it."

"Greeks get a bad rap on this campus, but they can be pretty cool if you have an open mind. Winters can get cold and lonely up here. You might as well go to some parties and hang with some sorority sisters, right?"

"As opposed to the guys in the Linux t-shirts and flannel?" Jamie laughed.

"The fact that you even know the *word* 'Linux' scares me. Fortunately, I have the answer." Fritz slapped him on the back. "We're having our first party of the quarter on Friday. You can come with me and check it out."

"I guess I could-"

"Trust me, this is a much sought-after invitation. You shouldn't pass it up."

"All right. I'm down for that."

"Good!" Fritz suddenly turned serious. "I hope you don't drink though."

Jamie looked at him with curiosity.

"Phi Psi isn't about beer and loose women, son. It's about brotherhood and service to the community."

Jamie stared at him blankly.

"I'm just kidding with you man, it's all about the sweet sorority lovin'. Eat a good meal beforehand, cause it'll be a long night."

They walked up the stairs to the third floor. The phone in Fritz's room was ringing. He opened his door and answered it as Jamie stood out in the hallway.

"Yeah, I was just telling someone about it." Fritz pressed the handset against his chest and turned to Jamie. "Hey listen, I'll talk to you later man, okay?"

Jamie nodded and headed to his room as Fritz returned to his call. More people had arrived while they'd been at dinner. Most of the doors were propped open in the hall, and kids were walking back and forth between the rooms, talking or screaming at one another as they fought each other in online computer games. Jamie opened the door to his room and slipped inside. He turned on his desk light, took a couple of pills from the bottles on his dresser, and stretched out on his bed. He was here. Now what? He reached over and picked up his course schedule. The first class wasn't until ten in the morning. That left plenty of time to get in a workout and grab some books beforehand. He tossed the paper on the floor and picked up his camera, playing with the lens and looking through the viewfinder. He sat up and looked out the window into the snowy night. One or two people were wandering around the quad. A guy ran out from behind some trees, wielding a snowball, chasing a girl who laughed hysterically. Jamie peered through his camera, zooming in on them.

"Click," he whispered.

He stood, stripped down to his boxers, and pulled on a bathrobe. He'd bought one with a hood, which he pulled up over his head. He studied his reflection in the mirror for a second.

"Looks great, Tyson. That won't make anyone uncomfortable," he muttered to himself, but it was better than answering any more questions tonight.

Outside the window, snow was still falling. Wind whistled through the edges of the glass. He felt the cold air on his forehead as he ran his fingers though his hair, once again kneading the scars on his head. He was getting nervous about tomorrow. He was rusty when it came to talking to new people. A shower would warm him up and help him relax. He grabbed a towel and his shower kit and walked down the hall to the bathroom.

*  *  *

He woke at dawn. The snow had stopped, and a cold, gray light was just coming up over the trees. Jamie pulled on a sweat suit, put on his gloves and hat, and walked downstairs. The halls were silent as he passed each level in the building. Every door was closed. He pulled the hood over his head, blew hot air into his gloved fists, and stepped outside.

Frigid air burned his nostrils, stung his lungs. He loved it. The snow creaked under his feet like packed cornstarch. He stretched against a brick wall, steeling himself for the workout, then slowly jogged around the side of the building, headed up over the crest of the hill, and down towards the parking lots. Everything was draped with a thick white blanket. Random flakes floated in the air, suspended in front of him, swirling

away behind him as he cut through the stillness. The
street lights were still on, and Jamie watched the snow
showers set off by the glow. Two deer looked up at him
from between parked cars as he crossed the street into
the parking lot. They were digging through a half buried
McDonalds bag. The animals gazed at him calmly, then
went back to their frozen fries.

He ran a loop around campus, running through
the student lots, up towards the campus apartments, the
signs read Perkins and Colony, then back through the
residential neighborhoods. RIT had what struck him as
an odd balance of apartment buildings and industrial
office space. He passed a technology park, emblazoned
with the school's tiger mascot, turned south towards the
Riverknoll apartments and down through the academic
side of campus. All the paperwork he had read described
RIT as The Brick City, as though trying to instill nostalgia
in its students at an early age. "Remember our days at
The Brick City? Boy, those were good times, eh?" Now,
running through the campus, on the walkway the books
dubbed "The Quarter Mile," what came to mind was
communist Russia. The stark brick buildings towered
overhead like illustrations from an Ayn Rand novel, each
more sterile and imposing than the last. The occasional
smokestack shot out through a building's roof, smoke
and steam billowing up into the air, scattering clouds of
snowflakes. Even under a layer of fresh snow, this was a
bleak campus, but it would have to do. Trying times and
hostile surroundings produced great art. Right? He'd have
to remind himself of that.

The dorms were still sleepy as he arrived back at his floor, stretched in the lounge, then showered and dressed. He grabbed his backpack and a handful of meds, stuff his schedule in his back pocket, and left for the day.

His first meal at Gracie's was an important college lesson: no one got up early, and *NO ONE* ate breakfast. Except for a group of Japanese students, a hunchbacked girl with thick, smeary glasses, and several engineering students, he had the place to himself. Every clink of a plate or clang of silverware echoed throughout the room. The radio played soft jazz in the background as he helped himself to a bowl of Wheaties, orange juice, and fruit. He sat at his table in the corner, his chewing and his thoughts far too loud for his own comfort.

Finished with breakfast, Jamie walked over to the academic side, where the students with unwanted morning classes wandered the campus like grouchy, Cabbage-Patch-Kid zombies, all dressed in sweatpants and hooded shirts, the drawstrings pulled tight, like baby bonnets. He went to the bookstore and found more lethargic students groggily bumping into one another as they struggled to forms words and sentences, feeling their ways through stupors brought on by deep or all too brief sleep. Jamie found his books, gasped at the prices, then waited in the long lines for the registers. When he had finally been rung out, he worked his way out of the store, maneuvering around a group of students, each member carrying a thirty-six-ounce coffee mug, mumbling how tired they were.

He was early for his first class, and sat on a bench

looking down the length of the hall. Students in winter coats filed past him, letting in blasts of cold air as they shoved their way through the double doors. Jamie took out a notebook and pen, turned to a fresh page, and looked down the corridor. He hesitated. He'd attempted to sketch off and on since the operation, but it had never gone well. Though occasionally timid, Jamie's movements were once again fluid and unfailing. His hands and body were steady. Yet, he was still unable to draw. It was like two wires were crossed in his head. He could pick out images and understand the mechanics needed to translate them to paper, but somewhere between his eyes and his hand, the signals became confused. Maybe it was lack of practice; inactivity had caked the workings of his brain with a thick coat of rust. He just needed to work at it and the old skills would return to him. He hoped. Jamie blinked and looked down at the notebook, beginning to draw. He glanced up, pulling the pen towards him as he compared picture to page. His hands quivered slightly, the line becoming a squiggle down the paper. He slowed his movements, focusing intensely on the tip of the pen as it careened back and forth on the page, shifting the lines away from their intended destinations, throwing the image askew. He stopped, again looked down the hallway, and again lowered his pen to the paper. Still his hand refused to cooperate. Jamie shot a look around him, then forced the tip of the pen into the paper as hard as he could, tearing the page and grinding a line across the sheets underneath. He pulled up on the pen and smashed it down onto the notebook, where the tip ruptured, splattering red ink across the white surface. Then he slammed the notebook shut.

Jamie's first photo class was anticlimactic at best. It wasn't that it was uninspiring, it just was what it was, the first class, in which students meet professor and the professor gives them the rundown of what they're in for.

In this case, the professor was a short, gray haired woman with a distinct Southwest flare about her. She wore large turquoise rings, a hefty silver and stone necklace, and billowing clothes of deep red and brown fabric. When she spoke, her voice had the breathy sound of words forced out over smoke-hardened vocal chords. Jamie could almost see the puffs of ash breaking loose from her lungs and fluttering out with each syllable. Officially, she was Professor Taylor, but she said to call her "Judy."

Judy was a great fan of the Xerox machine, handing out piles of pamphlets on everything from F-stops, to light meters, to department policies. She continually licked the tip of her index finger as she flipped through several massive, swaying towers of quarterly assignments. When everything had been passed out, she gave a dismissive invitation for questions, then directed them to their first assignment, working with photos using a manipulation program on the computer.

"If any of you have used Photoshop, then you have a bit of an advantage; if you haven't, the pamphlet I passed out should be all you need." She hoisted a massive packet of papers above her head for emphasis, then dropped her arms with visible relief. "If no one has any questions, I'll leave you in the hands of our student assistant to take a tour and learn the lay of the land."

The assistant was an unpleasant character from the photo cage, a young man named Victor, with spiked black hair, a ring dangling from his nose, and deep, black bags under his eyes, who made a point of calling a mopey "What's up?" to every upperclassmen who passed the tour. The woeful cry of the second year student burdened with the task of showing the newbies the ropes. Victor took them through the school's massive facilities, which included dozens of photo studios, darkrooms, locker bays, and digital photo setups. Then he filled them in on the complex process involved in checking out every piece of equipment available at the photo cage, the underlying message of which seemed to be:

"You break it, you bought it."

Everything seemed to be worth several hundred dollars.

"We have ten high end digital camera backs. They cost a near mint," Victor said flatly. "Freshman aren't allowed to check those out. You guys get to choose from these cameras over here." Victor waved a baggy-sleeved arm toward a shelf of camera packages. "They're old, but they work fine. Once again, parts are scarce, and repairs are expensive, so, you break it-"

"You bought it?" Jamie interrupted him.

Victor turned towards him, a mangy cat appraising a squeak toy. He flexed his jaw, "Yeah."

The class looked on in silence. Jamie hadn't even meant to speak. This guy just pissed him off. Something about him rubbed him the wrong way, and before he knew it, he had made his first enemy.

Victor looked pissed. "Once again, freshman have to wait a while for things. If an upperclassmen or a grad student needs anything you're signed up for, they have first dibs. If they have equipment to check in, you *will* have to let them in. You can fight it, but you won't be doing yourself any favors by making enemies."

This guy was a prick. Jamie knew it, the rest of his group knew it. He could see several of them stifling smirks. Jamie glanced around the group. Unfortunately, there weren't many interesting girls in the class -- two or three showed promise, but they had a distinct edge that Jamie found off-putting. One in particular, a tall girl with a smoking body, seemed incapable of smiling; she just kept pulling her cell phone out every three minutes to check for text messages, then scowling when she saw who had or hadn't contacted her. When Jamie started going at old Victor, he caught the cell phone girl lifting her head to shoot him an indignant glance. Her lips were clenched shut, a straight line across her mouth. No movement, not even the slightest curl at the corner of her lips. Jamie looked at the other girls, sizing them up. One resembled Grimace from the McDonalds Happy Meal commercials. She looked like she'd just bitten into a cookie and found a moldy nut. Another had a Kid Rock beard. Another had an *enormous* ass! One girl with short spiky hair was laughing. She looked pretty cool. Jamie craned his neck to get a better look, but one glance at her wardrobe warned him off. A girl with a pink t-shirt with the silhouette of a cat reading "I wanna pet your pussy" probably didn't want anything he had to offer. Shit. He turned and focused his frustration on Victor, who continued with his condescending spiel, emphasizing the word "freshman" in every sentence. Jamie lowered his head and looked up at their tour guide with wicked eyes.

"I'm gonna enjoy pissing you off Vic," he muttered under his breath.

* * *

The guy in the back was cute. Kelli kept peering toward the corner to get a peek at him. Nice build, not an ounce of fat, a little scruffy, with dark brown eyes, and a sort of... menace about him. She smiled. All right, not menace, but damn... he was intense. Like he was taking everything in, sizing everyone up. He looked over and she glanced down at her nails, then dug around in her backpack for a pen. A moment later he was pulling out a notebook, doodling. His eyes narrowed under a wool cap. She looked at the hat. Normally she didn't go for that kind of look, too Eminem *8 Mile*, but this guy was just... she laughed and looked away.

Jamie rolled his eyes up, watching the girl across the way. She had to be an art student. She had that look, only... better. Her hair was jet black, with a few scattered patches of deep red highlights among the twisted strands. She wore heavy black eye makeup, bordering on goth, but with a nice, inviting angle. She turned to the side, and he caught a better glimpse of her profile. She was *beautiful*. His eyes slowly slid down her body, hanging close against the curves, down to her waist that just… barely… peeked out from the space between her jeans and her tank top. She leaned forward and the edge of her shirt slid ever so slightly up her back. His mouth went dry.

BAM!

A man in a tweed coat and khakis walked in, slamming a book down on the desk at the front of the room. The entire class spun around to face him. The man turned, rubbing his hands together quickly.

"Okay! So this is Media and the Mind. Welcome to it."

Kelli watched the man in the coat, who leaned back against the desk and lifted himself onto it lightly, training his eyes on the audience. He was in his late forties, in good shape, with a boyish face, and salt and pepper hair, more salt than pepper, and white at the temples. This guy was cute too.

"So, the question I'd like answered, is just what exactly is on your dirty little minds? No doubt all sorts of dark, wonderful stuff, much of it placed there *by* the media, or bubbling up from your own grubby little hearts, ready and waiting for you to send out into the world *through* your own form of media. You're all art and photo majors, correct? Raise your hands if that's a yes"

He looked up as nearly everyone in the room raised their hands.

"That's what I thought. And everyone here has a dirty mind?" He looked around expectantly. No hands went up, and he grinned, nodding his head. "Suspicion confirmed."

The class laughed, and he stood up, walking around his desk to a white board at the front of the room. He picked up a marker and wrote his name on the board.

"So, let's pretend we're in an old high school movie. I am Professor Ryan, and for the next ten weeks we'll be discussing a whole bunch of things, all off which, I hope, will be related to the media, and the purpose, message, and motivation behind everything we can possibly think of."

He swept his arm across the room dramatically. Then looked up with a grin.

"Damn," Kelli thought to herself. "This guy really is cute."

"You're all in media. Whether you think of it that way or not, everyone in this room works with some form of communication. Everything you create is sending out a message. The medium you choose to work in, on its own, sends a message. Who here is a photographer?"

Half the class raised their hands. Kelli noticed the intense guy was part of that group. Ryan nodded.

"Who here is an artist or sculptor?"

Another quarter of the room raised their hands. Jamie kept his in his lap.

"Writers?" Professor Ryan raised his hand, and a handful of other students did likewise. "And who here is a filmmaker?"

Jamie watched as Kelli raised her hand. Christ. Even the angle of her wrist was cute.

"Lets talk about this. That is a wide range of art forms. Would anyone say that sculpting is the same as writing?" He waited a beat. "What about film? Is film the same as writing? You can use both to tell a story, make things up, make people get caught up in a love affair, or a thriller..."

He started walking down the aisle, looking from student to student.

"Michelangelo painted the Sistine Chapel before any of our fathers' fathers were born. Why? Food? Rent? Sure. He was on commission. Was he creating propaganda for the church? Certainly. But what is it that was he trying to say? Why is it that that ceiling, with the fancy paint job, stands out as one of the marvels of artistic creation?"

Ryan looked around, then whipped his head towards Jamie.

"What is it? Why did he paint it? Why not just write something on a scroll and hammer it up to the ceiling?"

The class laughed.

"You think it's funny, but really, why is a painting the accepted medium for that message? And why is it that *that church,* with *that image*, has withstood the tests of time?" He put his hands in his pockets and stood up straight. "Is it because Michelangelo had something utterly unique to express? Maybe." He spun on his heal and walked back to the front. "Is it that he did it better than anyone else before him? Quite possibly. In fact, lets go out on a limb—*absolutely!* No one could have done it better. But did Michelangelo ever write anything?"

Ryan pointed to a boy in the front row, who looked around and shrugged his shoulders.

"The history books tells us Michelangelo was also a poet. But do any of you know any of his pieces?" He pointed at Kelli. "You, Ms.-?"

"Petronio."

"Please recite that famous poem by Michelangelo."

Kelli felt her face getting red. "Uh, I don't know one-"

Ryan stared at her incredulously. "You don't know one."

He started back up the aisle, once again stopping beside Jamie, staring into his eyes intently.

"What about you? *You* must know it."

Jamie smiled. "I don't."

The professor again stood there, stone silent. Then he spun around again, throwing up his arms.

"I don't know it either! He must have written pure shit!" The class laughed. "But damn, talk about some fucking great paintings! And I hear he made a couple of decent sculptures as well. So that's another question, why did he choose paintings for some pieces, and sculpture for others? I dunno, but when you see them, they just make sense."

The room was quiet. Someone coughed gently. Ryan stood in the aisle for a beat, then walked up to the front of the room.

"So that's the point of this class. We will discuss the choices behind each form of media. Each medium has its own inherent message, each idea in our heads needs a different way to take flight, and each of our minds works in a different way. Consider what you're thinking right now, consider the words that have spouted out from my mouth, traveled through the air, into your ears, and been absorbed by your brains -- hopefully. I'm using speech now, but I could write it down." He motioned to Kelli. "Or Ms. Petronio here could make a film about it. And every form would add its own elements to the message. And what exactly is the message? Am I just some stuffed shirt, full of shit, spouting out here like a smart ass? Yeah, pretty much. But I've got a point, you'll see."

Ryan looked around the room, enjoying their confused faces. This was the best part of the quarter.

"So, my little media masters. Here is your assignment. I want you to think about what you study, and what you consider yourselves *to be*; writers, photographers, cartoonists, whatever. Think about your medium, and what your life purpose is. What is it that makes *your mind unique?*" He pulled a hand out of his pocket, stabbing at the air with a finger. "For some of you, this will be harder than for others. Do what it takes to get in the necessary place. If you've got some pot, smoke it. If you've got the means, get drunk this weekend. I'm sure you or someone you know has a black light in their rooms. Drink. Smoke. Stare up at some glow in the dark stars under a blacklight. Let's get deep and get heavy. I'll join you in this research. If you have any more questions, I will be at the Pig 'n Whistle tomorrow night, downing white Russians and considering my place in the communications lexicon, trying to figure out where it all went horribly wrong."

Ryan studied each of their faces. That hot girl in the front row was lapping it up. The little stooly next to her didn't have a clue. A few of them seemed to be laughing it off. The kid in the back row with the hat had an all-too-knowing expression. He couldn't read him.

"So, lets dig into your dark psyches and start coming up with some answers." He picked up his book and headed for the door. "Have fun. Think deep. And get a little fucked up, will ya?"

Ryan walked out the door without saying another word. Everyone sat there for a moment, then they looked around at one another. An older woman, probably in her forties, dressed in a denim Winnie the Pooh jacket, looked pretty upset.

"That's it?" she muttered. "This is bullshit."

Jamie laughed to himself. The rest of the people in the room were getting their things together hesitantly, unsure if the professor was coming back at any moment. The girl in the front row tossed her hair to the side and looked back at him suddenly. Their eyes locked for a moment. As always, Jamie didn't blink, but he was nervous. The girl, she just stared back at him with that certain look in her eyes, that glimmer that told him things were bound to happen with them.

Kelli stood up, still giving him that look. The professor was a cutie, but she didn't want another one of those situations. She'd learned after the whole affair with her Pop Art professor. Older guys were too much trouble, whether they were married or not, the thrill always ran out, and they ended up wanting her to be something she wasn't. No. It was time for someone younger, and the guy in the back was just what she was looking for. She stared him down, giving him the message: before she'd fuck him, she was gonna fuck *with* him. It was always better that way.

The girl headed towards the door, and Jamie hurried to catch up to her. The Winnie the Pooh lady stood up in front of him, gathering her things together, blocking his way as she complained to the girl beside her.

"This had better not be a waste of my money. I had a guy like this last quarter, and I told my husband we are not working two jobs to pay for this hippy, liberal nonsense."

Jamie shoved past the woman and out into the corridor. He looked both ways down the hall, but the girl was gone.

# CHAPTER TWO
# COLLEGE LIFE

College dorms are like space stations orbiting the planet, their inhabitants studying history and current events with finely tuned instruments and unforgiving eyes, all the while remaining safely isolated from the very events they're busy observing for meaning. But that's the way it should be. That's the only environment where youthful idealism has the space and ability to grow, while still letting students find their footing in the turbulent emotions of adulthood. In college, pot-bellied computer programmers and goth art students can happily argue the merits of communism with self-assured business majors, while in real life, those same artists and tech guys are doomed to customer service departments, working *under* the very individuals to whom they now preach. Where else can actions and emotions be more immediate and biting? A person can watch *The Simpsons* with a group in the lounge one moment, feeling a complete sense of community, only to walk down a quiet hallway to their room, and be overcome with an utter sense of isolation. Polar emotions experienced in a matter of seconds.

Maybe it was the price you paid for creativity, but such feelings were never alien to Jamie. Even throughout high school he'd had a sense of walking through life in a daze, oddly detached from the events playing out around him. Hell, maybe it was the Parkinsons, but somehow he doubted it. Well before he ever felt symptoms of the disease, Jamie had the sense of viewing life through old windows, the warped glass magnifying certain events, bringing them forward in his vision, affecting him in ways others around him were not always aware of, while other parts of life, certain social encounters, seemed to have completely escaped his attention.

While he was definitely excited to finally be in school, Jamie was still feeling that sense of detached loneliness. Most likely it came from starting classes in the second quarter, after everyone around him had already been on campus ten weeks. They'd made their friends, learned the lay of the land, possibly enjoyed the first lays of their lives, and life had suddenly stepped on the gas, whisking them into the next chapters of their individual stories. Yeah, it was only ten weeks, but to paraphrase Ferris Bueller, life moves pretty fast in college, and Jamie had the distinct feeling of leaping onto the roof of a speeding train while the other passengers were already settled into their seats.

He walked back through campus after class. Students were huddled outside the library, chatting with friends, lighting up cigarettes, and self consciously exhaling plumes of smoke as they watched the crowds wander by. Aside from the smell of that smoky sweet first drag on a cigarette, which always reminded him of his father, Jamie despised smokers. Now their instant sense of community bugged him even more. Sure, smoking butts looked cool, gave them something do with fidgeting hands, but he focused on the soot and the yellow film on their fingers. Disgusting. He wondered if he could pick a pack up on campus anywhere.

He passed another group of smokers outside the gym, several of whom pulled out lighters just as he approached, and the burst of tobacco as they lit up damn near convinced him to skip his workout and swing by a gas station instead. He entered the building and showed the kid at the gate his student ID. The gym was teaming with people who were the polar opposite of smokers. No droopy eyes and crinkled, gray skin. These folks were pink, and healthy, and firm. These were the folks on campus having sex, and Jamie's envy immediately shifted again. He got a towel from a cute blond at the reception desk, changed in the locker room, and followed a herd of frat guys to the weight room.

He stretched on the mats by the entrance and observed the crowd filing in and out. As with most gyms, one wall was covered in mirrors, and Jamie watched knowingly as guys and girls alike snuck peeks at one another and then themselves in the glass. The frat guys were the worst, their eyes constantly shifting from girls, to guys, to themselves, sizing up their targets, then comparing their own bodies to their perceived competition. Jamie felt the tingle of curious eyes as he tightened the strings on his hooded sweatshirt. Eventually, he might keep his head uncovered, but he hoped his hair might grow in before he'd have to respond to curious stares.

He did a round of exercises on the machines, then worked forty minutes on the elliptical trainer. A television was tuned to CNN in front of the aerobic stations. Jamie watched a segment with Elton John discussing his newest pacemaker. That was followed by a piece on a high school student who'd recently lost an arm and both legs, but had begun running marathons with the aid of space-aged prosthetic legs. Jesus. How did these people do it? His own experience had been a nightmare, but to start running marathons with titanium legs was unimaginable. This kid was amazing. Jamie turned the resistance up on his machine and picked up the pace for another five minutes. By the time he stepped off the machine he'd sweated through his sweatshirt. He wiped the machine down with a towel and went back to the stretching mats.

"I wonder if they'll want to do a story on me," he mused.

It was probably only a matter of time before Price and the university would start sending out press releases, trying to get some glory for their groundbreaking new treatment. Jamie knew what they were waiting for, however. They wanted to be sure their little miracle was the real thing. They wanted him to get settled in school, grow back his hair, become a little more photogenic, a little more productive, then they'd no doubt call in the camera crews and pitch their story. They were playing it safe, waiting to see if something was gonna go haywire.

No sense putting him on *60 Minutes,* showing him all pale and weak, only to have the implant fail, and watch "this promising young man" become a vegetable on national TV.

Jamie stretched on the mats. His eyes were stinging. He realized he'd been staring again. He blinked hard, then looked out at his hands as they stretched out to his toes. His fingers were still steady. He glanced over at a girl across the room who was jogging on a treadmill. She had nice, firm breasts, held tightly with a pink sports bra, but they were still bouncing just enough to get his imagination going. She was cute, sort of a Jennifer Aniston look. He put his head down, switched legs, and continued stretching.

He walked into the locker room after his workout, grabbed his towel, and headed for the showers. He was feeling good. His body was moving naturally, no sense of sluggishness. There was someone in the stall to the left, so he took the one by the far right wall, stripped off his clothes, and pulled the curtain behind him. He stepped under the scorching hot spray, lathering up with a combination shower gel/shampoo from the dispenser on the wall. The workout had gotten his blood pumping, he could feel his dick getting hard. He opened his eyes and looked down. This one wasn't gonna go away on its own, no ugly librarian images would do the trick this time. He pulled the curtain shut tightly and closed his eyes. The girl from the media class popped into his head. He remembered that look she'd given him as they got up to leave. Damn. He lathered up one hand and started stroking himself, picturing her walking towards him, pressing up against him. She was her turning her back on him, bending over the table in front of him. Jamie imagined his hands on her hips as he felt the hot water on his skin...

He opened his eyes and rinsed off, checking to be sure the curtain was still tightly closed and no one had seen what he'd been doing. He lathered up the rest of his body as he grew limp again, but he couldn't stop thinking about that girl from class. He had to say something to her next week. That look she'd given him was unmistakable, but he didn't want to take any chances.

Jamie picked up a sandwich at The Corner Store in the tunnels, then headed back to his room. The dorms had that lonely feeling again. Everyone was in an evening class, huddled in the lounges, or cruising back and forth between their rooms, but there was just an overall quiet feeling in the air. Jamie went past Fritz's room, but the door was shut, so he continued down to his dorm and closed the door behind him.

He sat on his bed and unwrapped his sandwich, the cellophane crinkling quietly. He closed his eyes, chewing slowly, picturing the implant in his head, wondering what it looked like nestled into those tissues, deep in the darkness of his brain. He pictured it sparking and humming, keeping everything in line, fighting to maintain control. Now and then an errant signal tried to break through, and the implant shot it down with a wild, spidery blast of electricity, like something from Frankenstein's lab. Suddenly, Jamie remembered that scene from The Bride of Frankenstein, where the creature finds the old blind man in the cabin who tells him, "Before you arrived, I was all alone."

"Alone bad," the Creature rumbled. "Friend good."

Jamie stopped chewing, got up, and went over to his dresser. He opened the canisters for his meds and took a pill from each, swallowing them as he stepped out into the hallway to take a drink from the fountain. No one was near his door, but he could hear voices around the corner. He needed to get to know some of these people, but somehow he wasn't in the mood tonight. He walked back into his room, locking the door behind him.

Jamie finished his sandwich and stretched out on his bed. Why the hell was he thinking of that stupid old movie? And why was it making him so damn depressed? He rolled over, stared at the brick wall by his bed, then closed his eyes. Gradually, his breathing deepened, and he fell asleep.

\* \* \*

The events after the accident had always been a blur. He remembered bright lights and the feeling of a latex glove on his forehead as the doctor pulled the glass from his eyes. He remembered a long period when everything was black, and he felt cloth bandages over his eyes. He'd drifted in and out of sleep, waking only to the sounds of his own breathing. Then slowly, he heard the voices of adults in the background. He heard his mother and father talking. No, not his father, someone else - Uncle Matt, whose voice had the same gentle murmur, but just a slightly higher pitch, fewer cigarettes, more herbal tea. They were talking about something. But the words came out like wheezing mumbles, characters from a *Peanuts* cartoon. The voices faded in and out like the sound of his own breathing.

Then he was awake, the bandages had been removed, and he was alone. Other than the smells, and the echoing silence, all he recalled was a giant purple elephant, spinning in front of him, an insane smile on its face. It was laughing at him.

*   *   *

Kelli reached over and twisted the volume knob on her stereo. She didn't feel like hearing Christie and her boyfriend fucking in the next room just yet. It was too early. She had enjoyed Thanksgiving break, reading in bed at night, free from her suite mate's steady moaning and the slamming of a bed against the adjoining wall. She looked at the clock - 9 a.m. and they were at it already. Jesus, if the girl had a ten o'clock class, she could barely make it to the shower before she left, but if Joe was in the mood -- and when wasn't he? -- the two of them were bright eyed and bushy tailed, animals in an entirely inappropriate petting zoo.

She took a couple of beer bottles from the foot of her bed and tossed them in the trash. Administration had made RIT a dry campus in the first month of the school year, after one of this year's freshmen drank a dingy full of Olde English and did a face-plant off a third floor balcony, but most of the people she knew had elaborate ways of smuggling the stuff in. It was like the dawning of a new prohibition era, only everyone was an underage Al Capone, squirreling booze into the dorms in gym bags, padding the bottles in rolled up socks. Will had snuck these bottles in by slipping them down his boxers. Even as she'd sipped from the long neck bottles, she'd shuddered to think how his depraved little brain would interpret it. He was her friend, and a decent guy, but he certainly wasn't the first pile of bones she'd toss herself at. He was fun to hang out with and talk movies, but aside from their studies in film, he was kind of your typical…film geek, which sort of said it all. He had a serious crush on her, and she'd have to give it the kibosh shortly - he didn't know what girls wanted, let alone what *she* wanted in a guy.

"Shit." She couldn't think about that now.

She had to get some food in her stomach and try to get some work done. Maybe take a stab at that script for the two-quarter project. Will would probably be stopping by later to see if she wanted to go to the movies. She wanted to feel like she had accomplished something on the first day of the new quarter.

A low wailing noise was coming from the next room, followed by grunting, and the sound of that dreaded bed frame creaking and thumping against a wall. Jesus. She needed to get some action soon, or she was liable to hop in with Christie and Joe for an impromptu threesome. Worse yet, she might throw common sense to the wind and have a go with Will. That would be a mistake. Kelli cranked the volume on the stereo still higher, then hopped up on the window sill, spinning her feet around 'til she was scrunched up in the window frame. She looked out over the quad. The sky was bright gray, practically white, the sun was just barely burning through the clouds in spots. It looked like nuclear winter. She bent her head, looking ten floors down at the ants hurrying to the academic.

Then she spotted someone in a familiar wool cap. The guy from her Media and the Mind class. She leaned forward, watching him walking past. She was sure it was him. Something about that guy was incredibly appealing. She'd been thinking about him all day yesterday, and she hadn't even *spoken* to him; he could sound like Mickey Mouse. What was it? He'd just been sitting there doodling in a notebook and she couldn't stop fantasizing about him. She pulled her hand to her face and bit down on the end of her pinky.

"He can doodle me any time he likes," she muttered.

\* \* \*

It was Friday and Jamie didn't have classes. He again woke early, feeling somewhat dazed. He'd had strange dreams during the night, and though he couldn't remember what they'd involved, the images were still nagging at the back of his mind. He decided to skip his run and just get out of the building. He grabbed his backpack and camera and headed for the door.

The quads were quieter than the previous morning. The wind was much stronger, whistling between the buildings, leaving the people around him leaning at forty-five degree angles as the air held them upright. He watched an art student as he struggled to carry a large, flat, cardboard package. The wind kept whipping the cardboard back and forth in the guy's arms. Suddenly, another blast snatched the package from his hands, twirled it in the air like a basketball on the almighty Globetrotter's invisible hand, and hurled it down on the icy sidewalk. The cardboard tore open as a stained glass window inside exploded in a shower of blue and red shards. Jamie spun down and to the side, throwing his hands to his head, shielding his eyes as needles of glass sprayed back over the Quarter Mile. In his mind, he could see the box hitting the ground, saw a sparkling cloud of slivers floating through the air. He stayed crouched on the sidewalk until the tinkling of falling glass had stopped. When he looked up, the clouds had broken, and luminescent glass shards were shimmering on the snow-covered walkway. Jamie turned his head toward the student, who stood in shock, looking out over his destroyed project. Dropping his arms in defeat, he picked up the mangled pieces of cardboard, and trudged away. Jamie waited a few moments, then pulled the camera from his backpack, crouched to the ground, and snapped a few pictures of the ground - a surreal picture of sky blue and blood red, sparkling over the blinding white landscape.

The image of that broken window stuck with him for the rest of the day. He went to lunch at the student union, all the while seeing that first cloud of glass as it burst from the package like a parachute snapping open in the wind. He decided to go over to the photo building and see if he could play around with the images on one of the computers.

He was disappointed that Victor, the photo cage prick, wasn't at the counter when he got there. Maybe pissing that guy off would get him out of the weird funk he seemed to have slipped into. The girl at the counter told him he could check out a computer in the imaging center, or just grab a work station in the lab downstairs. Jamie went down to the next floor and found a machine in a dimly lit corner. He logged on and downloaded the images from his camera, then clicked on Photoshop and started going through the pictures slowly. The images weren't exactly what he'd had in mind. He had been imagining the explosion of glass, and had forgotten that he hadn't actually photographed it, just got a fleeting glimpse before his eyes had instinctively snapped shut. He kept going through the images. Several of them were still fairly striking. The sunlight was piercing as it reflected off the glass. He stared into the image, his eyes going fuzzy.

Jamie snapped awake suddenly as someone coughed behind him. He turned and saw a tall, bald guy with a beard standing behind him, giving him a funny look. Jamie's eyes had been open, but he must have zoned out completely.

"We're gonna be closing the labs up in a few minutes. We need you to shut everything down.

Jamie looked at the clock. It was after eight.

"Oh, I'm sorry. I didn't realize it was so late."

He packed up his things quickly and left. It was

dark outside as he exited the building. He'd gotten there at three. Must have been more tired than he realized. It didn't feel like he had been sleeping. It was just a feeling as though he had completely spaced out for a few minutes. A few *hours* was more like it. Oh shit. He'd forgotten his meds. But those shouldn't have made a difference. Well, maybe with his motor skills, but not with his head. And even then, they were more as a precaution than anything else.

"Calm down, Jamie!" he muttered to himself.

He was overanalyzing it. He was just tired. Either way, he'd better get back and take those meds. He picked up the pace a little, noting that he was once again out of sync with the rest of the campus. A few students were walking along beside him, but overall the Quarter Mile was quiet. When he reached the residential side he cut through Greek Row, where things seemed to be livening up. Music was blaring from open windows, he could hear people laughing and joking inside. He passed a group of Abercrombie guys whipping snowballs at each other, their missiles continually missing their targets and exploding into chunks of ice at they hit the sides of buildings. Jamie tensed up, reluctant to get hit in the head by an errant iceball. He turned off Greek Row and trudged into the quad outside a dorm tower.

A couple was standing back in the trees outside the entrance to Jamie's. They held each other, kissing passionately, oblivious to his presence. He unlocked the door and hurried up the stairs, looking at his watch as he got to the floor. He was twelve hours overdue for his medication.

He opened his door, grabbed the canisters and headed for the fountain. He'd just thrown back the pills with a big gulp of water, when he heard Fritz calling his name and saw him coming down the hall towards him with a broad grin on his face.

"TGIF, buddy! TGIF!"

Jamie wiped his mouth and pulled off his gloves. "What's up man?"

"Not too much," Fritz replied. "I knocked on your door this morning, but you must have had an early class."

"Nah, I'm off on Fridays."

"Oh, you must have been sleeping then."

"Nope, I got up pretty early."

Fritz seemed puzzled. "Did you have work or something?"

Jamie shook his head.

"Then, I don't get it."

"I just felt like getting out."

Fritz looked at him blankly for a moment, then blinked his eyes and shuddered. "So anyway. We're having a kick-off party at the house tonight."

"Oh yeah?"

"It should be a pretty good time. You still interested in coming?"

Jamie nodded his head. "Sure. What time?"

"Its starts when it starts, but I was thinking we could get something to eat and head over around nine."

"Sounds good."

Fritz looked over, studying him. "How are things

going so far?"

"Not too bad. Had my first few classes."

"You met anyone on the floor?"

"No, I haven't gotten around to introducing myself yet."

"Great, we were just getting a group together." Fritz turned and called down the hall. "Yo, Dougie!"

A tall, beanpole kid came over. He was wearing a brown Virginia Beach sweatshirt, with a crewcut and thick wire-frame glasses. Fritz smacked him on the shoulder and he cringed slightly, forcing an uncomfortable smile.

"Doug, this is Jamie. Jamie, Doug."

"How's it going man?" Jamie asked as he squeezed the guy's hand, feeling bones shifting and popping under dry, flaky skin.

"Hey, wassup?" Doug said with a quick chin bob and a slow Snoop Dogg demeanor.

Fritz faked a punch to Doug's stomach, and the boy's face scrunched inward. This was not a young man who savored physical contact. "Dougie! Everyone ready to go?"

"Yeah, we were just trying to get Sandi off the phone."

"Oh, just forget her. Let's go." Fritz saw Doug's look of shock and added, "I'm just kidding with you man. Sandi's a great girl. As your RA, I can tell these things about people. Come on, let's head out."

Fritz threw an arm around Doug and led him down the hall. They passed an open doorway, where a skeletal girl stood talking on the phone. Fritz banged on the doorway to her room shouting "Yo, Sandi, we're rolling out!!"

Sandi pressed her hand over the phone. "I'll meet you over there."

"Sure you will," Fritz muttered as he continued into the lounge.

Jamie eyed Sandi's face as he passed, deciding that she must have been cute at one point, even a few months earlier, but had clearly succumbed to some anorexic demon. She turned her back on the door and he noticed her sweatpants: "Duke" was silk-screened across the butt. For some reason this stupid style was a huge turn-on for him. Go figure. But sadly, it seemed this particular Duke had seen better days. What had once stood as a plump, proud beacon of academic excellence was now sadly deflated, reading simply "UK," with two sunken characters resembling parentheses on either side of the British abbreviation. Jamie lowered his head, saying a silent prayer for the departed posterior.

A group of ten students was gathered in the lounge, holding their winter coats and watching *The Simpsons.* A tall, kind of goofy guy with a goatee was guffawing at the show, turning now and then to smack another much shorter kid on the back.

"Oh shit!" The guy bellowed, "that is too fucking funny."

The small guy scowled every time he got hit. This seemed like a floor that valued its personal space.

Fritz walked up to the smaller kid and turned him towards Jamie.

"Will, this is Jamie, the new guy."

They shook hands.

"And this," Fritz continued, turning towards the goateed guy, "This is my old roommate, Arlin." Fritz smacked Arlin on the shoulder. Arlin spun and punched him back much harder.

Jamie nodded his head as Fritz quickly pointed down a row of people. "That's Arlin's girlfriend, Vanessa. That's Vicky, Chris, Jen, Teresa, Nick, Steve, and that's Will's roommate, Gabe."

Gabe spun around and looked at Jamie with a curious expression. "Hey," he said slowly. "Weren't you just in the labs about a half hour ago?"

It was the guy from the computer lab who had woken him up.

Jamie was caught off guard. "Oh, yeah. That was me."

Gabe laughed. "Are you all right, dude? I thought you were epileptic or something."

"Oh no, I'm fine. Fell asleep for a few minutes I guess."

"Well, I was just glad you weren't having a seizure. I'm telling you, I had some girl have a seizure in there last quarter, really tore up a whack-um tablet. Fell on the floor, ripped the wires from the back of the thing, and smashed in the top."

"Geez…"

"But cool. Glad you're all right."

Fritz gave Jamie a funny look as he watched the exchange, then shot a quick glance up and down the hall. "So anyway, there are a few folks missing, but you'll meet them eventually."

Arlin smacked his hands together. "Okay, lets go!"

The gang headed down the hall. Arlin pounded on the door outside Sandi's room again, and she turned, flashing a look of sheer annoyance. "Get off the phooooone!" Arlin bellowed.

Jamie let the group move ahead of him a ways, then he followed behind. Gabe fell into step beside him.

"The folks Fritz said were missing live in these two rooms on the end." He pointed to two rooms on the left. " One is Steve's roommate Rob. He's screwing that girl Teresa behind his girlfriend's back. By the way, Steve, don't bother messing with that guy. He's an asshole."

"Oh yeah?"

"Yeah. I don't say that often, but in his case, it's the truth."

"Who else didn't I meet?"

"Uh, let's see." Gabe looked down the hall again. "Well, there's this girl, Ming Na, at the end off the hall, who I swear is like some guy's concubine. There's Doug's roommate Chris. He's in the same frat as Fritz. But he's *never* here."

They headed down the concrete stairway, the group's footsteps echoing ahead of them. Jamie shouted over the noise. "It seems like a pretty cool floor."

"Yeah, its not bad. People get pissed at each other now and then, but—" He trailed off as they walked outside.

Arlin was running up ahead, holding a couple of snowballs over Vanessa's head. She did not seem amused.

"Arlin, if you do it, I will fucking kill you!"

This seemed to goad him on, and he started tapping them on top on her head gently.

"Stop it! I'm telling you! Don't start with me! Not tonight."

"Those two fight a lot." Gabe said. "But they have *a lot* of makeup sex too. He's in the single next to your room, so I hope you have thick walls."

"Does she live on this floor?"

"Nah, she's a sophomore. She lived in the dorms her freshman year, but she's back at home now. She basically lives with Arlin though."

"What's Fritz like?"

"Oh, he's chill. Real relaxed RA. As long as no one makes a scene, he doesn't care what people are up to."

"Cool."

This guy, Gabe, was kind of a gossip, but he was making Jamie feel more comfortable. They got to Gracie's and filed inside, giving their meal cards to an older woman who sat in front of an enormous old cash register. She carefully compared each picture to the person before letting them inside. Every time she swiped a card through the scanner on the register, she'd give her chin a sort of frustrated jolt to the side, sending a tremor up to the top of her blue beehived hair.

"This is Esther." Gabe whispered. "Just smile, don't make any funny moves, and you should be fine."

They stepped up in line and Esther turned to Gabe with an accusatory expression.

"Good evening, Esther."

Esther eyed him carefully, cocking one brow as she looked from card to person. "Turn your head."

Gabe graciously turned to the side. "How are you this evening?"

"I'm fine," she muttered as she waved him through.

Jamie handed the woman his card and stood at attention. She studied him for a moment, then lowered the card without a word, and nodded. He and Gabe rounded the corner and headed up the long ramp to the food service area. The place was packed.

'So this is when people come here to eat,' Jamie thought to himself.

The rest of the group had fanned out to various food lines. Jamie left Gabe and wandered over to get a sandwich. He grabbed a tray and took a place in line, slowly arching his neck around as he watched people streaming into the cafeteria. He was growing accustomed to the polar extremes of the student body: beside grungy, paint-covered art students, finely groomed preppy business majors held hands with their significant others. Socially inept computer engineers stared down at brown plastic trays, not looking up, not moving a muscle, as though studying a line of code engraved in the ancient platters. Jamie was watching just such an individual at the salad bar, carefully selecting the perfect Saran-wrap-entombed jello, when he saw the girl from his Media and the Mind class walking by in the back of the room. Jamie turned his head to watch her pass, just as Fritz came up beside him.

"Don't get the grilled cheese."

"What?" Jamie was annoyed, trying to peer around him. "Why not?"

"Just trust me, man. It's bad. Get something else."

"Okay."

"You still down for the party tonight?"

"Oh yeah, I forgot all about it. Yeah, I'm totally down."

"All right. Well, you and I have been given a special mission. Top secret. High priority."

"What?"

"Beer duty."

"What, we have to serve it?"

"No, we have to get it. Don't worry, I'm twenty-one. But, I need help picking it up in my car."

"How much beer are we getting?"

"Couple kegs."

Jamie didn't want to do it.

"You know, I'm only eighteen."

"That's not even an issue. This is an honor. The brothers usually fight over who gets the chance to pick it up each week."

"Yeah, I'm sure they do."

"Unfortunately, they're all busy making preparations for tonight's festivities. Can you help us out?"

No sense getting off on the wrong foot.

"Yeah, not a problem."

"Cool man."

Jamie glanced around, wondering where that girl had gone. Ah well, he'd see her in class on Monday. He and Fritz made their way through the line, then headed to a long table by the windows, where the rest of their floor was seated. They found room at the end. The table was in a debate regarding the merits of the Matt Groening television canon. Everyone seemed to agree that between *The Simpsons* and *Futurama,* Homer and company had the upper hand, but the real issue was whether or not *Futurama* was "for shit," as Steve put it, or whether it was a sometimes funny show, but just lacking when compared to its predecessor, as Nick seemed to think. Jamie looked at Nick for a moment, and decided he was most definitely the target audience for *Futurama*. The guy was a monochromatic double for Martin Scorcese. Everything, from his flannel shirt to his khakis to his Vans sneakers, was a medium beige. Not too bright, not too dark, sort of a sandstone chameleon outfit. Jamie glanced down at the kid's tray, noting that every food item he had selected matched his clothing ensemble. Even the *tray* matched. He spoke in a sort of high-pitched voice that sounded, well, exactly like Martin Scorsese. Jamie wasn't an expert on the two shows under discussion, but he was curious to hear this guy's viewpoint, as it promised to be an illuminating look at more than just his perspective on a mainstream TV program, but also a glimpse into the mind of a man whose brain seemed to process only one color. Yet before Nick could complete his argument, Steve began bellowing over him, growing louder and louder.

"What the hell are you *talking* about?! That show is terrible!"

"All I'm saying," Nick started, "is that it has some funny moments."

"It sucks!"

"It isn't supposed to be compared to the other show, it's just trying to exist on it's own-"

"It's terrible. If you have to *try* to enjoy something, then that means it sucks. IT. SUCKS."

Nick made a move as if to speak again, then sat there with his mouth partially open. He turned his head, picked up a brown sandwich, and began eating quietly.

"Steve's a real asshole." Fritz said to Jamie out of the corner of his mouth.

"So I gather."

Fritz sighed heavily. "Next they'll start up the great Mac vs. PC argument. They haven't jumped into that one in a while now."

Jamie looked around the table. Gabe and Will were deep in discussion next to Nick. Vicky was talking with Teresa a few seats away. Arlin and Vanessa were carrying on their mix of fighting and foreplay as they tussled over the remainder of a Belgian waffle, then began feeding it to each other in sticky finger-fulls, their faces becoming dripping masks of maple syrup.

*Sickening.*

"Any questions about the rest of the floor?" Fritz asked.

"Anything else I should know?" Jamie responded.

"Well, I can give you a one or two sentence profile of each if you like."

"Sounds good."

"Will and Gabe are roommates, both film majors. Arlin and Vanessa are sexaholics-"

"Yep, heard that from Gabe on the way over."

"Word gets around fast. I hope you have thick walls." Fritz muttered. "Vicky wants to be Oprah. Nick is a software engine. Nuff said. Oh, and Teresa is a nymphomaniac. She's screwed around with most guys on the floor."

"Oh really? "Jamie perked up. " Have you slept with her?"

Fritz smiled and picked up his Jello-O cup. "No comment."

Jamie glanced down the table, seeing Will look away from the conversation. Jamie turned to follow Will's gaze. The girl from Media and the Mind was taking her tray to the exit. Will shot his hand up, waving to her. She turned at the last moment, giving him an absentminded wave in return and started to turn away, only, at the last minute she saw Jamie. Their eyes locked for a millisecond, and she stopped, turned around, and came back to the table

\* \* \*

She wasn't going to talk to him. She felt bad about it, but hanging out with a guy for two nights in a row, when she had no desire to date him, well, it was starting to take its toll, especially when she could hear her roommate having mind-blowing, tantric, Kama Sutra sex in the next room. Kelli prided herself on not being the girl who ditches decent guys in search of something better, but tonight, she really needed more than a 50s comedy and several hours of uncomfortable silence and pleading eyes. She still didn't know how to finagle her way out

of this situation, so she was just gonna absentmindedly
wave to him on her way out, then not answer her phone
or come to the door if he stopped by later. You know,
be grown up and mature about the situation. Then Kelli
noticed the guy from class sitting at Will's table. What's
more, he was watching her with obvious fascination. It
might cost her another night, but the time could pay off
in heavy dividends in the near future. She walked over
to the table, feeling Jamie's eyes on her. She had to make
this quick. Just go over, exchange a few words, and get
out of there. Keep that air of mystery, but establish some
approachability with the mystery guy at the table.

It was quick and painless. Yes, they would hang out
again, Will had a DVD with a "real nice print" of *One,
Two, Three*, he'd stop by around ten. She thought she'd
handled it nicely. Short and sweet, with just enough
detachment to keep herself interesting. Maybe a tad too
theatrical with her departure, flipping her hair to one side
with a bit too much force, but she'd recovered with a nice
sway in her step, and a knowing glance over her shoulder.

She replayed the scene in her mind. The feeling
of his gaze, the eye contact as she walked away. Damn.
He was hot. Muscular and compact, but with a funny
glimmer in his brown eyes. A buff guy who still
understood all the jokes. But, what was the deal with that
hat?

\* \* \*

The girl rounded the corner by the exit, and Jamie
dropped his fork on his plate. There was no mistaking

that look she'd given him. He grabbed his tray and stood up.

" What do you say we get going?"

Fritz looked up at him as Jamie started up the aisle. By the time he'd tossed his tray onto the conveyor belt at the exit and run down the stairs, the girl was gone. Jamie stood in the lobby, looking from side to side, then headed for the door. The courtyard in front of the building was empty. She had disappeared.

Fritz came out the door a moment later, looking irritated.

"What was that all about?"

Jamie looked from side to side desperately, then threw his hands in the air. "Just getting ready to party, man. Just getting ready to party."

"That's what I like to hear, kid!"

\* \* \*

They'd arrived at the location of Fritz's "beer hookup" around 8:30. The guy's home was essentially a small, well-rotted shack behind the liquor store on Jefferson Avenue, the four-lane street which ran past the RIT entrance. The building was a white cinderblock structure, with a well worn, moss-striated roof. The eaves sagged from years of snow and neglect. The windows were filled with signs for Labatt Blue, Saranac, and Bud. Sun-faded cardboard cutouts of volley ball models stood pressed against the glass, happily hoisting foamy mugs of bleached-out brew. Fritz drove around the side of the building, parking his enormous '74 Cutless in the back to "keep the cops from seeing us."

"I thought you were twenty one," Jamie asked.

"I am. I just don't want someone to see us loading up a couple of kegs and driving back to campus."

After several bangs on the shack's door, they were greeted by an enormously obese man in a skin tight undershirt. At first, Jamie had mistaken the t-shirt for a severe farmer's tan, before realizing it was a garment so form-fitting it had become a sort of a fish belly-colored second skin. The fact that the man answered the door brandishing a Sherlock Holmes pipe and a glass of red wine momentarily threw him for a loop. Jamie blinked, struggling to reconcile the dapper accoutrements with their slovenly owner.

What Fritz had described as a "couple kegs" proved to be four, and since their dealer was three sheets to the wind, they had no help moving the enormous metal cylinders to Fritz's car. After several false starts, they managed to maneuver two of the kegs into the trunk, and the other two in the back seat, strapping them in like passengers, and setting a paper bag full of plastic cups on top of each. Fritz thought the bags made the kegs look like people seated in the back, Jamie felt they made them extremely conspicuous as they turned out onto Jefferson and took back roads on their way back to campus.

"Is there a law about an underage driver transporting this much booze?"

"Probably, but it's leftover from pilgrim days. Besides, any cop we pass will just think we have a couple of fat asses in the back seat."

"And a couple of dumbasses in the front."

Jamie glanced in the rear view mirror, eyeing the tall, square "heads" on each keg. What on earth was this guy talking about? Unless Danny Devito was cast as Frankenstein's monster, these short, rotund little passengers with tall, square heads looked like nothing more than beer kegs they had no business transporting onto a dry campus.

After a tense back-road drive, during which they passed two campus security cars, they made it to the Phi Psi house. They pulled into the parking lot for the Perkins Student Apartments and Fritz flipped off the headlights, letting the Cutless coast to a stop beside a footpath that disappeared around the side of one building. He gave the horn a long honk and two quick blasts, then they sat in the silence for a moment, until several guys in football jerseys came running around the side.

Fritz got out of the car, and Jamie followed suit. The frat guys were all built, and all seemed to tower over Jamie. He glanced around uncomfortably, eyeing the pack of guys that walked toward them through the dark. As they came closer, he noticed that each had a nicknamed emblazoned across his jersey. A thin, red haired guy named "Big Red," pushed a hand truck in front of him. Fritz gave the guy a high five.

"Hey, what's up man?" Fritz turned to Jamie. "This is Chris, Doug's roommate from the floor."

"Hey," Jamie said.

"What's up?" Chris replied with a head nod.

Two other guys, "Ron Jeremy" and "Slick Willy,"

appeared. Jamie didn't ponder the origins of the monikers.

"These guys are Joe and and Matt." Fritz continued.

The brothers grunted their hellos and shook Jamie's hand. He fumbled with their complicated handshake maneuvers, but no one seemed to notice. In a few minutes "Ron" and "Willy" had unloaded the kegs and rolled them around the side of the building. Music poured from the back windows of one of the apartments, growing consistently louder. Fritz handed Jamie the keys and pointed him to a spot at the end of the lot.

"You sure you want me driving your car, man?"

"Don't worry about it," Fritz said. "Just lock it up, we'll be walking back tonight, trust me."

With that, Fritz turned and headed off with the rest of the guys. Jamie started the car and slowly shifted it into gear. The car bucked backward with a screech. Jamie stomped on the brakes, then ever so slowly backed out into the parking lot. A few more jolting turns and gear changes and the car drifted to a stop at the end of the lot. He rolled up the windows, locked the doors, and jogged back to the apartments, feeling more self-conscious by the minute. A group of girls walked out in front of him as he started down the pathway. He watched them as they continued up ahead. One of them was a tall blond. Jamie's eye wandered to her tiny, sashaying waist. She was gorgeous. The other two were equally attractive, one with Asian features, the other a curly-haired redhead. They were dressed to party, in form-fitting jeans, tank tops, and heavy eye makeup. Jamie focused on the blond, feeling a shiver of excitement. This was his first college party. Let the games begin.

The girls continued on up ahead, and he realized they were headed for the same party. The music from the apartment drowned out their laughter. They got to the steps at the entrance of the building, where a group of frat guys stood, leaning against the railing, some of them smoking cigarettes, all of them holding plastic beer cups. The girls approached the steps, instantly greeted with smiles. One guy reached out, grabbing the blond girl around the waist and pulling her toward him. She turned and lunged at him eagerly, grabbing his shoulders as the two of them fell back into the bushes. So much for that one, Jamie thought to himself. The other girls, seeing their friend disappear, headed into the apartment. The frat brothers turned, watching admiringly as the girls walked away. Jamie approached the steps quietly, barely noticed as he headed inside.

There were apartments on either side of the lobby, and a stairway straight ahead that led up to two additional units. Partygoers were wandering in and out of the open doors. The place was hot from the closely packed bodies. Jamie headed into the first door on the right, shoving past a line of revelers as they held their plastic beer cups overhead. He made it through the living room and into the kitchen, where he saw Fritz standing at a table, a keg tap in one hand, filling cups. Jamie worked his way against the tide and stopped at the keg. The music was deafening, the cigarette smoke thick. Fritz shouted something to him as he approached, but Jamie couldn't hear a word he said. Fritz slapped him on the back, handed him a beer overflowing with foam. Jamie nodded and stepped back. He leaned against a wall and took a sip of his drink. He was gonna have to get drunk. Very drunk.

Fritz leaned forward, screaming into Jamie's ear. "There are some fucking hotties here tonight!!"

"Oh yeah!" Jamie agreed.

Fritz bobbed his head, his body language making it clear that he couldn't hear a word Jamie was saying, and it wasn't important either way.

Jamie threw his head back and chugged his beer, then he went back for another. He started to rock on his feet, waiting for the alcohol to kick in, needing to loosen up. Fritz motioned towards the door and led Jamie through the crowd, laughing and joking with his fraternity brothers as they went along. Jamie chugged his second beer, slowly feeling the dizzy, numb sensation he was looking for. He recognized a girl walking past them into the apartment as they stepped out onto the front steps. It was the girl he'd seen the first night at the Commons, the Courtney Cox lookalike.

Fritz spotted her and smiled. "Yo, Erica!"

She flashed him a sexy smile as she continued into the apartment. "Hey, Fritz."

Jamie spun around, the room swirling in his peripheral vision. "You know that girl?"

"We all know that girl, dude."

"I was checking her out at the Commons the other night," Jamie shouted, sounding a bit too shrill for his own comfort.

Fritz smiled. "Yeah. I know. You like her."

"Hell, yeah I do."

"You wanna get with her?"

Jamie looked at him, taking a pensive sip from his beer. "Yeah, of course I would. Why?"

"Say no more man."

"What are you talking about?"

Fritz just laughed and bummed a smoke off of one of his fraternity brothers. He took a drag and again made the round of introductions. The guys nodded their heads at Jamie and continued talking amongst themselves. Jamie leaned back against the door, downing his drink, and trying his best to look casual. He gazed up at the moon through the bare branches overhead and thought of that girl Erica, his blood pumping with nervous excitement.

The night drifted by. Fritz made the rounds, leaving Jamie standing alone to start awkward conversations with whoever was nearby. He eyed the girls filing past, giggling in groups or shrieking with laughter as they were carried off by fraternity brothers, who hoisted them over the crowds and disappeared into back bedrooms. Jamie watched two girls who stood alone, looking uncomfortable as they brushed hair out of their eyes and sipped their drinks, all the while scanning the crowd. Fritz appeared, handed them freshly filled cups off brew and patted Jamie on the back.

"You having fun yet?" Fritz asked Jamie as he floated past.

"Oh yeah," Jamie said. "Don't worry about me."

Time was passing in that manner unique to college

parties, and Jamie found himself in a happy, drunken state, in which talking becomes fast and loose, and coherence is not an issue. He stood outside the building with Fritz and his friends, rattling off jokes, and, judging from the laughter, successfully cracking up the other brothers.

Fritz slapped him on the back. "Is this the guy or what?"

Jamie laughed along with them, but he couldn't remember what he had just said. Then he turned, and saw Erica walking past. She peeked over her shoulder at him as she slipped inside. Jamie looked over at Fritz, who was watching with a smirk. He hoisted his cup, downed the rest of his beer, and handed it to Jamie.

"Why don't you go get us a couple more beers man?"

"Okay…" Jamie said curiously.

He headed into the apartment, stumbling around the crowd, whose ranks were thinning now as the people that weren't making out in the shadows began to pair up and head off to their private destinations. Jamie staggered into the kitchen and refilled Fritz's glass. The keg was running out. He was just starting to fill his own cup when the spigot started burping foam. Just as well, he was wasted. He turned for the door, but got caught behind a group of guys who were doing tequila shots off their girlfriends' chests. As he stood behind the other onlookers, watching the guys lick salt from the girls' sweaty skin, he felt a pair of hands sliding down his shoulders. He spun around, startled, and found himself face to face with Erica, who pushed him against the wall. Beer sloshed onto his pants and down his shirt. She glanced down, smiling deviously.

"Is that for me?" she asked, already wrapping her fingers around the cup.

"Sure," Jamie replied.

She took the beer with an impish smile, chugged it, and threw the cup against the wall as she lunged at him. She kissed him roughly, her tongue in his mouth, her teeth on his lips. Jamie struggled to keep up. The room was spinning, the music drowning out the sounds of everyone around them. He felt himself getting aroused. Then, just as suddenly, he felt Erica's fingers running over the bulge in his jeans. Next thing he knew she was whispering in his ear, and leading him into the bathroom.

Erica pulled him inside, closing the door behind them. The bathroom was dark, the only light coming from a red nightlight over the sink. Erica pushed him against the counter and stood back, watching him for a moment. She stepped forward and kissed him again, her tongue lingering in the corner of his mouth before she bit down on his lower lip. He flinched and she stopped, looking into his eyes with a devilish sparkle. She slipped her hands up to his face, running her fingers over the stubble, then she slid them up to his hat. She started to play with the edge of the cap, slipping her fingertips under the band.

"Why do you still have this on?" she whispered.

Jamie put his hand on her wrist, keeping her from removing the hat. He kissed her and she lowered her hands, running them down his back and around to the front. He felt her fingers fumbling with the button on his jeans, then she stopped, changing direction as she reached down and pulled her beer-soaked shirt up over her head. She threw the shirt on the floor, and stood back, letting Jamie size up her bare breasts. He noticed her hard nipples, was about to comment, but she was already on top of him, pulling off his shirt and pressing her chest against his. Then he felt her hand slip down his jeans. His breath caught in his throat as she slid the zipper down on his pants, and he felt her hands on him. He closed his eyes as he felt her breath on his skin, when he again opened them, she was on her knees in front of him, her fingers running back and forth over his dick. He looked straight ahead, then lolled his head drunkenly to the side, his eyes locking on the glowing red nightlight over the sink. He narrowed his eyes. It was a porcelain Jesus nightlight, giving him the thumbs up and smiling at a baby held happily in the crook of his elbow. These frat guys had a weird sense off humor. Jamie stared up at the ceiling, closing his eyes, waiting for the feel of her lips on him. Then her fingers stopped moving. Jamie looked down slowly. Erica was leaning back on her feet, her face slack and pale. She stared up at him, then turned, and vomited across the bathroom floor.

* * *

It had been a long night. Will had shown up at her dorm at ten o'clock sharp. Christie and Joe had just completed one of their three hour "romantic interludes," and the sounds of their lovemaking had left

Kelli depressed and restless. She was just contemplating slipping into the bath with her vibrating rubber ducky, when the suite's doorbell rang. She walked out into the living room, relieved to see that her suite mates had slipped out for the time being. She opened the door, the sight of Will instantly pulling the rug out from under her libido.

"Ta da!" he exclaimed, holding out a DVD case.

"Wow. That's looks great," she said, taking it from his hands.

They walked into her room and slipped into their well established routine. She turned on the TV and put the disc into the player. He pulled two beers from his cargo pants and pried the caps off on the edge of her dresser, while Kelli grabbed several pillows out of the closet, and threw them on the floor. She gave Will the blue one. He liked the blue one.

Jesus.

She felt like slapping herself in the head. Was this like a marriage or something?

They'd been friends since their freshman year, but never anything more. Will had long established that he wished to change that, but it was not meant to be.

Until September, Kelli had been dating a guy from back home, and they'd carried on a long distance relationship for the better part of eighteen months. At the start of the year, as she was leaving for Rochester, he'd told her he was tired of making the trip, that he was starting to see someone else. Oddly, it hadn't fazed her. She enjoyed his visits, but they were never a perfect match. After the first year, their sex life had begun a slow but steady slide into limbo. They'd get around to it once a week when he came up to visit her at school, but by the end of her freshman year, the visits had begun stretching from every weekend, to every other weekend, to once a month. By the time she'd come home for the summer, they were living all but separate lives. Her first weekend back, it had all felt normal again. She'd skipped out on her folks and stayed at his house for the weekend, where they'd all but devoured each other, but it was short lived. The rest of the summer their lovemaking was sporadic as the tension between them grew. By September the end was in sight, and when he stopped by her house the night before she went back to school, she'd known it was coming. Truth be told, she was relieved, excited by the possibility of meeting someone new. Finding something better.

Of course, once Will picked up on her lack of weekend guests, his visits to the suite became a daily routine. By October, he'd all but roped her into weekly movie marathons in her room, or trips to the Little Theater downtown. Since they were both film majors, going to the movies had always been a regular part of their friendship, but somewhere along the line it had begun bordering on something else. Kelli wasn't sure how to get out of it, but she knew a deadline was fast approaching. This pattern of several movies a weekend, and zero romance, was driving her through the roof. Unfortunately, though she had a more than willing male companion every weekend, she knew it wouldn't work, and she had no desire to give it a try. So, they watched movies, each of them glancing at the other out of the corner of their eyes. Will wondering how he would make his move, Kelli wondering how she would dodge it.

Rather than *One, Two, Three*, Will had gone with *Sabrina*. A shrewd choice. Had he chosen the 1995 remake (and who would?), Will's intentions would have been all too clear, and pathetic, but the selection of the 1954 original carried layers of hidden meaning. They were both films geeks; he would undoubtedly have weighed all the factors in his mind, just as Kelli found herself doing as she sipped her beer and watched the opening credits. Whereas the remake with Harrison Ford and Greg Kinnear wreaked of the shameless attempt to fashion a modern date movie from a romantic comedy, the version with William Holden and Humphrey Bogart was not just more complex and believable, but a simple film classic. They were both Billy Wilder fans, which almost invited them to ignore the plot of a woman choosing the diamond in the rough over the playful cad, but she knew of Will's fondness for Humphrey Bogart. Half his film quotes came from *Casablanca*, and the subtext of Audrey Hepburn making the unlikely choice and going with the stodgier, more serious suitor was hard to ignore. She and Will were reaching the danger zone; he'd be showing up with *When Harry Met Sally* any day now, and when that happened, they would have to have a talk.

She knew how the night would end. Once the movie was over, they'd sit there for a minute or two, til she got up and turned on the lights. She'd see him watching her out of the corner of his eye, wondering how to proceed next. Then she would go over to her bed and sit down with her back against the wall. They'd talk a little bit about the movie, with many long, meaningful pauses generously dispersed throughout the exchange, then, they'd either sit there, locked in a battle of wills until one of them fell asleep, or pretended to, or she'd fake a yawn, exaggerate exhaustion, and tell him she had work in the morning. This had been her tactic for the better part of two months. Once in September she had honestly fallen asleep, and had awoken to find Will curled up on the floor, pretending to be passed out, yet when she quietly turned her head a few minutes later, she caught his eyes quickly snapping shut. She lay awake for the rest of the night, fearing the moment he would summon the courage to boldly climb into bed beside her. In the end, she'd gotten up around 5:30, snuck into the bathroom to change, and snuck out of the suite, leaving a note saying she'd gone to the library to work on a paper. She'd actually spent four hours drinking coffee at Gracie's and reading, before sneaking back to her room around eleven. Happy to see that Will had left, she'd gone back to sleep. Neither of them had ever mentioned the incident.

They'd been about halfway through the movie when she sensed Will glancing at her now and then. She'd been considering asking him about the guy in the hat who she'd seen with Will's group at dinner, but thought it best to wait. She knew he'd only get quiet, making things more awkward.

Kelli began stifling exaggerated yawns, preparing for the sleepy performance to come.

* * *

Fritz slipped on the icy sidewalk, falling into a frozen mudpuddle and laughing drunkenly. He and Jamie were walking back to the dorms in the dark, having left the car back at the parking lot. Jamie went over to help him to his feet, almost going down with him as their feet slid in circles on the frozen ground.

"Oh shit," Fritz gasped.

"Come on, the last thing we need is to both crack our heads open."

"Wait- wait- wait- wait- wait- wait- wait!" Fritz fired off as he held his hand up to keep Jamie at bay. "I can get up by myself." He dropped his head in concentration, summoned his strength for one sober moment, and pushed himself up off the ground with his fists. He stood with a very slight stagger, and threw his arm around Jamie's shoulder.

"You okay there, buddy?' Jamie asked him.

"No," Fritz slurred. "No I'm not. I disappointed for you man. I thought Erica would hook you up."

"So you knew she was gonna do that?"

"What? Puke?" Fritz's face scrunched up in dismay. "Hell no!"

"No, I mean the other thing. Did you tell her I liked her?"

"Yeah, I thought she'd help you relax. That's like… her thing, you know man? She's like the samurai of blowjobs."

Jamie wasn't sure what to make of this.

"The samurai of blowjobs, huh?"

Fritz waved his arm like a pinwheel. "I'm telling you, she's the best." He staggered on for a moment. "Ah well, maybe next time."

"No, don't worry about it, man. I don't really wanna hook up with a girl like that."

Fritz turned to him, puzzled.

"But that's the beauty of it. She's not looking for anything more. She just loves giving em."

"Really, I'm fine."

They were trudging up the hill towards their dorm. Jamie looked at his watch. It was two in the morning.

"Dude, how we gonna get in?"

"It's cool," Fritz answered. "Just be cool. If we see anyone from campus safety, we just…act…sober…" He paused dramatically, his hands held aloft in cautious glee.

"They're gonna know we're drunk."

"No man. No. Just relax."

Jamie looked around the quad. It seemed pretty quiet, but every so often a car drove by on the road that looped around past the dorms. He expected to see a campus safety car at any moment.

"Trust me," Fritz continued. "It's a piece of cake."

Apparently it was, though Jamie felt sure they'd be stopped at any moment. They arrived at the building, fumbled with their keys, and stomped up the stairs to their floor. Fritz was by far the drunker of the two, leaning against the smooth walls in the hallway as his feet carried him down the hall. They stopped at his room and he opened the door.

"Hold on a second buddy," he said, holding up his

index finger. "Just let me grab something, just let me..."

Fritz trailed off as he disappeared in his room. Jamie continued down the hall to the water fountain. A moment later Fritz staggered down after him, holding out a couple off white caplets.

"Here, take these."

"What are they?" Jamie asked.

"Vitamin C. Trust me man, they'll help with your hangover tomorrow."

Jamie accepted the pills and swallowed them with a gulp of water from the fountain. Fritz did the same, then leaned back against the wall as he slid to the floor. Jamie looked down at him.

"You sure you're okay man?"

"I'm fine. I'm fine," Fritz slurred. "Sit down for a while."

"You don't want to sleep?"

"Nahhhhhh. I'm not tired. Let's talk."

As he spoke, Fritz's head lolled from side to side, heavy with fatigue. Jamie hesitated, then sat across from him, reclining against the opposite wall. Fritz stared down at the floor for a minute, then slowly looked up, locking Jamie in his gaze. Jamie looked at him apprehensively. Fritz stared right back.

"Why did you have that operation?" Fritz pointed to Jamie's head. "What was wrong with you?"

Jamie hesitated, wondering if Fritz would even remember their conversation tomorrow. He sat with his mouth poised to speak, debating, then decided what the hell?

" I have a pretty severe case of Parkinson's Disease, one that just kept getting worse. My doc decided we had to try something new."

"And what was that?"

"Implanting a sort of pacemaker in my brain to help clear up the signals in my head."

"Parkinson's is the one that makes you shake around, right?" Fritz asked.

Jamie nodded his head. "Among other things."

"Wow."

Fritz looked up at Jamie's hat, then turned and looked down the hallway suspiciously. Jamie watched him with a half smile.

"Does it work?" Fritz asked conspiratorily.

"It seems to so far." Jamie replied. "I'm here aren't I?"

"How does it get power?"

"Well, it sounds funny, but it has something like a fifty year battery."

Fritz raised a wavering finger in the air, a look of drunken disbelief crossing his face as he pointed at Jamie's head "You're telling me you've got, like, a *Duracell* up there?"

Jamie laughed. 'Yep."

"Damn." Fritz stared at him again. "Tell *that* story to chicks. That's a foolproof way to get yourself laid."

"Yeah, right."

"Just tell 'em it powers your vibrating feature!"

"Well, it didn't work any wonders tonight."

"Whatever!" Fritz waved his hand in impatience.

"She's a different story. And you didn't even try it yet. Girls will think that's cool. But-" He stopped short.

"What?" Jamie asked.

"Are you bullshitting me? You're not gonna go crazy like *The Terminator* or anything are you?"

"No, I'm not. And I'm not bullshitting you either."

"That is so fucking cool!"

The two of them sat there for a moment. Jamie was far more sober than Fritz, but even he was starting to feel the weight of the night's activities. His eyes were drooping. Then he heard footsteps coming up the stairs, and turned to see Will trudge around the corner looking extremely disgruntled. He was holding a DVD in his hand. Fritz turned to the hallway and shouted to him, his voice echoing in the empty corridor..

"Yo, Will! What's happening?"

Jamie kicked him, and Fritz caught himself, lowering his voice to a whisper.

"What's happening man?" he whispered.

"Not much," Will muttered as he continued down the hall.

Fritz bobbed his head back towards Jamie.

"Girl troubles?"

Jamie nodded knowingly. "Hey listen... About that implant thing. Can you try to keep that to yourself?"

Fritz nodded his head. "Of course man. Of course." He held up his hand. "My bird is my wand."

Jamie blinked but decided to let that pass.

'I appreciate it," he replied.

Fritz slumped back against the wall, his eyes

fluttering shut.

"Let's call it a night." Jamie said as he staggered to his feet.

"Sounds good to me."

Fritz started to stand, then stumbled to the side. Jamie caught his arm and helped him to his feet. Fritz walked a wiggling line to the door of his room, then spun around, saluted Jamie, and closed the door. Jamie stood in the hallway for a moment. He was alone again. He walked down the hall to the bathroom. The bright fluorescent lights stung his drunken eyes. He blinked a couple of times, adjusting to the flickering lights, then walked over to the sink and splashed water in his face. He looked up at his reflection, then reached up, pulled off his cap, and studied the long, dark scars. He wondered if Fritz had believed him. Even to him, the implant sounded a bit farfetched. He lifted a handful of water to his head, running his fingers over the bumpy surface, feeling the water trickling down the sides of his face.

\* \* \*

Fritz's vitamin C capsules eased the pain of the next day's hangover, but something, most likely the massive quantities of alcohol, had played strange tricks of the mind all night. Jamie woke constantly, struggling to discern between a steady stream of nightmares and reality. It didn't help that each dream sequence began with Jamie being jolted awake, obscuring the line between sleep and awakening . His first impulse was to fear for the implant -- An infection or rejection was poisoning his mind, forcing disturbing and unwanted imagery to the surface. No. It was just the alcohol. He was hung over. He had to remember that, he was *just* hung over.

The first of the nightmares came soon after he fell asleep. He'd gone into the bathroom, washed his face, then stumbled into his room and collapsed face down on the bed. A few hours later, in his dream, he awoke to a soft scratching at the door of his room. There was a high-pitched sound in the background, a sort of wailing moan, then the rumble of someone banging his fists on a wooden surface. In the dream, Jamie sat up in bed, walked over to the door, and saw a man's shadow moving back and forth in the dim rectangle of light that spread out across the carpet. Jamie looked through the peephole, but saw nothing. He stood there for a moment, his hand on the knob, bracing himself to throw it open. His heart beat heavily in his chest, his breathing was dry and painful, the taste of rust rose up in the back of his throat. When he finally swept the door open, the hallway was empty. He stepped out into the corridor and looked around. No one. Jamie had awoken from this dream disoriented, but quickly fell back to sleep.

In the second dream, he again awoke to the sounds of scratching on the door. He stood, and again saw the same restless, pacing shadow. This time he was angry. He lunged for the door and ripped it open. Again, the hallway was empty. He stepped outside, looking from side to side. The lights were dim. All the doors were closed. Silence. Jamie hesitated, then went back into his room, closing the door behind him. He leaned forward slowly as he closed the door, peeking through the peephole at the empty hallway. No sooner did his eye focus on the space outside, than the face of a man, his features obscured by a black cloak, lunged at him through the peephole. The man's icy blue eyes glared at him through the glass, twitching wildly. The moaning noise returned, undulating through the door as the man tried to shove it open. Jamie smashed his shoulder against the heavy door, trying to close it, but the man's strength all but overpowered him. Jamie heard another strange howling, grunting noise, and suddenly realized it was the sound of his own guttural terror. He took a final lunge and slammed the door shut. He was just reaching for the lock with his finger, when he awoke, letting out a final gasp as he sat bolt upright in his bed.

The last dream, though far less violent, had really spooked him. Jamie's eyes had popped open. A mist of sweat ran down the sides of his face. Again he heard the moaning and the sounds of scratching, but when his eyes flicked towards the door, there was no pacing shadow at the bottom. He tried to sit up, but his body wouldn't respond. He tried to turn his head to the door, but it wouldn't move. The room became silent. His breathing, the scratching, the moans, everything stopped, like a conductor had drawn a finger across his throat, silencing each element of the assembled mass. Jamie felt blood pumping in his chest, pulsing at his temples. His eyes scanned the room. Moonlight shone in through the edges of the curtains, casting bands of light and dark over his bed and down the walls of the room. Then he saw a movement in the shadows, someone stepping out from the corner, dressed entirely in black, walking towards him. Jamie lay there, transfixed. Then the wailing began, and he saw the figure's eyes, icy blue, almost white, staring at him as they came closer and closer and…

Jamie had woken for the last time after that dream. By then his room had grown lighter with the rising sun. He lay on his back, afraid to move, for fear his body would prove unwilling to cooperate. His eyes went to the clock on his desk. It was just after ten. His eyes scanned the room. Nothing but bare walls, scattered clothing, and books. He took a deep breath, then sat up, swinging his legs over the edge of the bed and crouching with his elbows on his knees, his head in his hands. He clenched his toes, digging into the industrial carpet on the floor, feeling the bumpy concrete beneath. His fingers clutched fistfuls of his hair, wiry and course. His skin felt clammy and damp, his entire body was coated in a film of dried sweat. Jamie stood and paced the room, stretching his arms, feeling his muscles pulling taught against his bones. He scooped up his shower bucket and a change of clothes and left the room.

A group of girls walked past him as he headed down the hallway. The television murmured from the lounge around the corner. One or two doors were propped open. It was the first time Jamie had seen any signs of life in the morning. Of course, it was the first time he'd gotten up later than seven since he'd arrived on campus. He staggered into the bathroom and stepped into the shower stall closest to the wall, locking the door behind him. He stripped off his clothing, running his hands over his arms and chest, still feeling detached from his body after the dream. He looked down at his limp penis, and remembered the aborted blowjob from the previous night. He hadn't had sex in over a year. One of the many areas of his life that had been cut off. He turned on the hot water, absentmindedly cupping his dick with one hand as he tested the water temperature with the other. He stepped under the stream of hot water and ran his hands through his hair, stepping forward to let the hot water spray into his face. He breathed in the steam and leaned against the wall with one hand.

He considered going to the gym or running, but didn't think he'd be up for it. It probably wasn't the best idea drinking so much; he obviously couldn't handle it as well as he used to. The dreams were his body telling him to take it easy. He soaped himself up and stood under the coursing hot water. He thought back to the last dream, to being paralyzed in his bed. That had actually happened to him once, right before his mother took him to Dr. Price's office for the first time. He'd kept the problem in the art studio to himself for close to a month, that is, until the incident with the alarm clock.

He'd stayed up late the night before, sketching in his notebook and watching Letterman and Conan until close to 2 a.m. He'd always wondered if fatigue might have triggered it. When the alarm went off the next morning he'd tried to roll over to switch it off, but he couldn't move. Just as in the dream, his body wouldn't listen. He was completely paralyzed. The alarm had continued buzzing, growing louder and louder until he heard his mother's voice calling for him to get up. He heard her footsteps clomping down the hallway toward his room. Then the tremors began. He'd finally managed to turn his head towards the door when his body began to shiver, only it didn't pass like the chill from a draft or that first gust of fall: it continued rattling his body. He could hear the sheets on his bed shifting and whipping back and forth. His mother stepped into the room, framed by the doorway, as her jaw fell open. Jamie had been unable to move, simply looking up at her as she became hysterical. That was the first day he met Dr. Price, and the first time he ever heard of early onset Parkinson's. All in all, it had been a pretty shitty day.

Now he stood in the shower, breathing in the hot steam, imagining it billowing into his lungs. He pictured curls of vapor swirling through his skull, relaxing the tissues in his head. Then he closed his eyes, and tried to envision the implant, buried deep, deep inside his brain -- he saw it suspended in place, and tried to picture the tiny metal barbs clenching the tissues, all the while sending out little jolts of electricity, keeping him from going apeshit. He opened his eyes suddenly, turned off the water, and dried himself quickly. After dressing, he realized he'd forgotten to bring a hat or sweatshirt with him. The scars were always pink and swollen after a shower. He stepped out of the stall, picked up his things, and hurried down the hallway, back to his room, before anyone had a chance to notice him.

The rest of the weekend passed strangely. Jamie

stayed in his room for most of the morning, trying unsuccessfully to do some drawing, before throwing his sketchbook against the wall in disgust, and going out with his camera in the afternoon. He came back in the evening, just as the group from the floor was heading out to the Commons for dinner. The food was a nice change of pace from Gracie's, and he had a chance to talk with a couple more people from the floor. That guy Nick, who had had the *Futurama* vs. *Simpsons* debate with Steve on Friday, turned out to be a pretty humorous guy, albeit it a tad extreme. As Gabe put it "He's a software engineer... Boy is he ever a software engineer."

Apparently the highlight of the last four years of Nick's life was an event that took place the previous spring, when Bill Gates was at a technology conference in Europe. As Gates and his entourage were entering a hotel before a lecture, an unseen protestor had managed to slip past security, stepping out from behind a column, and smacking ole Bill in the face with a cream pie. Someone had captured the entire event on video and posted it online, and according to Nick, it was the greatest piece of news footage ever recorded. Just recounting the look on Mr. Gates' face, and his enraged rant as he walked inside, scraping pie filling from his glasses, sent Nick into gales of laughter. Then, in a grave voice, he'd confessed that the greatest drawback to the video was that it had forced him to install Microsoft Windows on his computer in order to play the clip back. Afterwards Jamie had turned to Gabe for explanation, and learned that Nick was an apostle of the church of Linux, a free operating system created in the

80's by some computer student in Europe.

"Don't even *ask* me how I learned the history of Linux." Gabe muttered. "Nick despises Microsoft with a passion. If you want to get him started, ask him about either Microsoft Windows or Pepsi. He'll be ranting for at least an hour. He loves Pepsi. He *hates* Windows."

"What about Apple?" Jamie asked.

"He hates them, too," Gabe replied. Then he shrugged his shoulders. "I dunno. Like I said, he's a software engineer."

Jamie nodded his head, he'd have to chew that one over. He glanced around the table and asked Gabe more questions about the group. Gabe and Will were both Juniors, as were Vicky and Nick. Arlin and Fritz were in their fourth years of five year programs. Jamie was one of the few freshmen on the floor. Apparently there had been another one, some strange kid at the end of the hall named Elliott, who used to walk around shirtless, inviting the girls into his room for a beer.

"He was creepy," Gabe said. "Picture Elliot from *E.T.,* take off the red sweatshirt, swap the Reeses Pieces for a pack of Milwaukee's Best, and you have Elliott."

Around Halloween it turned out Elliot's seventeen year old girlfriend back home was pregnant, and he disappeared overnight. A week later some relatives arrived, packed up his stuff, and left.

Gabe seemed to have the inside scoop on everyone. Probably best to avoid the guy's questions, not reveal anything he didn't want getting out.

Someone suggested getting a movie after dinner.

Fritz, who remained under the weather from the night before, was recruited to drive to Blockbuster. When he got back from the store, Gabe and Will had lifted the lounge couches up on cinder blocks, and had hooked up an elaborate series of speakers. Apparently they'd done that a lot the previous year, but Will had been trying to hook up with a girl from his classes all fall, so the floor movie nights had been on hiatus.

"He's been pretty moody lately," Gabe said. "I think his plan went off track this weekend."

Jamie had a feeling he knew who the girl was. He looked over at Will, who was working behind the TV, a humorless expression on his face. This could get messy.

Saturday night proved to be a good time. No one drank since they were out in the lounge. Gabe had picked up the original *Star Wars* trilogy, and between installments, they would run to The Corner Store in the tunnels to grab snacks and junk food. *Return of the Jedi* wrapped up by two in the morning, and the group disbanded.

Jamie went to sleep feeling apprehensive, but there were no more nightmares. The next morning he dragged himself to the gym, then spent the rest of the day working on a class assignment. By Sunday night, people were busy working in their rooms. Nick wandered the halls, Pepsi bottle in hand, talking to anyone who left their doors open. Fritz had a big report due for his main biotechnology class, but was procrastinating, playing battle games on the computer network with Chris at the end of the hall. Jamie went into his room, closed the door, and did his assignment for Media and the Mind. Namely, he lay on his back, with his feet propped up on the wall, and pondered his career goals. Despite the implant, it looked like he'd be sticking with photography for a while longer. He looked to the corner, where his sketchbook had landed after bouncing off the wall. Maybe he'd give it a try again, but it could wait for now. He was getting ideas for his Fine Art  photography class, and thought he might do some shooting the next evening. Maybe Victor would be working at the cage and he could do his best to piss that guy off. He laughed to himself, then walked over to take his meds.

He was feeling good.

He hoped it would last.

# CHAPTER THREE
## THE MIND

The second class was always the most interesting. He got a kick out of the first meeting, but the second was when he got to see what these folks were made of, see how they thought. That was simple enough to interpret, he just took note of the students that bothered coming back.

Karl Ryan had been at this for twenty-two years, and past experience had taught him that an empty chair in the second session inevitably represented a transient student currently standing in the Registrar's office, withdrawing from his Media and the Mind course. His assignment to get stoned and ponder the future was the first of many turning points. It tended to level out the audience intellectually; those unable to see past the "sticker price" of the class, usually students returning to college after a long break from academia, had greater difficulty swallowing the prospect of such a loosely structured, admittedly "out there" method of instruction, and were usually gone by the start of the second week. Others, who saw it as a simple gut class, requiring no work or commitment, usually sat in the front row for the second session, grinning like they'd just found a signed blank check, yet they too would inevitably fade away, the level of personal analysis and theory becoming too much for them as the quarter progressed.

Then, there was the group of students that got it, the ones truly interested in considering their areas of study and analyzing what the purpose of their life's work might be. Owing to the subject matter, and the temperament of the students who stayed, Ryan usually found himself with a lecture hall full of art students. This suited him just fine, as they invariably proved themselves the most interesting individuals on campus. Filmmakers, photographers, artists, and writers, *these* were his people.

"Looking a bit more spacious in here today," he called out, as he marched into the classroom and tossed his books on the desk. There was a light wave of laughter. "The others must be out convincing their friends to sign up. Well, if they don't show, we'll chalk it up as their loss."

Jamie was sitting in the back row again. He glanced around the room. The woman in the Winnie the Pooh jacket was gone, as were the people she'd been sitting with in the previous class. Will's hot friend was back, but she'd switched seats, now sitting a couple rows in front of him. He arched his neck around for a better view. She still looked amazing. It was strange, her appeal was completely different from the women he was usually attracted to. Jenny, his high school girlfriend with the belatedly discovered penchant for bedding football all stars, had been a tall, rail-thin blond, with a classic WASP look - gorgeous by any stretch of the imagination, but, certainly not exotic. Even that girl Erica, who'd now lost all appeal, was basically normal looking – smooth skin, slightly frizzy hair, a general party-girl manner. But the girl two rows up, she had an altogether different thing going on. She was... scary. It wasn't just the dark eye makeup, or the clothing, it was the whole package. She sat in an aggressive manner, legs tensed, elbows turned outward, as if ready to spring forward at a moment's notice and rip off your head. Jamie never thought he'd feel this way, but he liked it. He watched her intently now as she listened to the lecture, chewing on the end of her pen absentmindedly. It was sexy; nothing wrong with a little oral fixation.

Professor Ryan walked up the row, moving his arm like an orchestra conductor as he spoke. "I trust you've all followed the first assignment closely, and I'm looking forward to discussing your conclusions with you today. From there, we'll just see how things go." He scanned the room, looking for the faces he had picked out during the previous session. He knew choosing favorites was officially a "no no," but over the years, Ryan had found he could tell within the first few meetings which students would keep the discussions interesting. He noted the girl in the middle of the lecture hall. She'd been in the front row last time and he'd found his eyes wandering to the patch of skin between the bottom of her shirt and the top of her low-rise jeans. He turned to her, disappointed to see there was no skin on display today. He stopped at the end of her row and she looked up at him.

"Tell me Miss-"

"Petronio," Kelli said.

"What is your major?"

"Film."

"What area of film?"

"All of it."

"All of it," Professor Ryan paused. "Meaning?"

Kelli looked at him strangely.

"Is there a specific part of the process your prefer?"

"I don't know. I like when it's done?" she said.

"So, you don't like the actual process, so much as the experience of watching the finished product."

"Yeah, I guess so."

"Why?" Ryan asked loudly.

"I like to watch how the audience reacts. See if they understand what I was trying to say?"

"Which is?'

Kelli felt like she was giving stupid answers. Her face was feeling hot.

"Well... it varies, I guess. I just want to see if my original idea comes out in the film. If it's a comedy I want people to laugh. If it's non-fiction, I want to see if I gave them enough information to understand the topic."

"So, in a lot of ways, you're involved in several different forms of communication. Do you write?"

Kelli nodded.

"Direct?"

She nodded.

"Shoot and edit-"

She smiled. "Yes."

"Wow," Ryan turned to the audience. "take note of this young lady fellas." He turned to Jamie suddenly. "And what do you do?"

Jamie coughed. "I'm a photo major."

"Are you a photo major, or a photographer?" Ryan asked.

That was a strange question. "I suppose I'm an... artist who's working in photography."

"Ooooooh, an artist. But again, not a photographer?"

Jamie hesitated. "I'm not entirely sure, actually."

"Why not a painter or a sculptor like Michelangelo?" Ryan said with a distinct edge in his voice. "It sounds like that's more the way you fancy yourself."

"I had a slight change of plans."

"Oh, I see." Ryan said sharply. "Care to elaborate?"

"No..." Jamie said.

Ryan threw up his hands in a manner or dismissal. "Fair enough," he said, as he walked down the aisle and sat atop the desk at the front of the room. "An artist has no need to explain."

Kelli turned her head, catching a glimpse of Jamie out of the corner of her eye. He glanced up at her, and she held the gaze for a beat, before returning to the professor.

"As I said on Thursday, you are all working in some form of media. Which is to say, you are all learning how to use very powerful, very persuasive forms of communication. Look at the headlines in today's newspaper. The president is caught with his pants around his ankles Monday, it's in tomorrow's headlines Tuesday, Wednesday's headline is about the stock market crashing as a result." There was a murmur through the room.

"In the past, politics was a guy going from town to town, speaking from the back of a train. Today, it's the guy who knows how to grab the headlines, and not for getting caught with his dick in his hand." He paused for emphasis. "Hitler was a master of media," he pointed to Kelli. "Do you know Leni Riefenstahl?"

"Yes."

"Who was she?"

"Hitler's filmmaker."

"Triumph of the Will!" Ryan shouted. "Blitzkrieg! The tank! And the movie camera! Which was the greater weapon?"

Kelli stared at him, unsure if he wanted an answer.

"The movie camera! *Media!* Hitler's long dead, but that fucking film is still around. *Mein Kampf?* The writing's terrible, but his book is still out there, the insane rantings intact, sitting on shelves, waiting to be read. Go to Amazon and you can order a copy! Right now, some kid is sitting in a Starbucks, digesting that garbage," Ryan looked around the room. He had their attention. "A movie, and a book, both historical documents,  both powerful, and both potentially dangerous pieces of communication, ways of carrying across the ideas of a long dead madman. Six million Jews died from thoughts that quickly gained momentum in part from those two forms of media. They should be preserved, and they should be studied, and they should stand as a warning. The world might be a different place today if Adolf Hitler had not been such a master of manipulating the media."

Ryan sat on the desk quietly for a moment. Someone

stifled a cough. He stared down at the floor as though deep in thought.

"But then there are positive things about media. Not only can it be used to propagate horrible, evil ideas, it can also help make people aware of them. Picasso's Guernica did this. News crews and filmmakers have done this with Vietnam. Think of that war and what do you see? The child burned by napalm. The man with the gun to his head. *Platoon?* War… Peace…" He looked up. "What about love? How many of you learned about love from a Beatles song, or a movie. Woody Allen? *When Harry Met Sally?*"

Jamie's attention was torn between fantasies of the girl, and thoughts about what this guy was saying. He might be a bit heavy on the theatrics, but this professor was interesting. For him, painting had always been his first choice; now, through narrowed options, he was studying photography. There were similarities and there were differences, and in many ways, there were benefits to each. He looked over at Kelli. If he were painting her in the nude, it would take his full concentration, and hours of time. If he were taking a photo of her, it would take a few minutes, and leave plenty of time for lovemaking. Priorities. It was lot to consider.

"This will be the primary concern of the course. Hopefully, by the time we're finished here in ten weeks, you'll all have some new perspectives on the mediums you have chosen, and why. Ten weeks is a short period in which to develop a complete philosophy, and its an even shorter time to consider just what the hell you all want to do with your lives, what you want to say, to whom, and in what manner, but it will be worth it."

Ryan turned to a red-haired girl in the front and again began the rundown of what she studied, how she had chosen to do so. The rest of the class continued along the lines of this discussion, and Kelli found herself getting sucked into the topic. Her professors lightly touched on these issues in her film courses, but Professor Ryan had a way of making it seem passionate and vital. She imagined he might be a bit like Dylan Thomas in the fifties. Booming, big ideas, a voice to match, and a boyish disposition to draw in the women. No wonder all those college girls were always crawling into bed with him. The angry passion about works of art was just, *hot*. Throw in some shaggy hair and a sly grin and you had a major aphrodisiac. Her mind was torn, bouncing back and forth between the professor in front and the guy in the hat behind her. It was like a fantasy. She gave the upper hand to the student. He'd given a strange response to the professor's last question, grunting a short "No-," but the attitude with which he'd spoken was virtually dripping sex appeal. Maybe that was even *more* appealing, a man of few words, just actions. He had a charm she couldn't put her finger on, a seductive spark in his eyes, like he could taste her blood after biting down on her lip.

The next time she saw him, that sparkle would be gone.

# CHAPTER FOUR
## THE ACCIDENT

Jamie did not go home the day the bandages were removed. When he awoke, his mother walked to his bedside and told him what had happened, or what they thought had happened; the details were hazy.

After carrying his young son into the emergency room, frantically filling out paperwork, and calling Lynn as the ER attendants wheeled Jamie away, Jeff had sat down in the waiting room. He'd been unable to reach his wife, leaving a message on the answering machine with directions to come to the University hospital. Then, amidst the chaos of the hospital, he had leaned back in his chair, his hands to his head, and wordlessly slumped to the floor.

When Lynn arrived an hour later, she was met at the admissions window by a nurse with a blank expression. Yes, someone had brought in a young boy who had been in a car accident, but the boy's condition was unknown, and the father himself had been admitted shortly afterward. She had no information as to what had happened to him, or where he had been taken. Lynn had attempted to reason with the woman, pressing her for further information, but gaining little ground.

"I told you ma'am, I don't know where he is."

"Well find out!" Lynnn screamed. "It shouldn't be so difficult!"

The nurse turned around, throwing up her arms and tilting her head to a fellow attendant, who ignored the expression, and looked right at Lynn, saying, "Just a moment Mrs. Pepper, I'll take you to him."

Jeff had been sprawled out on the waiting room floor when they found him. His face and hands were stone cold. A thin stream of blood trickled from his ear. He was initially unresponsive, taking several minutes to regain even a listless degree of consciousness. By the time Lynn arrived he had been x-rayed and undergone a brain scan. Now he lay in a hospital bed, sedated, as the doctors filled Lynn in on what they knew, which didn't boil down to much. His condition was unclear. He had suffered a head injury in the collision, which had smashed his head into the driver's side window. There were no lacerations or puncture wounds on his head and face, but the scan revealed very slight internal bleeding, a thin sheet of blood had pooled on the surface of his brain, yet not enough to justify surgery. Not yet anyway. Aside from waiting for the blood to disperse, there was little else that they could do.

Lynn took the news calmly, no stranger to traumatic environments and situations, and certainly no stranger to emergency rooms in general after years of following rock stars and their exploits, but despite every effort to maintain a professional aura, this was different. She was sober. The patient was not some coked up front man who had tumbled from a hotel balcony. At that moment, the two people for whom she cared most in this world were stretched out in hospital beds. She got up and crossed the hall to the children's ward, where Jamie had also been sedated after eye surgery. His hands were stretched out, his tiny fingers curled upwards. She walked over, kissed him on his damp forehead, then walked out into the hallway and called her brother-in-law.

# CHAPTER FIVE

Jamie felt sick. He'd been sitting in the computer lab all evening, experimenting with images of the broken window. Once or twice he'd blinked and looked around, feeling the way he had the night Gabe startled him awake to say the labs were closing, as though he were continually drifting in and out of sleep. Fortunately, Gabe wasn't working tonight to again observe his strange behavior. Jamie had made sure he ate after leaving the gym. His meal should have held him over, preventing a hunger headache, but something was not right. He went back through his memory of the day. He'd taken his meds at all the right times, yet it felt as though someone were squeezing in the sides of his head like a balloon. Jamie lifted his hands to his temples, propping his elbows up on the edge of the table. He looked down at his lap, glimmers of light sparkled along the edges of his vision. His ears were ringing. The room was twisting and bending. The next thing he knew, Kelli was whispering in his ear, pressing his face against her chest.

He hadn't seen her sitting in the back corner of the room, typing up a paper. The report wasn't due for a week, but Kelli hated the class, and had decided to complete the assignment so she could stop obsessing over it. She was about half way through when she'd noticed him sitting down at a computer in the front of the room. Kelli pulled her chair forward, craning around the monitor to see what he was doing. She'd been hoping Professor Ryan would press him for his name earlier in class earlier that day, but surprisingly, he'd been let off the hook. Now he was sitting across the room, his head held in his hands, looking much the worse for wear. Was he having a panic attack or something? Overwhelmed by an assignment? People with their heads in their hands were not an uncommon sight on campus, but after an hour, she began to worry about him. His ever-present cap had grown dark with perspiration and sweat was dripping down the back of his neck.  He slumped forward suddenly, his slack face pooling on the desktop. She hesitated, glanced around the room, then got up and slowly went over to him.

He was breathing heavily, long, deep sighs that seemed to catch in his throat, then slowly wheeze out through his mouth.

"Excuse me," she whispered.

No response. Kelli reached a hand out and placed it on his shoulder, shaking him gently. Still nothing.

"Are you all right?" she said louder.

Jamie's eyes fluttered open. She crouched down to look him in the face. He stared through her, eyelids drooping heavily.

"Are you sick? Can I help you?"

Jamie sat up slowly, his head tipping backwards. Kelli kept her hands on his shoulders. He was soaking wet. She could feel the moisture seeping through his clothing. His body was solid. The muscles in his back grew tense under her fingertips as his body swayed in the chair. Then his head fell forward. She caught him, pulling him towards her chest. Her hand shot up to the back of his head, cradling him against her. He was boiling hot.

"What's wrong? What's the matter?"

Nothing.

"Are you sick? Do you have a headache?"

She felt him nod his head against her chest.

"You have a headache? A migraine?"

Slowly, his mouth began to move, barely a tremble in his lips, but he didn't say a word. Kelli looked around the room. It was practically empty, save for a tiny Asian girl sitting at the assistance desk.

"Do you need help getting back to your dorm?"

Jamie again nodded his head. Kelli surveyed his work area. He had a backpack, a notepad, and a digital camera spread out.

"All right, let me get your stuff together and we can go."

She helped Jamie place his head down on the desk, and quickly gathered everything together, slipping his things into the backpack. She checked the computer, then shut it down.

"I'll be right back," she whispered.

She went back to her seat to gather up her own

things. When she returned, Jamie was nearly incoherent. She pressed her hand against his shoulder.

"Okay, let's try to get up."

Jamie set his legs apart, then forced himself to stand quickly. Kelli stepped forward as he swayed unsteadily. She held their backpacks in her left hand, and reached around him with her right arm. He leaned against her. Kelli could again feel his muscular body tensing and moving against her, but it was barely capable of supporting his own weight. She prepared herself in case his legs gave out.

"All right, here we go."

They slowly made their way out of the room, walking past the assistant at the desk, who didn't even glance up at them. Out in the hallway they began to trudge down the long, empty corridor. He was not looking good. His face had gone completely white now.

"What's your name?" she asked him. "We have a class together, but I don't know your name."

He took a gulp of air, and exhaled, "Jamie-"

"Jamie," she repeated. "Well Jamie, where are we headed? What dorm do you live in?"

"Gibson."

The hallway opened up into a large foyer. Kelli looked out the window, and saw snow falling outside. Damn.

"It looks terrible out there."

No response.

"I don't know if we'll make it if we go now."

Again, he said nothing. He had stopped, and was

once more swaying on his feet. She looked up at his face, the eyes were closed, his mouth hung open.

"Do you need to wait?"

No response.

Then, he fell forward. She barely caught him, dropping the backpacks as she angled her body to hold him up. She led him to a row of benches in the entryway. They stopped at the end of a long bench, where she turned him around, holding him steady as he sat down and fell backwards, stretching out on his back. She leaned forward, looking into his face. He was out. She again looked around. There was no one in sight. It was almost eleven o'clock. She bent down beside him, breathing in his smell, a spicy mix of cologne and deodorant.

"I'll be right back, Jamie."

She walked down the hallway to the bathroom, where she pulled several paper towels from the dispenser and ran them under steaming hot water, then she ran back and placed the steaming towels on his face. He reached up and pulled them down over his nose and mouth, inhaling deeply. She went back and soaked more paper towels in hot water. When she returned, the first towels had cooled. She crouched down and replaced them, then sat still, watching him.

"Is that helping at all?"

He said nothing, just continued breathing deeply, his eyes still closed.

Time drifted.

~

Jamie was still feeling out of it. His head was throbbing. It felt like he had a fever. He was vaguely aware that Kelli was helping him, but he was too sick to enjoy her attention. The towels helped, but he still felt terrible. He couldn't tell if the responses he was giving to her questions were even coming out, or if he was simply hearing them in his mind. She must have heard him, as she left again, and came back with more hot towels.

They were in the foyer of the photo building for more than an hour. Finally, Jamie seemed to be recovering, and Kelli brought him some snack mix from one of the vending machines.

"Try eating some of this," she said. holding the bag out to him. "The salt always helps me when I have headaches."

He sat up, taking a handful of the mix in his shaky hands. He brought it to his mouth and chewed slowly. The skin around his eyes hung heavy with exhaustion, but a sparkle had at last returned to the dark green irises.

"Thank you," he said softly.

"No problem."

They sat wordlessly for several more minutes. Finally, Kelli stood and walked over to the window. She wiped fog from the glass and peered out into the courtyard, shielding the glare from the glass as she stared at the pools of light under the walkway lamps. The snow had slowed, but only slightly. Who knew if conditions would be getting any better, or any worse.

"Think you can make it back to the residential side?"

Kelli asked as she turned to Jamie.

His eyes opened and closed slowly, then he leaned forward and got to his feet. Kelli went to him, grabbing hold of his elbow. She looked at his eyes, but they were staring at the ground. He glanced over at her and nodded his head.

"Let's give it a shot then," she replied.

The snow was still falling as they left the building and headed down the quarter mile towards to the dorms. The first breath of cold air sent a shiver of relief through Jamie's head, but the second seemed to hit his system the wrong way, and it wasn't long before he was feeling sick again. The heat and pain in his head were doubling by the minute, and with each new wave, his movements grew more and more labored. Each step on the frozen ground seemed to jar his brain, bringing the headache back in force. Kelli carried his backpack for him. Every so often he'd try to look up at her, or think of something to say, but mostly he watched his feet, trying to ignore the pain, hoping he could make it back to the dorm without throwing up.

Eventually, they reached Gibson Hall, where Jamie managed to fish the keys from his pocket as he leaned against the side of the building. They opened the door and started up the dark, narrow staircase, their footsteps echoing as they ascended. Kelli pushed over a heavy metal door on the third floor, and they were quickly engulfed in the smell of microwave popcorn and the low murmurs of conversation coming from open doorways. Kelli recognized the dorm; Jamie lived on the same floor as Will. That would explain his appearance at Gracie's on Friday. She looked around warily, hoping she wouldn't bump into her friend. Jamie had started getting worse about halfway back from the academic side. He wore that signature hat of his, but the cold air still must have frozen him to the bone as it chilled the sweat that was streaming down his face. Now, as he staggered down the hall beside her, she heard his dry, heavy breathing again - holding the air in for a brief moment, before exhaling slowly. He dug through his pockets and pulled out his keys. Kelli waited as he opened the door, switched on the light, and staggered inside. She followed him inside looking around the room curiously. It was dark. He had no posters on the wall. Very few books. No computer or TV. A row of prescription containers was lined up neatly on top of his dresser. She counted a half dozen of them.

Jamie pulled off his jacket and kicked off his shoes. He went straight to the dresser, twisted the caps off several of the canisters, and shook out a handful of pills.

"Do you need anything?" Kelli asked.

Jamie answered in a low whisper as he lurched toward the bed. "Could you get me some water?"

Kelli glanced around and picked up a cup by the door. She walked out into the hallway where she heard people's voices coming from the lounge around the corner, and suddenly recognized Will's voice carrying over the crowd. They hadn't seen each other since Friday, when he'd finally gone in for his move, and she'd stood up quickly, cutting the evening short, saying how exhausted she was. He hadn't stopped by since, and she wasn't ready to explain to him what she was doing on his floor tonight. She went over to the water fountain, filled the cup, and slipped back into the Jamie's room. He had stripped down to a pair of boxers, and was just pulling on shirt when she walked in. The room smelled like him. It was nice. He took the water and gulped down the pills, one after the other.

"Thanks," he said as he fell onto the bed.

There was a strange energy in the air. It was palpable, like the charge before two lovers go to bed for the first time. For a brief second, she almost thought she should take off a piece of her own clothing and climb in beside him. Jamie lay on his back, his eyes closed. She hesitated for a moment, then crouched down beside him.

"I'm going to leave now," she said softly.

There was no response. His breathing became steady. She studied his face for a moment. His skin glistened in the dim light. Except for the tightness at the edge of his eyes, he looked peaceful. She leaned forward, hesitated, then kissed him on the corner of his mouth.

He didn't move.

Kelli stood and went over to the door. She turned around, stealing one more look at him, then switched off the light and left.

*  *  *

His damaged eyes struggled to focus on the animal as it twirled in the air in front of him. The huge cartoon eyes opened and shut slowly, its mouth drew up in a leering, maniacal smirk. Jamie tried to scream, but his mouth would only let out a hiss of hot air. His head twisted sluggishly as he tried to move. The voices still mumbled in the background, but he couldn't understand what they were saying; the words all melted into a low murmur. Finally, the room stopped spinning, and he lay back. He was in a hospital room. The walls around him were bright yellow. The curtains were closed over the room's one window. He could hear a television in the hallway outside, Brian Williams was reading the news. It was nighttime. Jamie looked at the foot of the bed, where an enormous purple elephant was painted on the wall. It was an image he would never forget.

Then he heard the soft squeak of sneakers on linoleum and he turned his head. His mother stood in the doorway, her eyes red, her face streaked with tears. She didn't move, she just stood there, teetering on uncertain legs.

\* \* \*

He wasn't in class the next day, which worried her. Kelli had arrived late, in part to avoid an uncomfortable conversation about what had happened the previous night. It wasn't that she was afraid of what he might say, in fact, she was dying to have a moment alone with him, even if it was filled with awkward silences and uncomfortable glances. She didn't know if he would remember the kiss, or if he even knew it had occurred, but she was still apprehensive. Despite the odd nature of the previous night's events, it had been… exciting. She'd been fantasizing about him since that first day of class, when she'd given him that *look*, and even more so after she saw him at the table in Gracie's. The fact that he was with Will and his floor mates, putting him in the range of *possibility*, had sparked her imagination.

He was clearly an athletic, attractive guy, and after last night her view of him had only improved. She kept picturing his gaze as he looked up at her. He never blinked. He'd just open and close his eyes in a slow, deliberate movement, never an involuntary motion, as though the effort itself took all of his concentration. It was in the moments when he was visibly forcing himself to recover that she caught a glimpse of his personality -- as though he were looking at his pain in the distance, staring it down into submission. He wasn't a victim of the pain, he was fighting against it. Yet, the lines at the corners of his eyes, the look of consistent pressure, both told her that he'd been going through this for some time, that something in his life was slowly taking its toll on his body. He was like a young boy, holding his arm in pain after a fall from a tree, rubbing his elbow tenderly as he glared up through the enemy branches.

She understood what he felt, and she wanted to see him again.

~

He took the first bus from campus the next morning, switching on Mt. Hope and getting off at the University. He didn't want to get his mother involved, hoping there was no cause for concern. No use getting her worked up if he could check it out himself and avoid needless maternal hysteria. He stopped at the Dunkin Donuts on the corner, grabbed a classic glazed and an orange juice, and headed for the hospital. By nine o'clock he was sitting in the waiting room, eating breakfast and flipping through a magazine. He'd read most of these issues over the last year, but he still thumbed through the worn magazines, flipping the pages with nervous energy. He wasn't reading them, just staring through the paper, seeking distraction from the thoughts in his mind.

Beside the headaches, had he had any other symptoms? His body had never felt better. Aside from one or two episodes, he felt sharp mentally. He still found his mind racing with sexual anxiety, one of the more troublesome side effects of the meds. He still beat off constantly in the showers, but it was getting no better and no worse, and was certainly reduced from the height of his medicated periods. He was almost feeling normal again, whatever *normal* was these days. He might very well have had a simple migraine, no cause for alarm, but all the same, it had been off the charts. He'd only felt pain like that a handful of times in his life, and all but one of those events had been related to the damn Parkinson's and attempts to manage its effects.

No, he told himself, it was nothing. Just read the magazine. Read the magazine and don't worry.

Dr. Price walked through the door and into the waiting area. He was dressed in an overcoat and carrying a briefcase, his hair blew forward with the motion of the door. He took off his glasses and was wiping them with a cloth as he raised his head to speak to the receptionist. He paused as he spotted Jamie.

"Mr. Pepper." His jawline tightened. "How are you? Lets go into my office."

Jamie stood and followed him past the front desk and down the hall to his large, dimly lit office. Price walked around the room, setting his briefcase on the desk in front of him, running his fingers through his hair.

"Have a seat. Would you like some coffee?"

"No, thank you," Jamie replied.

Price glided over to the door and leaned out into the hallway.

"Ms. Oliver, a cup of coffee please."

He pulled his head back into the room, not waiting for a reply, then shrugged off his coat, hung it on the back of the door, and lurched to his desk. He stood behind his chair for a moment, hands clenched around the seat back, rocking it back and forth slowly.

Jamie noticed the white edges on the man's knuckles. He seemed unusually agitated.

"So, have you experienced some sort of a problem?" Price asked.

"Well, I hope not a problem really," Jamie said. "Just a concern."

Price looked at him expectantly.

"I had another headache last night."

"Like the ones after the surgery?"

Jamie hesitated. "Worse."

"How long did it last?"

"Hours. I'm better today, but I'm still feeling a little...off."

"Are you symptomatic?"

"No."

Price's face relaxed. "That's good." He sat down and leaned back in his chair. "Well then, let's talk about it, see if we can get to the bottom of things."

* * *

Kelli stopped by Jamie's room in the afternoon. She knocked on the door and waited, then knocked again. When there was still no answer, she pulled out a pad of paper, jotted down a quick note, and ripped out the page.

*Jamie-*
*Just wondering how you're doing.*
*Gimme a call sometime X4150*
*-Kelli (from Media and the Mind)*

She went back to the door but hesitated. For someone so brazen, she was suddenly nervous. It felt as if she was leaving a proposal under the door, but it was just a note. She was wondering how he was doing. After last night, it was a perfectly normal thing to do. 'I'm just wondering how you're doing. Call me.' But it didn't say 'call me,' it said 'call me *sometime*.' That was different. She knew it was. Call me meant... call me, we'll have a perfunctory sandwich together. Call me *sometime* meant...call me sometime, we'll have a good fuck and smoke cigarettes in bed. She smiled. That's what she was going for anyway.

Her stomach tightened with excitement.

She looked up and down the hallway, and slid the note under the door.

She stood up quickly, eager to make her escape, and hurried down the hall. Around the corner, she ran into a tall guy with glasses as he came up the stairs. He looked at her and put out his hand.

"How you doing? I'm Fritz."

*　*　*

The tests were not missed. Jamie had taken them all before, had hated them as much then as he did now. But he had to smoke out the problem. Drag it out into the open and get it over with. The bottom had fallen out of his stomach, and it made him angry. If anything came up that showed the implant was having adverse effects on his brain, or any other parts of his nervous system, it would have to be removed. Yet, as Dr. Price had pointed out so many times before, removal of the implant was unspeakably risky, and all but irreversible. The trauma to the brain was great, and the scarring involved in both implantation and removal made second and third procedures increasingly dangerous and unlikely. Price compared it to sugar in the gas tank. Once it's in there, you can never get it out and make things run like they used to. In most cases, the machine is a junker.

Fortunately, the results were good, or seemed to be. Jamie was back on campus by five o'clock. He felt guilty letting another day go by without exercising, but he knew it was better to take it easy than risk major problems by pushing his body when it needed a breather. Price reduced his meds, told him to keep a lookout for any symptoms that might show their faces again, but as far as he could tell, the headache had simply been a benign, albeit painful, migraine.

"We've gotta remind ourselves," the good doctor had said, "that not every ailment is a sign of the apocalypse. You're still susceptible to the same run-of-the-mill ailments that face the average Joe."

Jamie was trying very hard to believe that as he got off the bus and headed for his dorm. He still had his doubts, but he pushed them to the back of his mind as he walked up to his floor to find the usual dinner group congregating in the lounge.

Arlin looked up. "Yo man! You coming to dinner?"

"Yeah, sure," Jamie replied.

Fritz was just stepping out into the hall as Jamie reached his room.

"Hey, some girl stopped by looking for you earlier."

"Oh *really*," Jamie asked. "What did she look like?"

"She was pretty hot. A little bit scary. I was kidding around with her and she told me to 'go fuck myself.'"

Jamie gave him an odd look. "Oh yeah?"

"Cute though. I've seen her once or twice before. I think Will knows her."

Jamie nodded. " I know exactly who you're talking about."

"You hookin' up with that girl?" Fritz said with a smirk. "Very nicely done, man."

Jamie ignored him. "You going to dinner?"

"Yep, another Gracie's meal. The sacrifices a resident advisor's gotta make. I *really* wish your freshman meal plans let you eat at the Commons more often!"

Fritz headed down the hall as Jamie ducked into his room. He flipped on the light, pulled a new prescription bottle from his pocket, shook out a pill, and popped it in his mouth. He lined up the containers on the dresser and turned to leave. Just as he was heading out the door, he glanced down and noticed a piece of paper on the floor. He picked it up and opened it quickly. His eyes ran down the page, and his pupils dilated.

～

Kelli was in a shitty mood. She'd come back to the dorms exhausted, only to hear the sounds of Christie and Joe fucking in the next room the moment she opened the door. She had to watch a movie for her Film Language paper, and was hoping to get it out of the way tonight, but *The Apartment* wasn't something you watched with the sounds of animal coupling going on in the background.

"Change of plans," she muttered as she tossed the DVD on her bed and walked out. She grabbed the edge of the door as she left, took one big step forward, and slammed it shut as hard as she could. It was unlikely those two rabbits would hear her angry tantrum, but it made her feel the tiniest bit better.

She walked over to The Commons, where she ate dinner and tried to outline the elusive script she'd been working on. Progress was slow as always. She looked around the room now and then. Every table was filled with groups of laughing kids, or girls eating dinner with their boyfriends; all smiling, or fighting, or wrapping their arms around their companions' necks. Aside from Will and the occasional casual friendships, she had a small circle of college friends. Dating someone long distance, dividing weekends between trips home and his visits to Rochester, hadn't helped her make any lasting connections at the school. She chewed on the end of her pen as she stared through the windows and out across the fields.

"Why the hell haven't I heard from him?" she thought to herself.

He probably wasn't interested, or maybe he had class tonight. Was he shriveled up in his dorm room, dead? No, that cocky asshole she'd bumped into in the hall said he'd gone off campus for the day. She tried to ask more, but he'd just turned on that frat boy "charm." It pissed her off. Ten seconds of his leers and sophomoric innuendo and she'd stormed out, shouting over her shoulder what he could do to himself. Now she wished she'd had a little more patience, if only to eke a bit more information out of him.

"Fuck him," she muttered again. "Fuck both of them."

But she didn't mean it. Not all of it anyway.

Her mind wasn't on the script. All she could think about was Jamie. What if he was trying to call her now while she was sitting here eating? Please, that'd be ridiculous. He obviously wasn't gonna call her.

Besides, she had the machine.

Still, he might not want to leave a message.

She hesitated.

"This is retarded."

She chewed on her pen, fighting to be logical.

"Screw it."

She picked up her tray and headed for the door.

Back at the dorm... Nothing. No messages. She couldn't tell if he had called. Thankfully, the lovebirds had gone on their way, probably in search of food to replenish their energy. She headed across the room, slipping off her shirt and jeans as she walked. The geeks across the quad were probably getting an eyeful. She knew there was a pack of computer geeks in the next tower who were constantly scanning the dorm windows for naked girls or fucking couples, but she very seldom closed the curtains. Even on the rare occasions she had a guy over, she tended to leave the windows open. Saw it as a humanitarian effort. Give em something to get their blood pumping. Tonight was different. She stuck her middle finger in the air as she walked past the window, giving an emphatic bob upwards as she pulled the curtains closed. She was just pulling on some sweats and a tank top when the main buzzer rang.

She walked out into the living room expecting Christie and Joe and some explanation of forgotten keys. Instead, she opened the door just as she was pulling on her shirt, and was greeted by Jamie, who stood there with a sexy smile on his face.

"Is this a bad time?" he asked.

She was caught off guard.

"Hi," Kelli replied.

"Hi."

God he was cute.

She brushed her hair away nervously.

Jamie looked at her, trying to seem relaxed. She had washed the makeup from her face, and her cheeks were flushed. The usual dark outlines around her eyes were gone. She was still cute though. *Cuter* even. Less intimidating.

"Is this a bad time?" he asked again.

"No. Not at all. Come on in."

She stood to the side to let him past, wrapping her arms up around her chest to keep warm.

Jamie stepped inside, glancing around the common area of the suite.

"I got your room number from your friend Will. He lives on my floor."

"Oh yeah. I thought I recognized it when I took you to your room."

Kelli pressed her fingers into her ribs, suddenly aware that she wasn't wearing a bra. She rubbed her hands up and down over her arms, the nervous energy warming her.

"I just wanted to thank you for your help last night. I really appreciate it."

She nodded as he spoke. "No problem, I was glad I could do it."

Jamie continued, "I thought maybe I could take you out for coffee sometime."

"Oh, you don't have to do that. I'm just glad you're

okay."

"Yeah, I'm fine. Just a headache. I get them from stress sometimes."

Kelli cocked her head to the side. "Not to be rude, but that seemed like more than just a headache."

Jamie shifted his weight from one foot to the other. "Well, to be honest, that was one of the worst ones I've had, but I think it's just from starting classes and getting used to things here-"

Kelli stepped backwards, toward her room, as the wind whistled outside the windows. Her skin rippled suddenly. She felt her nipples pressing against the front of her tank top.

"I'm sorry, I just need to grab a sweatshirt. Do you wanna sit down?"

"Sure." Jamie ambled over to the couch.

Kelli disappeared, emerging a moment later, pulling a sweatshirt over her head. "Do you want a beer or anything? I have a couple drinks someone smuggled over."

"Nah, I'm okay."

"You sure? Cause I'm gonna nab one."

"I'm fine

Kelli walked over to a mini fridge and pulled out a bottle. She popped the lid off on the side of the table and sat down.

"So, are you a freshman this year?"

"Yeah. I'm getting a bit of a late start. I missed the first quarter."

Jamie watched Kelli take a long sip of beer. She swallowed and pulled her legs up onto the couch, crossing them, and holding the bottle in her lap.

"Why'd you miss the first quarter?"

She watched his eyes glance down to her body and return to her face. He was nervous, which somehow made her calm.

Jamie hesitated. "Well, it's sort of a long story. Kind of a medical thing-"

"I'm sorry," Kelli cut him off. "That's none of my business."

"I don't mind-"

"Seriously, forget I asked. Please."

They sat silently for a minute.

"How do you like RIT so far?"

"It's cool. Still getting used to the classes and everything, but so far so good."

"You're in photo?"

"Yep." He bobbed his head slowly.

There was another awkward silence. Jamie looked over at the coffee table, where Kelli had tossed *The Apartment.* He leaned forward and picked it up.

"Hey, I love that movie. Is this yours?"

"Oh yeah, I was just gonna watch that for one of my classes."

She watched as he read the back of the case.

Another gust of wind blew outside again, and he looked up towards the windows. She curled up in her sweats, glad to be inside.

"Did you wanna hang out and watch it with me?"

\* \* \*

Kelli's mouth was soft, and warm, and aggressive. Her lips tasted of fresh water, with a twist, as her tongue hit his like vodka - sharp, and clean, and utterly intoxicating.

When they did kiss, it came naturally, the next step in an easy conversation. The night drifted by strangely and easily, with no sense of time passing, or moments slipping from one into the next. The movie ended and they fell into conversation, all of the previous hesitation stripped away. They talked more about the previous night, then slowly circled around to school and classes, before somehow crossing the threshold, leaving small talk behind, and stepping into the realm that *is* college. Talk of classes gave way to thoughts on life and love, work and purpose. It was the type of exchange exclusive to youth, and only possible in the late night hours, when self-consciousness and embarrassment are held at bay, and people are more honest than they could ever think possible during the day. Jamie recounted his first days at school, which made Kelli remember her first year at RIT. She told him about her roommate and the constant noises from the next room, which led to talk of sex, which strangely wasn't awkward or embarrassing. Both felt the inevitable tingle as they went into their views on loving and fucking, the important differences between the two. Each felt the rush of blood, the shift of breath, but it didn't change the mood of the night. It all felt somehow inevitable, and as such, there was no need to rush. Then, late in the night, after the sounds of partygoers had died out in the halls, and all they could hear was the wind outside, Kelli moved towards him, placing her hand on his leg, pulling herself against him. He turned to face her, and in an instant, everything changed. She saw the light flash in his eyes just before he closed them. He felt the brush of her hair as it ran against his face. Then, they were kissing.

He was calm and deliberate. Again, no anxiety. No hurry. His five o'clock shadow tickled Kelli's lips, and she bit his mouth softly, savoring the tingle that raced through her body. She felt his hand on her side, pressing against her ribs, then sliding up to her breast. His fingers cupped the back of her neck, tangling in her hair. She ran her fingers over the prickly skin near the bottom of his cap and pulled him close. He wrapped his arms around her, pushed her back into the cushions. Her hands dropped from his neck to his shoulders, feeling the tight muscles, before sliding down his back. His body slipped between her legs and she spread them further apart, felt him hard against her. Kelli pulled her head back, looking into his puzzled eyes. He leaned towards her, but she again pulled away. He tilted his head questioningly. Kelli slowly stood up, and took his hand. Without a word, she led him into her room.

The wind was howling outside as Kelli closed the door, locked it, and went over to her dresser. Jamie sat on the bed and watched her light a match, the hot flash filling the room as she lit two candles and set them on a dish. Kelli stood with her back to him, blew out the match, and turned around. The candles glowed softly behind her. She dropped her hands to the bottom of her shirt, twirled her fingers in the fabric, and pulled it up over her head, taking the tank top underneath with it. Jamie's eyes moved slowly from her belly button, to her full breasts, the nipples small and hard, up to her neck and her mouth, where white teeth sparkled as she bit her lower lip. She gave him a small, wicked smile as she approached him. The closer she came, the more she slipped into silhouette. Jamie watched the perfect outline of her body as she moved toward him. Her hands settled on his hips, then slid slowly upwards, pulling off his shirt. She shoved him back onto the bed and fell on top of him, kissing him on the neck, sliding her tongue up to his ear, then back to his mouth. She gave him a long, slow kiss, then pulled a heavy blanket over them as she rolled him over and wrapped her legs around his back.

Outside, snow was falling, whipping past the walls of the cold brick building. The constant wind roared through campus, swirling in the woods and pelting the walkways. Ice crackled on the glass of Kelli's window, ricocheting into the darkness, as all the while warm light glowed around the edges of the curtains pulled tight against the darkness.

* * *

They didn't have sex that first night. Not because they didn't want to. If pushed a hair further, they would

145

undoubtedly have gone for it, but things were different. Through all the hormones and kissing and hours of conversation, something else was passing between them. Something deeper, beyond either of their abilities to sense what was happening. Truth be told, if things had gone differently they would have fucked each other's brains out that night, and then, who knows, things might have worked, they might not have, but on that first night, Kelli did something that changed things in a way she never could have expected. As she pulled the blanket over them, she kissed Jamie hard on the mouth, then reached up, and removed his hat.

He saw her looking at him, her mouth hanging open. For a moment he couldn't tell what had happened, then he saw where she was looking, and felt the unfamiliar sensation of air on his bare head. He started to speak, then stopped, closing his mouth tightly. Kelli's lips pressed together as her eyes moved over the dark scars criss-crossing the top of his head. She reached up and slowly, gently, placed her fingers on the thick, raised ridges. The skin was ropy and hard against her fingertips. The marks looked painful and fresh on his scalp. She didn't know what they were from, and after a moment, she knew she didn't need to know, not yet. She slid her hand over the top of his head and down the back of his neck. She pulled him closer, kissing him long and hard, and then, eventually, they slept.

For the first time in weeks, Jamie had no dreams.

He slept through the night, waking once or twice to find Kelli lying against him, her arms wrapped around him. When he moved, she pulled him closer, burying her face against his chest. He pressed his mouth against the side of her head, smelling her hair and kissing her softly. Her bare skin was warm against his, but even still, a shiver ran up his back. He pulled the blankets tighter around them and fell back to sleep.

The room was lit by soft light filtering in through the edges of the curtains. He was alone in the bed, but he could hear sounds in the next room. Kelli was taking a shower. He looked around the room, taking in the details of someone else's space. There were lots of film books scattered in piles around the room. CDs leaned against the walls in stacks and against one another in precariously high towers. The walls were covered with movie posters, but none of the usual suspects, the *Scarfaces* and the *Say Anythings* that he saw through so many dorm windows when he walked the quarter mile. Kelli's posters were all for old Billy Wilder and Woody Allen movies, the largest featured Jackie Gleason as he lined up a shot in *The Hustler.* Every chair arm and lampshade had an item of clothing hanging from it. The most intimate items seemed to be the most prominently displayed. A collection of bras hung from the foot of the bed. Panties were scattered on the floor and atop her dresser by the dozen. Jamie fell back onto the bed and rolled over, burying his head in the pillow. He took a deep breath, smelling Kelli on the pillows. Then, from the other room he heard the squeak of the shower being turned off. He listened carefully. Silence. He was just about to get up and put on his shirt when he heard the door open and turned to see Kelli walking into the room with a towel wrapped around her.

"Hi," he said softly.

She looked him in the eyes.

"Hi."

Kelli closed the door behind her, giving it an extra push 'til the latch clicked, then she turned and stared at him. She reached her hand up to the towel and with one swift movement untucked the edge. It fell away, revealing her body, pink and warm from the shower. Jamie's eyes ran up to her smile. She came towards him as he stood up from the bed. He set his hands on her waist and leaned down to kiss her, but she put her hands on his chest and pushed him back abruptly. He looked at her as if he'd done something wrong. She smirked, and her hands went for his belt buckle. She slid the leather through the metal loop and unfastened the button at his waist. Her fingers moved down the front of his jeans, undoing each of the buttons. She raised her hands to the waist of his pants and brought them down, bringing his boxers with them. She stood and kissed him again, all the while leading him to the bed, where she sat on the edge and looked up at him.

"You wanna fuck?"

He didn't know if he said anything. He just found himself on top of her, kissing her on the mouth and up and down her neck. She caught her breath as he ran his tongue up to her earlobe, then gently took it in his teeth. She pushed him away, rolled him onto his back, and reached up to a shelf above the bed where she took down a condom. He watched as she tore open the wrapper, placed it on the head of his cock, and rolled it down the shaft, her fingers tickling the hairs at the base, making him harder. Kelli looked him in the eyes as she straddled his body and lowered herself down over him. He pressed his hands around her waist and held her tightly as she moved against him, her mouth open, exhaling quiet moans. She leaned towards him, her breasts rubbing against his chest as she kissed him slowly, her tongue lingering against his. Jamie slipped his hands down her back as she picked up the rhythm. He raised his hips to meet her and she gasped. He gazed up at her face through the hair that tumbled down towards him. Her eyes were closed. They moved faster. The bed frame thumped against the cinder block wall behind them. Then he came, his body tensing, growing rigid... falling limp. Kelli rolled off of him, her fingers between her legs as she rubbed herself quickly. Jamie watched as she shivered, then became quiet. Her fingers slowed as her mouth tightened and her head turned upwards. And then she was still, curled up on her side, her hand pressed between her legs.

They lay for a while in silence, listening to the radiator popping and hissing. Then Kelli opened her eyes, looking at him with a devilish smile, before standing and leading him into the bathroom. They showered together, the steam filling the room, scorching their lungs, as Kelli stood behind him, running her soapy hands ran over his body and pressing her lips against his shoulder.

Afterwards, they dressed and took the tunnels to

Jamie's building, where Kelli waited downstairs as he ran up to take his medication. He was overdue. Then they headed to Gracie's, ate an anxious, impatient breakfast, and left, walking through the snowy quads between the buildings, both of them hyper with sex.

They took the back stairs in Kelli's building, pausing at her floor where she pushed him against the wall in the stairwell. She kissed him gently as she ran her hand under the bottom of his shirt, feeling his stomach muscles, dipping below the waist of his jeans, brushing against him in his boxers. Jamie leaned forward and kissed her. She bit his lip gently. Then they came out on her floor, where Kelli unlocked the door to the suite and led him back into her room.

"Now," she whispered. "We make love."

And they did. And it was different. Not better. Not worse. Just slower, more intense. She stared into his eyes as he moved inside her. He felt her body responding to his, tightening and squeezing, pulling him in and warming to his touch. Kelli was more sensitive this time and Jamie found himself fighting to catch up. All he could hear were the sounds of their breathing, of Kelli's moans, as they both came closer and closer, and then he felt it: Something in the back of his head popped and white light washed in through the corners of his vision. Everything fell silent as his senses went numb. When he opened his eyes, he was lying on top of her, shaking and exhausted. He rolled over and lay beside her. Kelli opened her eyes and looked at him.

"That was amazing."

"Yeah," he said, remembering the fireworks he'd just seen in his head. "It was."

# CHAPTER SIX

Jeff was different after the accident. The doctors kept him in the hospital for two days to monitor him for changes; when his condition seemed stable, they released him from care. At first, things had seemed normal, though in hindsight, perhaps not so normal as far as Jeff Pepper was concerned. It wasn't that he was a morose man; he just wasn't a happy man, not an outwardly happy man at any rate. He had his interests and his passions, but something in his personality always kept him standing back, watching and waiting for the other shoe to drop. This aspect of his personality had always served him well professionally, but it made his personal life a bit more difficult.

When he and Lynn first met, Jeff's coarse edges had proven the greatest hurdle in their courtship. As an actively neurotic writer, he was all but impossible to live with. He was always turning his thoughts inside out, struggling to make sense of behaviors the typical person merely wrote off as life's puzzles. As the years went on, Lynn's influence had, for a time, helped to curb some of his more obsessive tendencies, while maintaining just enough of his edge to preserve "the bite" that gave his writing such inexplicable appeal. For a time, the majority of his work involved a series of productions for TV - strange, almost campy flights of fancy, many of them philosophical mysteries for Public Television, which only increased his audience, but at the same time bred talk of his selling out, going soft with age. Later, as Jamie grew older, and Lynn and Jeff's marriage again went through a rough patch, they both retreated into their work. Lynn shifted gears and turned to fiction, writing her two poorly received novels. Jeff on the other hand returned to the topics of his youth, regaining his manic style, and building on it. His writing again grew increasingly esoteric, and with his style apparently revived, the popularity of his plays and films increased exponentially. At the time of the accident, Jeff was at the height of his popularity, and as men at the height of success are prone to do, he turned his sights on the past, and returned to his most famous work, the novel he'd written in college that had sealed his reputation from the beginning. The week before the accident, Jeff signed a high profile deal to publish a sequel to *Dub Taylor* - a book which his proposal described as a continuation of the story, picking up twenty five years later, with the iconic young college student now a disillusioned professor at a liberal arts college. Aside from the brief outline Jeff submitted to the publisher, neither he, nor his editor, had any idea what the book would entail. But the prospect of a sequel was irresistible, and the day of the accident, a check for a near-record author advance arrived at the house, just as Jeff and Jamie were climbing into the car and heading off to the movies. It would be two years before any new writing would see the light of day.

As the creator of *Dub Taylor* and other dark, cult pieces, Jeff Pepper had a rather unique outlook on life. Always civil and polite, but often prone to excitable outbursts and extreme viewpoints, Jeff Pepper would never have been described as carefree. Yet, for the first week after the accident, the only word to describe him was *gleeful*. In fact, he was damn near manic in his sudden and overflowing appreciation for life and all that it had to offer. Yet, by the end of the week, he had begun a quick and steady slide into a deep depression, one that he would cling to for years, despite treatment, therapy, medications, and the best efforts of his family. From the moment of the accident, Jeff Pepper would never publish another book, produce another play, or pen another film, at least, not in his lifetime. The last years of his life were a cloud of unclear, undefined disappointments, and severe unhappiness. He went through a series of therapists and counselors, trying for years to shake off the kind of depression Churchill referred to as "the black dog." Yet aside from intermittent and illusory improvement, the dog would be forever at his heels.

For two years after the accident, Jamie's life was punctuated by moments of panic and dread. He and his mother had arrived home numerous times to find small, white envelopes taped to the front door or sitting on the kitchen counter. On every occasion, Lynn had opened the letters in a panic, rushed to the phone to call the police, and taken off in her car. Hours later, his parents would either return home together, his father looking weary and defeated, his mother visibly shaken, or Lynn would walk in the door alone, pour herself a glass of wine, and tell Jamie that his father would "be gone for a while."

But Jeff Pepper never did get better.

On New Year's Day, when Jamie was ten, his mother came home after the most recent incident soaked with rain, her face slacken. She came into the house, stared through the doorway at Jamie, who was sitting in front of the television in the living room, then went into the kitchen and poured a glass of wine. When she didn't return, Jamie went through the house looking for her. He found her sitting at his father's desk, one hand on the typewriter, the other pressed to her forehead. The wine glass sat empty on the edge of the desk. Jamie stood in the doorway and she turned to him slowly.

"Jamie," Lynn said. "I'm afraid Daddy won't be coming home."

# CHAPTER SEVEN

"Are you any relation to Jeff Pepper?"

It was a question Jamie had been asked countless times before. When he was younger, people would stop him on the street, commenting on the striking resemblance he bore to "that odd writer in town…" And as he grew older, the similarities between them only increased. He had his father's features, the smooth, boyish face, the narrow nose and slightly furrowed brow. His eyes were the same deep shade of green as Jeff's. Jamie's mother often commented on the almost frightening echoes in their mannerisms as well. Even after the symptoms of Jamie's PD became constant, there were flashes when his movements were unmistakably those of his father. Many times in later years, Lynn had looked out the window as Jamie approached the house and felt a sudden shiver ripple up her spine, thinking for the briefest moment that she was seeing a dead man returning home. They had the same stride, the same unusual lightness in their limbs. In college, many of Jeff's classmates had pegged him as homosexual, owing to the wispy quality of his hands and arms, which were always somewhat tensed, elevated ever so slightly towards his chest, as if held by strings. His soft, even voice added to this misperception. After the publication of *Dub Taylor,* a book whose main character was almost universally seen as an autobiographical portrait of the author, the novel's bisexual undertones only cast further speculation as to Jeff Pepper's sexual predilections. Truth be told, there was little in Jeff Pepper's most famous work that offered insight into the life of the author himself, and both his friends and family knew that the only man who held romantic interest for him, was himself. Like his son, Jeff was enchanted by women, obsessed with them, but before women, his first love was and always would be his own psyche, a fact that made his marriage to Jamie's mother all the more difficult over the years. Not that any relationship between writers has ever been easy, but Jeff's self-assaulting criticism and determination to "find the truth" in his work, were not only completely contrary to Lynn's journalistic sensibilities, but they tested her ability to take his obsessions seriously. Preternatural navel gazing, that's what she dubbed it during their more unhinged arguments. Yet, unlike Jamie, Lynn understood what made her husband's work great, or what made others feel that way. But, perhaps more in line with her son's later impressions of Jeff's writing, she increasingly had the feeling that some of her husband's work, as well as his mental struggles, were an overly romanticized "tempest in a teapot." Still, as with most relationships, their careers had little bearing on their feelings, and they did love each other, greatly, which is was why Jeff's final period of depression and his ultimate disappearance, remained an event Lynn had never stopped turning over in her mind.

Jamie, on the other hand, had long ago embraced his father's myth. Though unable to fully comprehend the impact of Jeff's work, let alone the appeal, he had, for the greater portion of his life, attempted to adopt his father's obsessions. Yet, aside from his voice and mannerisms, the two could not have had more different personalities.

Jamie was calm, quiet. True, he had an undeniable introspective streak, a tendency to pick away at a question in his mind, but unlike his father, Jamie also had the ability to arrive, if not at an answer, than at a point of acceptance. If he couldn't put a question to sleep, he had no problem setting it loose in the wilds of his mind. Jeff, on the other hand, felt any question about human behavior, world events, or his own motivations *had* to be understood, taken apart, and analyzed on the spot. If not now, when? He could not accept that certain aspects of life were simply incomprehensible. As a result, his life and work were a pure reflection of the unbearable inner turmoil that raged inside his head.

Tragic writers are the stuff of legend. Papa Hemingway, Dylan Thomas, Edgar Allen Poe, the greater the turmoil in the author's work, the more the scholars seem to take note, picking apart each of their pieces, looking for answers and insights into life and its workings. The thing with Jeff Pepper was that aside from his last couple of years, his was not a classically tragic life. Despite the darker tone of his works, his career and popularity were more along the lines of Woody Allen, had Allen written *The Catcher in the Rye* in college before making

*Annie Hall* and *Manhattan*. Yet, after the accident, Jeff's life had taken an unexpected turn, and with it, his career gained the weight of tragedy from which literary and pop culture legends are made.

It was not an uncommon question to come up, and when it did, Jamie usually tried to brush it away as quickly, and as gracefully as possible. He understood the fascination, if not the fanaticism, and he tried to answer as politely as his father had when he was growing up. Still, the attention had always made him uncomfortable. This time, the source of the question had surprised him.

"Are you any relation to Jeff Pepper?" Professor Ryan asked.

Class had just started, and Jamie and Kelli were sitting down at the front table, running late after an early morning quickie had taken longer than expected. Ryan let the class wait as he sat silently on the front desk for a few moments. He stared down at the class list, then he looked up, locking directly on Jamie and uttering that familiar question. Jamie should have known his luck would run out sooner or later. In three weeks on campus, no one had made mention of his last name, or taken note of his resemblance to a certain literary cult figure. He'd briefly stopped by Gabe and Will's room the night before, and watched Will warily as he poured over notes from one of his classes. Jamie was still on edge around the guy after learning more about his infatuation with Kelli, but he was trying to smooth things over to avoid any tensions. Jamie had just launched into a conversation with Gabe over the latest floor gossip, when in midsentence he'd looked at the shelf above Will's desk and noticed a copy of *Dub Taylor*. His mind went blank for a moment before he was able to return to the conversation and quietly make his exit. Since then, every time he saw Will, Jamie had been waiting for him to make some mention of his father. It still hadn't happened. Even Kelli had not yet made the connection.

Now he was caught off guard. The mood in the room changed immediately. Jamie could physically feel his classmates' eyes watching him. He couldn't see Kelli's expression, but he heard the wooden chair beside him creak softly as she shifted towards him. After an uncomfortably long pause, Jamie regained his speech.

"Yeah," he replied. "He was my father."

Professor Ryan nodded his head slowly. "He was a good guy."

Jamie waited for him to continue, expecting the usual comments about the book or the movies, or at least the whispered "It's a shame what happened." But instead, Ryan just stood up, walked up the aisle to the back of the room, and asked someone in the back row what movies he had seen that weekend. The answer launched the professor into a lecture on the mass media and the phenomenon of weekend box office. But Jamie's concentration was shot. For the rest of the two hour lecture, all he could think about was Professor Ryan's comment. He could feel Kelli looking over at him, and he tried to talk to her, turning his head to whisper comments about the class, but he couldn't focus on what was being discussed.

At the end of the lecture, as they were filing out of

the room, Professor Ryan called him over.

"I knew your father," he said matter of factly. "I worked with him on a couple of his shows."

Jamie looked at him blankly. Kelli watched them out of the corner of her eye, then walked past and waited in the hallway.

"Which shows? Jamie asked.

"It was that whole series he did with the anti-social police detective character, Brick Ransom. I worked on the animated sequences. I was on that show for a couple of years in fact."

"Yeah, those were pretty popular."

Professor Ryan was gathering up his books, pulling on his jacket. He studied Jamie for a moment.

"They were brilliant."

Jamie nodded his head slowly. The Professor looked at him closely, almost staring through him.

"You remind me of him, a lot." Ryan said, as he tucked his books under one arm and walked out of the room.

* * *

"So I guess I'm the one who has to bring this up."

Kelli was stretched out on her back, her feet dangling over the edge of the bed. She was dressed in sweatpants and a sweat-soaked tanktop. They'd just come back from the gym. Jamie lay on the floor, one hand held to his head. He was feeling odd after his workout. Professor Ryan's comments had caught him off guard. He knew the guy liked to throw people curve balls, but the way he'd brought up his father, and their odd exchange after class had twisted Jamie's mind in on itself. Going to the gym had helped, but he still felt somewhat removed from his senses, as though the tiny hairs on his head were dancing in place. He didn't like it.

"I said, I guess I have to be the one to bring this up," Kelli repeated.

"Bring what up?"

"You know what."

Jamie sat up and looked at her.

"What do you want to talk about, the books or the movies?"

Kelli stared back at him, her eyes narrowed.

"*Neither.*"

"Come on. Just ask. I don't know much about the guy, but I can tell you more than you'll read in the books, probably. Lets get it over with."

"Don't be an asshole. I'm just wondering if you're upset."

Jamie lay back on the floor again. He was quiet for a moment.

"Nah. I'm used to it."

"I didn't know," Kelli said. "If that matters to you--"

"Do you know who he was?"

She didn't say anything, only stood up and walked over to a shelf of books. Shoving several away, she tossed one across the room. It slammed down on the floor to Jamie's side. He turned his head and looked at the book's spine. *Dub Taylor.*

"It's a great book," she said.

"So I've been told."

"I meant I didn't know he was your father. And quite frankly, I don't give a shit. I was just worried it was supposed to be secret."

"No, not a secret. Just…" he trailed off. "Just not the only thing I want people to know me for."

Kelli walked back to the couch and sat behind him, spreading her legs on either side of him. She leaned down, wrapping her arms around his neck and kissing him behind his ear. She could taste salt on his skin from the workout.

"Do you remember him?"

"Yeah, I remember. I was ten when it happened. He didn't start going nuts until I was eight. But we still had some good times."

Kelli sat up, raised her hands to the back of Jamie's neck, and kneaded the tensed muscles. He sighed softly. The sounds of the dorms echoed out in the hallways. Two girls yelled at each other over the volume of music blasting from their rooms a few doors away. Kelli slowly massaged the bristly skin at the bottom of his cap, then she slipped her fingers under the edge and pulled it off. He still grew tense whenever she removed his hat, breathing in suddenly, then visibly willing his body to relax. The scars still surprised her. She was getting used to them, but hadn't asked him for an explanation, not yet. She was waiting for him to bring them up himself.

"He was in therapy for years, but we knew it was coming. He'd leave us suicide notes, then disappear--"

He stopped abruptly. The sounds of footsteps came

rumbling down the hall as two people ran past the door. A girl's hysterical laughter echoed down the corridor.

"I just can't help remembering things when I meet someone who knew him."

"Were those shows Professor Ryan talked about filmed in town?"

Jamie nodded. "Yep. They did a lot of his stuff at WXXI here in town.

"You know, we watched a few of those in my classes last year. They're amazing."

"Yeah, I always like the TV stuff."

Kelli leaned down and kissed him on the head.

"I never got the books though," he said after a few minutes.

"I loved the first one. The second one was a little..."

"Fucked up?" Jamie asked. "Who writes their suicide into a book? It's so--"

Kelli waited for him to finish. He remained silent.

"So, that was true?" she added.

He nodded his head.

"Yeah, they found his car in the ferry parking lot."

"But did they ever find *him*?"

"No, but his credit card had a charge for a ticket. He got on at one end, didn't get off at the other. If there was any doubt, the book cleared that up for us nicely."

Kelli had read the sequel to *Dub Taylor* a few years ago. She didn't want to tell Jamie how much the first one had meant to her, to sound like a cliché, but she still saw it as a touchstone reading experience. There were a lot of comparisons between Dub Taylor and

Holden Caulfield, which she could understand. It was probably unavoidable. People were always looking for the next character with whom they could identify, and the attitude and excitement of Jeff Pepper's book made comparisons irresistible. She liked *Dub Taylor* better, had actually read it three times, most recently that fall after she and Mike had broken up. She first read it in high school, then, despite warnings from everyone, she'd read the sequel, called simply *Dub*. She remembered hearing about the book when she was younger. It had been tied up in lawsuits for years. *Dub,* as it was published, was not a completed work. In fact, until Jeff Pepper disappeared, no one really knew how much of it had even been written. As Jamie had alluded, the major controversy surrounding the posthumous work, was that Jamie's father had written his own suicide into the storyline. Whereas he had always strongly denied any similarities between his most famous character and himself in the original, in the sequel, Jeff had very thinly disguised elements of his own life, even going so far as to give Dub's son the name Jamie. In the aftermath of Jeff's disappearance, the news of the second book's existence had kicked off a media frenzy, during which Jamie's mother had tried to block publication, claiming it was the right of the author's estate to give final approval. Ultimately, complications with the advance for the book, along with the costs of Jeff's on-and-off treatment for the two years during which the fractured work was completed, forced Lynn to give in and allow it to be released. Morbid curiosity and a sincere hunger for the continuation of a cultural milestone, sent sales soaring. But such high anticipation, combined with the incoherent, rambling nature of the product itself, made the critical response more vicious than warranted. The most infamously lurid connection between fact and fiction was the character's own suicide, committed on New Year's day; it seemed both Jeff Pepper and the fictional Dub Taylor had chosen a leap from the Toronto ferry into the icy winter waters as the ideal way to stop the voices they had both come to hear in their heads. Jeff Pepper's car was ultimately found parked at the Toronto ferry terminal, and several witnesses later recalled seeing the famous writer on board the boat the day of his disappearance. Interestingly, unlike the family of the book's main character, Jamie and Lynn Pepper never felt the sad relief that the fictional Taylor clan experience when the body of the long-unstable main character washes up on shore. For one thing, Jeff Pepper's body was never found. For a time Lynn darkly joked that it was a good thing Jeff had killed himself, cause the reviews for his final book, which *The New York Times* summed up as "the insane, raging words of a once-great writer," would have killed him.

Kelli stared at the top of Jamie's head. She wondered what was he was thinking. Despite everything, she was feeling an undeniable excitement welling up in her arms and legs, and she was immediately disgusted with herself. The response she felt was probably the exact one Jamie had hoped to avoid in the first place. Who wouldn't despise the constant shadow of a dead parent? He must have resented the man terribly. Kelli pushed her questions to the back of her mind. She would wait for Jamie to tell her what he was thinking, just as she would wait for him to bring up the details of the scars on his head.

Jamie sighed and looked up at her. She leaned her head down, looked him in the eyes, and kissed him.

He knew she'd been looking at his scars again. She had still said nothing about them. He wanted to talk to her about them soon, but for now, he just wanted to be with her. He closed his eyes, and suddenly had an image of the piece of metal, suspended in his head. His eyes shot open, and he looked at her again. The air in the room was growing heavy with questions.

He knew when he went to sleep that night, the nightmares would be back.

# CHAPTER EIGHT

Jamie lay awake. His bare arm was pressed against the damp, warm skin on Kelli's naked back. Her body was pressed against him, her face buried against the side of his neck. He could hear her breathing softly.

Winter quarter was going quickly, just as Kelli had said it would. After the ten-day break at Thanksgiving, there were just three weeks of the new quarter's classes before everyone again scattered for Christmas break. Professors hated the arrangement, felt it disrupted their classes and gave the students a distracted manner, as though the first three weeks didn't count. For some, that was definitely true. Most saw it as the more relaxed portion of the year before the long, gray midwinter that stretched out until spring. For those in new relationships however, it was a period fraught with anticipation and uncertainty. For Kelli and Jamie, there was no fear of things falling by the wayside as they separated for the holidays, no concern that either would meet someone else or lose interest, but simply an anxiousness at being separated, if only for another ten days. Kelli had begun staying in his room almost nightly, and their relationship had grown much more intense, both physically, and emotionally, than either would ever have expected. Though they never put too fine a point on it, both felt more attached to the other than they cared to admit. During the days, they found their minds drifting towards the other, their bodies tingling and responding to the memories of what they had done together that morning, and the night before. Kelli would sit in her classes, nuzzling her nose under the collar of the shirt she'd swiped from Jamie's chair. Jamie would think of things he wanted to tell her, or that he definitely wanted to avoid, then he'd bring them up anyway, unable to keep them to himself.

Jamie thought rekindling his sex life would ease the hyper-sexuality that had continued, even with the reduction of his meds, but it seemed to have the opposite effect. There was an electricity in his veins that he'd never felt before, an almost singleminded need to fuck his brains out. Fortunately, Kelli seemed to have the same intentions.

Yet, he couldn't shake the feeling that the other shoe was waiting to drop. After that first event, with the silence and the flashes of light while they had been making love, there had been repeated incidents, after which he always had the dreams.

They weren't always the same, just similar in mood - a feeling of dread, and then, cold terror. Visions of the man with the icy blue eyes came at him from the shadows. He'd wake with a start, relieved to find Kelli's arms wrapped around him in the dark, the wind whistling on the other side of the building's concrete wall. He held her tighter on those nights, nearly clenching his teeth as he squeezed his arms around her. It was a sense of calm he hadn't realized had been missing in his life.

He'd read articles about people in constant pain, ones who'd had surgery to remove tumors, or cancer, and felt a relief they'd never known they needed. He knew pain. Knew how it felt to have something intruding in your body. He lifted his hand to his head. They say pain is your body's way of telling you something is wrong. Are nightmares the same? His body was still cooperating with him, but he had the feeling he was fighting off confusion. Things were still going well, but he sensed that it was taking a bit more concentration for him to keep his thoughts in order. He considered seeing Dr. Price over vacation, but he wasn't yet sure there was a reason to do so.

The night crept by slowly, with that strange sense of drifting in and out of sleep. When light started filtering in through the blinds, crawling across the floor toward him, Jamie couldn't tell if he had slept at all, wasn't sure if he had even closed his eyes. He could hear people's alarms going off; they'd stop, then go off again nine minutes later. Clearly a floor fond of its "snooze" buttons. Eventually, doors began opening, and bare feet trod down the hallway to the bathrooms.

Jamie heard Will's voice as he called something to Sandi; he'd taken to flirting with the girl after he first saw Kelli leave Jamie's room the previous weekend. Things were strange among the three of them. The guy had never really spoken to him, so Jamie couldn't honestly see a difference, but both Gabe and Kelli noted that Will seemed genuinely pissed off. They tried to stay at her place more frequently, but dealing with Christie and Joe seemed like an unnecessary annoyance, and as he argued, they couldn't let someone else's feelings come into play with their decisions. Personally, he thought Will was a pain in the ass; it bothered him to see Kelli so upset by the tension it was causing.

He sat and watched her, lying on her side with her face buried in the pillow. A door slammed in the hall and her eyes flickered open. She looked up at him.

"Fuck you."

"What?!" Jamie asked, pleading innocence.

"You know I hate it when you watch me sleep."

"I can't help it."

"Yes you can."

He took a breath and fell back against the mattress. Kelli closed her eyes again, then let out a frustrated grumble and got up, shivering in the cold as she pulled on one of Jamie's sweatshirts and opened the door to the hallway. Jamie watched her slip out the door, then turned his head when he heard the latch click shut. He lay on his back, looking up at the sky through the upturned blinds. It looked cold. He was still staring out the window when he heard her return and lock the door. He didn't turn his head to look at her.

"Do you have to go?" he asked.

She walked over and kissed him on the temple.

"You know I do."

"You could stay here and have Christmas with me

and my mother."

"I think that might be a bit premature."

"Then come for dinner this weekend."

"All right."

"And then stay…"

"How about this?" Kelli said as she ran her hand down his chest, slipping her fingers under the edge of the blanket. "I come to your house for dinner this weekend--" She brushed her fingers against him as she kissed him on the lips. "Then I go home for Christmas--" She slid one leg under the covers, straddling him. "The next day, I take the train up from New York-" She hesitated for a moment, then lowered herself down over him "and we spend New Year's and the rest of the break here in the dorms, just the two of us."

Jamie ran his hands down her back, wrapped them around the back of her thighs, and stood suddenly, lifting her with him. Kelli laughed as he pressed her back against the wall.

"Do you like that idea?" she asked him.

Jamie kissed her eyes, and held her gaze when she opened them again.

"Sounds fantastic."

* * *

The floor threw an improvised Christmas party on the last day of classes. Fritz took a portion of the activities money from student housing and bought an eight-foot sub sandwich from Dibella's, along with some cakes and soda from Wegman's. A few people brought gifts and exchanged them in the corners. As they sat around the room eating cake and talking about their Christmas plans, Will came over to Kelli, quietly asking if he could see her for a moment. She glanced at Jamie, then walked down the hall with Will. Gabe walked over as Jamie watched them turn the corner.

"You live here in town, right?" Gabe asked.

Jamie turned to him, his attention split.

"Yeah, I'm from Rochester."

"What are you doing for the break?"

"Uh," He turned to Gabe, not wanting to seem jealous as Will and Kelli disappeared around the corner. "No plans, relaxing at home, might come back a little early and hang with Fritz."

"When does he come back?"

"Two days before classes start. I guess RAs have to get back early in case anything comes up."

Gabe nodded his head, taking a pensive bite of his cake and looking away, as though contemplating the great responsibility of the resident advisor.

"Where are you from, Gabe?"

"Me? Long Island."

Jamie nodded, inexplicably stumped for conversation. He looked back down the hall and saw Kelli returning. She was carrying a paperback book in one hand and a crumpled up wad of wrapping paper in the other. She dropped the paper in the trash as she walked over to Jamie.

"Everything okay?" Jamie whispered in her ear.

She nodded her head bruskly. "Yeah, it's fine."

"What did he give you?"

She held up a copy of *A Prayer For Owen Meany.*

"Oh," he started. "Can I look at it?"

She lowered the book to her side. "Maybe later."

Will walked back down the hall, ducked into his dorm room, and walked out a moment later, coat in hand. He glanced at them dejectedly and left.

"What time you guys wanna leave?" Fritz asked as he walked over, slapping Jamie on the shoulder.

"Any time you're ready." Jamie replied.

Fritz had offered to drive them to Jamie's house. Jamie would drive Kelli to the station the next morning. He wasn't looking forward to it.

He turned to Kelli. "You all set?"

She nodded her head.

"I'll just make sure I have everything." He replied as he headed down the corridor.

The sounds of the party faded as he stepped into his room. He was already packed, but needed a moment to himself. He glanced around, looking over the prescription containers lined up on the dresser. He'd all but stopped taking them the last week, hoping it might clear his mind, but he was having the same daydreams and hallucinations as the previous summer -- his mind continually slipping into fantasies, his attention wandering, but his body behaving perfectly. He hadn't told Kelli anything, and so far, she hadn't noticed anything unusual in his behavior. Still, he was growing concerned. He'd have to ask Dr. Price about it, but was afraid he'd be reprimanded for messing with his dosages. That was something Price did not take lightly. Who knows, maybe drug fluctuations in his system were causing the problems, or maybe he was just extra horny lately. He doubted it though. He was still feeling good, but different somehow. He'd have to talk to Price. Probably better to take the meds with him. He ran his hand over the dresser, scooping up the containers and slipping them in his duffel bag.

Kelli slipped into the room. She walked up behind him and wrapped her arms around his chest, kissing him on the neck.

"You okay?" he asked again.

"Yeah, I just feel bad. You know…?"

Jamie turned and kissed her again. "There's nothing to feel bad about. This stuff happens."

"Would you be saying that if you were in Will's shoes?"

Jamie hesitated, started to speak, then stopped himself.

"You ready to go?" he asked.

Kelli knodded her head. "Absolutely."

# CHAPTER NINE
## CHRISTMAS

The snow scrunched under their feet, the crackling sound of bitter cold.

Jamie turned to Fritz, who seemed unnaturally quiet.

"What ya doing for break?"

"I don't know, man. Catch up with some of my high school buddies. Bang some honeys."

"Pig," Kelli cut in. "No 'honeys' want anything to do with you."

Fritz made a hissing cat noise, swiping at the air with a gloved hand.

"You *really* don't like me, do you?" he replied.

"If I gave you any thought, I probably wouldn't." Kelli said in her best Bogart voice.

"Huh?"

"Would you two stop?!" Jamie interrupted.

They walked on silently.

"What day do you think you'll be back?" Jamie asked.

"The thirtieth. You guys still coming back early?"

Jamie nodded. "Looks like it."

"That's cool." Fritz said, shooting Kelli a wary look.

"We can all hang out," Jamie continued. "Give the two of you some time to work out some of your issues."

Neither one of them responded.

\* \* \*

The car finally started to warm up just as they were pulling in the drive to Jamie's house. It was dark out. Kelli looked up at the moon through the passenger's window, then turned her eyes to the sheet of ice glazing the snow on the front lawn, over which the moon reflected in a bright white line. The house was lit up warmly in the background. It looked enormous.

"Shit man," Fritz whispered. "You live in a fucking palace."

"It looks bigger than it is, trust me." Jamie replied from the backseat.

"Yeah, sure it does."

Fritz lowered his head, peering out the window as they drove up the hill and curved around to the front walkway. The car stopped in front of the house, and Kelli opened the door, holding the seat forward for Jamie to get out.

"Did you wanna come inside?" Jamie asked.

Fritz looked at him, then over at Kelli, who leveled him with an icy look.

"Nah. Thanks, though. I wanna get back to the floor."

"You sure?"

Fritz nodded his head. "Yeah. Thanks for the invite

though.

Jamie leaned in and slapped him on the back, then gave him a strong handshake.

"Have a good Christmas, man."

"You too," Fritz replied. He waved a hand to Kelli. "Merry Christmas babe."

"Merry Christmas, pig," she shot back with a smirk.

Fritz revved the engine, spinning out the tires as he tore off down the driveway. Jamie put his arm around Kelli's shoulder as they headed for the house.

"Why do you hate that guy some much?"

"I don't *hate* him. He just bugs me. Intensely."

"Okay. Well then, why does he bug you so intensely?"

Kelli just sighed. "If I have to explain it, then there's really no point."

They walked up the steps to the front porch and pushed opened the heavy wooden door.

"Hello?" Jamie called inside.

There was no response. Kelli noted that his voice almost echoed back to them.

"Mom, you home?" he called again.

They stepped into the front entryway. Kelli looked around the room. Deep red carpet covered the floor around them, then curved and ran up an arched staircase to the next floor. Lamps and wall sconces filled the room with pools of warm light. It took her a moment to adjust to the posh surroundings. She'd forgotten about Jamie's father. Of course he and Jamie's mother would be rich. The thought simply hadn't crossed her mind. Jamie set their bags at the bottom of the stairs, then walked through a doorway and out of sight. Kelli heard him calling hello again. He returned a moment later.

"She must be out. I can take our stuff upstairs and show you around."

Kelli nodded her head. "This place is amazing."

"Yeah?" Jamie began, then trailed off. He picked up their bags and started up the stairs. "Anyway, she'll probably be back any minute."

Kelli followed him up the wide, curving staircase, which came out on a landing halfway up. A staircase on the left ran up to a third floor. A plaque at the bottom of stairs read *Come On Up – Everything else has gone wrong*.

Kelli stared at the sign.

"Wasn't that the title off one of--?"

"Yeah," Jamie interrupted her. "That's my father's office."

He switched on a row of lights that ran down the length of the red carpeted hall. A series of large, boldly colored paintings hung on the walls. Kelli studied them as Jamie whisked them down the corridor.

"Did you paint these?" she asked, breathless.

"Yeah."

"They're amazing!"

Jamie was slow to respond. "Thank you."

They stopped at a bedroom at the end of the hall. Jamie turned on the light and set their bags on one of two twin beds.

"Is this your room?" Kelli asked.

"No, mine is upstairs. I thought this one might be

182

better--"

"I want to stay in your room." Kelli interrupted him. He hesitated. "All right."

"Will your mother have a problem with that?"

"*My mother?*" he started to say. My mother was sleeping with rock stars and snorting cocaine when she was my age, he thought. "No," he continued. "She won't care."

He switched off the light and led her around the corner to a dark, narrow corridor. Kelli walked behind him as they slipped into the shadows, heading towards a doorway at the end of the hall.

"I'm sorry it's so dark," Jamie said over his shoulder. "The wiring in this hallway's been burned out for years."

Kelli reached into the darkness and put her hand on Jamie's shoulder. The door opened with a gentle squeak as they slipped inside. Jamie set their bags on the bed and crossed the room. Kelli watched his silhouette in the darkness.

"Just let me turn on a light."

"No, don't," she said. 'I like it this way."

She watched him stop in the middle of the room as she walked towards him. The room was dark and warm. She could just make out the outline of his face in the moonlight. She slipped her hands around his waist, pulled him towards her, and kissed him gently.

"I love you," she whispered.

He started to speak, but she brought her fingers to his mouth to quiet him. She reached down with her other hand, pressing it against the front of his pants, held it there, slowly rubbing her palm against him. She felt him getting hard - kissed him again, slower, biting his lip. She slid her hand under his t-shirt, felt the course hairs running down his abdomen. She tickled the skin softly, then brought her hands back to his waist, fingering the button. He caught his breath as she unfastened his pants, slowly slid down the zipper.

Jamie felt her hands sliding over him as she pulled his cock out into the open. The air was cool on the delicate skin. Kelli's warm fingers were around him, stroking up and down, teasing the head. Her eyes looked up at him, sparkling wickedly, as she went down on her knees in front of him. Jamie held his hands on the back of her head, twirling her hair in his fingers. He leaned his head back, heard the blood pumping in his ears. He wouldn't last long. Her mouth was so warm, and...

Jamie closed his eyes, and it happened, the flashes of light, the whirring hum, and the silence.

He came suddenly, his hands tensing at the back of her head as she held her mouth against him. She pressed her hand to his back, holding him in place as he tried to pull away. Then he was still. After a moment, she pulled her head back, closed her lips, and looked up at him. She stood, staring into his unblinking eyes as she wiped her mouth, smiled wickedly, then kissed him on the neck. He wrapped his arms around her, led her slowly to the edge of the bed. Kelli pressed her head against his chest.

They lay in the darkness.

"I'm gonna miss you," he said finally.

"I'll miss you too."

* * *

Jamie sat up suddenly. He had that strange sensation again, almost like being drunk - as though his vision, and his mind, were a few seconds out of sync with the motion of his body. He sat on the edge of the bed, then got up and went into the bathroom, where he closed the door behind him and turned on the tap in the sink, scooping handfuls of cold water up onto his face and rubbing his cheeks and eyes.

Kelli felt along the wall by the door, found the light switch and flipped it on. Nothing happened.

"Hey," she called over the sounds of splashing water through the door. "How do I turn on the lights?"

"That switch is messed up, like the one in the hall. There's a lamp on the dresser."

Kelli sat in the dark. Her eyes had yet to adjust to the light.

"Where's the dresser?" she muttered.

She stood and felt her way across the room, walking in baby steps 'til she bumped into something. She looked around the room, objects were slowing emerging from the darkness. She could just make out the edge of a lampshade glowing in the moonlight. She crouched down and flipped it on, only to recoil in terror at a grotesque sculpture bobbing its head up and down at her.

"Jesus Christ!"

The sounds of the water stopped.

"I'm guessing you found the lamp."

Kelli leaned forward, studying the bouncing dragon head. It was sculpted from clay and intricately decorated.

She looked at the symbols and markings, then stood and wandered the room. Paintings hung from the walls, and bizarre pieces of artwork sat on tabletops or crouched on shelves, as if ready to pounce. She studied a painting that hung over the dresser, the details along the edges were the same as the ones on the figures.

"These paintings are *unbelievable*."

She crossed the room and looked at several more canvases, all done in the same style as the pieces in the hallway. She looked at the dates; there was nothing from the last two years. An arrangement of framed photos hung to the side of the bedroom door; one was signed from the current year. The bathroom door creaked as Jamie stepped out into the room. He was wiping his face with a washcloth.

Kelli was still looking at the paintings as Jamie went over to the dresser and pulled out a shirt, removing the one he was wearing.

"This stuff is incredible. Why did you switch to photography?"

Jamie started to speak, then stopped, and pulled the shirt down over his head. He was just looking up at Kelli when a door slammed downstairs, and Lynn's voice called up to them.

"Hello? Anybody home?"

Jamie looked Kelli in the eyes, then shouted, "Yeah, we'll be right down!" He turned back to Kelli. "Can we talk about it later?"

When they came down the stairs, Lynn Pepper was

standing in the middle of the kitchen, pulling off a snow covered winter parka and hat. She turned to them with flushed cheeks, throwing her arms open.

"Hi!"

"Mrs. Pe-" Kelli started.

"Lynn," She interrupted. "You must be Kelli." She stepped forward, giving Kelli a hug. "I'd like to say I've heard so much about you, but Jamie has been keeping pretty mum."

Lynn turned to Jamie and gave him a quick hug.

"Hi Mom."

"I'll have dinner warmed up in a few minutes. I just finished a piece for the magazine and wanted to go for a quick loop around the golf course."

"You were playing golf?" Kelli asked.

"Oh no. No. Just cross country skiing. The golf course is great for it in the winter." Lynn stopped and pulled a pack from her back, rummaging through it and removing a large paper sack. She continued, "I swung by Rice's on the way home and got us something special for dinner."

"Lobster?" Jamie asked.

Lynn nodded.

"Do you need help with anything?" Kelli asked.

"No, you two sit down." Lynn tossed her gloves on a chair by the door. "Jamie can help me when it's time to pop these guys in the water. Do you want any wine? Jamie, you can have alcohol now, can't you?"

Jamie could feel Kelli watching him.

"Yeah, Mom," he said flatly.

They exchanged looks.

Lynn glanced at Kelli, then back to Jamie. "Well, why don't you run downstairs and grab us a bottle?"

Jamie left the room as Lynn took a covered dish from the fridge and set it down on the counter.

"So, Lynn, what were you working on today?" Kelli asked.

Lynn was a blur of action, sticking the dish in the microwave, pulling out a loaf of bread, and slicing it into wedges.

"Oh, just a piece on Bowie. A follow-up on how he's doing after the angioplasty." Lynn continued, "I've gotta say, it's a weird feeling when your rock Gods start having heart surgery, or dying."

"He's not dying is he?"

Lynn looked up at her.

"Who?"

"David Bowie."

"Him? No way. Not yet anyway. He's the healthiest of the lot, but he is getting up there now."

Jamie returned, carrying a bottle of red wine. He found a corkscrew in a cluttered drawer and popped the cork, deftly pouring three glasses of wine, giving one to Kelli as he arched an eyebrow and nodded towards Lynn.

"Mom loves Bowie. She thinks he's '*fabulous.*'"

Lynn looked up at Kelli, a twinkle in her eye.

"Isn't he?"

"Well, I don't know him that well."

"Mom, not everyone is as familiar with seventies rockstars as you."

"Yes, but she *is* a woman. Old or not, I mean, come on," she bobbed her head knowingly at Kelli. "Bowie is a very sexy man. He just has it. Whatever the hell *it* is."

The microwave beeped and Lynn pulled out the dish, gave it a quick once-over, and stuck it back in. She turned to Jamie and snapped her fingers.

"Where's my wine?"

He motioned to the glass sitting on the counter and she scooped it up, downing a long gulp.

"That makes the ride worth it." Lynn put her hand on Kelli's shoulder. "Come on, let's sit down. I want to know everything about you."

A fire crackled in the background as they sat and had their drinks. Lynn set out a plate of crackers and a block of cheese, which she attacked with a slicer the moment they sat down.

"So, where are you from Kelli?" she asked as she scarfed a cracker.

"From downstate, just outside New Paltz."

"Oh, you mean in all those "kill areas?"

"What?" Jamie asked.

"You know, all the towns down there are named things like Wallkill and Fishkill. I think it means river or something. Can't be good for tourism."

"Yeah, I don't know that it does wonders," Kelli laughed. "I'm actually from Fishkill. I grew up there."

"Do you have any brothers or sisters?"

Kelli nodded, "Three brothers. I'm the only girl."

"Three brothers? My God, it's a wonder you're not

sick to death of boys."

"Oh, I have my moments," Kelli replied, looking Jamie in the eye as she took a sip of her wine.

The fire sizzled and popped behind them.

"I love your house," Kelli said after a moment. "How long have you lived here?"

"Oh, Gosh, probably thirty years now. Jamie's father and I got this place right after we were married. Most of the look of the place is his doing."

Kelli looked around at the dark wood paneling and the walls of books and artwork. "Well, it's really inspiring. I could happily spend a month just looking through the books."

"Well, thank you. I've always liked it." Lynn sat forward suddenly. "You said it's inspiring. Can I ask what it is that you're studying?"

Jamie interrupted, "Do you feel like you're in a Lynn Pepper interview here?"

Kelli laughed.

Lynn turned her head to him, "What? I'm interested!"

"No, no. It's fine! I'm actually studying film. This is my second year at RIT."

"Film's good. Any specific area?"

"Unfortunately, I'm probably at the stage where I think I can be the next Nora Ephron."

"Why unfortunately? No reason you can't be."

"I just keep hearing how impossible it's gonna be to break in. So I feel kind of stupid when I say I want to be a director."

"But that's what you want to do," Lynn responded. "Don't let people convince you that you can't do it. That's part of the racket! When I was in school they did the same thing. Talk up the field, talk down to you; make you feel like you can study the medium and the craft, but you have no business shooting for the industry itself. They want you to think it's impossible, cause they don't want you stealing any of their thunder, or their opportunities! "

"Well, thank you, I appreciate that," Kelli replied.

"Besides," Lynn continued. "I know Nora. Maybe I can hook you two up for a pep talk."

Kelli's face froze in a half smile. "What?"

Jamie looked at her, nodding his head with a smile, first up and down, then from side to side.

Lynn stood suddenly. "I'd better check on dinner." She ran out of the room.

"Nora Ephron?" Kelli whispered to him.

"What can I say?" Jamie shrugged his shoulders.

"Jamie," Lynn shouted from the kitchen. "The water's boiling."

Jamie stood and leaned down to kiss Kelli on the forehead. "I'll be right back," he whispered. "I'm off to murder some lobsters."

"I see from insurance that you saw Dr. Price last month," Lynn remarked as he walked into the kitchen.

Jamie was quiet.

"Everything all right?" Lynn continued.

"Yeah. It's fine. I had a little thing. Nothing to worry about. He checked the dosages, checked the implant.

Thought it was from stress while I was getting my bearings with classes."

Lynn looked at him intently. "And what do *you* think it was from?"

"I think he was right. I missed a couple days of exercise. Could feel my brain tensing up like I was getting too worked up about classes. It hasn't happened since."

Lynn turned to the stove, where she pulled the lid from a massive pot of boiling water. "Well then, if you're not worried, I'm not worried."

"But," Jamie laughed, "you're still worried."

"Of course I am."

"Everything's fine, Mom. Stop. Save some panic for the future."

"You can pop in the lobsters now."

Jamie opened the paper bag on the countertop, looking down at the mass of greenish-red claws and feelers. "Say your prayers, fellas."

He flipped the bag end over end, dumping the lobsters on the counter, then picked them up one by one, and slipped them head first into the boiling water. He dropped the last one into the water, and watched as its eyes fogged over and air bubbles rumbled to the surface.

"Does she know what you've been through?" Lynn nodded towards the living room.

Jamie stared down into the water. "No. Not yet."

"Any reason you're waiting to tell her?"

"I don't want to jinx it."

Lynn nodded her head and marched out into the living room.

Dinner was simple and delicious. Scalloped potatoes, salad, and the lobsters, smothered in drawn butter. It was probably the butter, the ultimate indulgence. They sat at the table, washing each bite down with sips of red wine.

Lynn didn't cook much, but she knew her wine, or rather, she knew her late husband's wine, which had been aging in the house's cellar for a decade now, the majority of his collection slowly clicking into its prime years, which they might not have had time to do had Jeff and his less patient artist's temperment been at the helm. As it was, each bottle seemed better than the last, and at a time like tonight, as they sat around the table in the midst of a dark winter's night, a fire at one end of the room, hot food in their stomachs, trouble momentarily at bay, the wine tasted all that much better as it swirled in their glasses and burned its way ever so gently down their throats.

The wind grew louder as the evening went on. They had dessert and sat by the fire talking. Kelli turned the questions to Lynn, who answered quietly, occasionally deferring a response with a joke. Lynn mentioned Jamie's paintings once or twice, but that just led to questions of photography, and the when and the how, which left them scampering in squirrelly maneuvers to get the subject back on safe ground.

At midnight, Jamie got up to bring in the dishes, and looked out the window to see snow swirling in the air outside. He flipped on the porchlight and saw the white flakes billowing in under the awning and up over the steps. The wind roared against the sides of the house, gust after gust fighting to peel away the old wooden siding.

"It's getting late," Lynn called from the living room. "I'm gonna have to turn in."

Kelli stood and walked into the kitchen with the last of the dishes, which Jamie loaded into the washer. Lynn walked in close behind, setting her empty wine class on the counter with a gentle *ting*.

"Kelli, it was lovely meeting you."

"It was nice meeting you too."

Lynn yawned loudly. "I'll see you two in the morning. I trust Jamie to get you some towels and anything else you need."

"Good night, Mom."

Lynn slipped out of the room. They listened to her footsteps as she crossed the front entryway, then slowly made her way up the stairs. Kelli walked over to Jamie, looked him in the eyes, and gave him a long, deep kiss on the mouth.

They turned off the lights, strolled through the house to Jamie's room, and stood at the window, watching the snow as it tumbled down from the sky. The wind still rumbled as they slipped into bed, burrowed under the covers, and squeezed each other tighter with each gust outside.

"I love you," Kelli said once more in the darkness.

"I love you too."

The thermostat clicked on downstairs; hot water burbled up through the pipes and into the radiator, which popped and rumbled as it warmed the air. The window panes grew foggy from the heat inside. Then they kissed, and grew still, and fell fast asleep.

It would be one of Jamie's last peaceful nights.

The storm swept out during the night, leaving drifts of snow in its wake. The long, curving driveway was under at least four feet of it, which didn't get cleared until noon that day. They could hear the sounds of the snowplows going back and forth across the drive as they sat in the kitchen at breakfast.

"The roads are gonna be a nightmare, you know."

Kelli cradled a coffee mug in her hands. "You don't have to take me to the station. We can call a cab."

"Do you have to leave today?" Jamie asked. "You could always stay another night."

"I wish I could, but the folks are expecting me. They've gotta pick me up, then head out to the Island."

"You can't meet up with them out there?"

"Trust me, this is easier. I'll be back in a week. We'll have New Year's together in the dorms."

Jamie nodded. "That'll be great."

"Hey, we've still got a little time here. Let's make the most of it, not ruin the morning hoping for something else."

"I hope the trains are canceled," Jamie said.

"Thanks a lot."

When they could finally leave, Lynn waved from the front porch as they crept slowly down the length of the driveway. The old Buick's heater purred at their feet as the tires slipped in gripless circles, then caught hold and pulled the car out onto the main road. They passed several cars off on the side of the road, their lights flashing, the drivers sitting on the hoods, cell phones in hand, waiting for AAA to come and pull them out.

"See?" Jamie said. "You're putting my safety at risk."

He eased off the gas, watching the road ahead carefully.

"You've lived here eighteen years. I trust you to drive in this." Kelli replied, obviously knowing better.

There were a few other brave souls on the road, their headlights slipping away in the snowy haze ahead of them. Jamie pumped the brakes gently, keeping the car's momentum at bay. Once or twice, he took a turn with a bit too much oomph, the back end sweeping around with a little Dirty Harry swagger, but things went smoothly for the most part. They took the long stretch of road down Mt. Hope, past the cemetery, past the turn-off to the University of Rochester, then down into the center of town, where their conversation cut off suddenly. The station was almost in sight. Jamie cleared his throat and sighed.

"Just about there."

Kelli nodded.

"Think it'll be on time?"

She shook her head, "No idea."

The road curved to the right, then sliced through several cross streets. The lights were all in their favor. The snow was still falling as they turned into the parking lot and pulled into a space. Jamie killed the engine and they sat in silence for a moment. The car clicked and moaned as it settled. The air outside whispered icy thoughts.

They looked at each other, then turned and stepped out into the cold. Jamie pulled Kelli's bag from the backseat and walked around to the passenger side.

"Should we get this over with?"

She paused a moment, then nodded.

The terminal was about the same temperature indoors as it was out. Jamie waited with the bag as Kellie went up and bought her ticket. He turned and watched the few scattered people waiting for the train. An older woman sat at the far end, alone, an overflowing wire laundry cart beside her. Lord only knew if she had walked all the way here by herself. A heavy-set woman rested on a bench in the middle of the room, her son and daughter, both clad in purple bubble-jackets, ran around fighting. The little boy kept grabbing his sister's braided hair and throwing it back over her shoulders. The girl kept reaching behind her ears to sweep the braids back in front, brushing her hands down the twisted strands and scowling at him. Then he'd run over and do it again.

"Stop it!" the little girl shouted.

The mother seemed to ignore them as she looked through a wad of papers and glanced up at the clock. The little boy ran back towards his sister, again eyeing the braids intently. Then, just as he was reaching for the hair, his mother leaned forward in her seat and grabbed the back of his jacket, stopping him dead in his tracks. He made a whimpering noise as the collar caught his throat.

"Jeremy! Cut it out!" the woman hollered, then she dropped her hold on the jacket and went back to her paperwork.

Jeremy sat down and pouted.

A couple of Bukowski types stood by the vending machines, their hair shooting out in all directions, their faces blackened with dirt and stubble. Jamie thought of a Wiley E. Coyote cartoon where TNT had just blown up under the hapless protagonist's nose. Face by Acme.

A few remaining travelers waited out on the platform, their clothes rippling in the wind.

The snow seemed to be picking up force. The drive home wasn't gonna be any easier.

Jamie turned and watched Kelli at the ticket counter. She handed the teller her credit card and looked through her wallet, absentmindedly playing with a strand of her hair. He was going to miss her. Christ, was he ever going to miss her.

"It's just a week," he muttered to himself.

In a week they'd be back at the dorms. Fritz had given them the keys so they could sneak in before anyone else got back. Think of the fun the two of them would have in a massive, empty building. Creepy, sexy fun. He smiled. Just a week. Just a week. Then Kelli took her ticket from the teller and walked over to him. Their eyes locked as she swept a lock of hair behind her ear. It damn near killed him.

"I wish I was staying!" she said.

"I do too."

They were quiet. Then, without a word, they headed out the double doors and onto the platform. The snow was coming down harder. An icy gust of wind wheezed over the roof of the terminal, sweeping a cloud of snow down with it. Kelli stepped towards Jamie and ducked her head down against his side. He could smell her hair, could feel her warm cheek brush against his chin. He put his arms around her, pulled her tight against him. The train whistle sounded around the bend. A moment later, it was pulling into the station. The platform rumbled under their feet. Kelli looked up at him, her eyes a deep, shimmering blue. They kissed goodbye and she walked away, slipping into line with the other passengers.

The train stopped and a conductor came out and set a case of Rubbermaid steps down on the platform. He motioned towards a group of parka-clad departing passengers, who wobbled their way down the wiggly steps, then he turned to the next batch of passengers.

"All aboard!"

The group began boarding. Kelli waited for the woman with the two bubble-jacketed kids to herd them on board, then she slowly walked up the steps. She turned at the top and gave Jamie one last, long look, then waved her hand, and slipped inside. The rest of the passengers made their way on board, quickly on account of the cold, then the conductor made a series of announcements over the loudspeaker, his voice murmuring from the train's windows and drifting out into the icy air. Another announcement mumbled over the platform P.A. system and the doors to the train slid shut. The engine made an irritable, whining groan as the wheels slowly came to life, slipping on the metal rails, then catching hold and pulling the train forward with a flinty squeal.

Jamie stood on the platform, watching the cars

rumble away. Then, in a wink, the snow clouds swallowed all signs of the train. He listened as the sounds faded to silence. A gust of wind murmured around him as he turned and cut through the station to his car.

The drive home was nerve-wracking. The road conditions were deteriorating swiftly. Jamie flipped on his lights and found himself testing the brakes every few feet, afraid to pick up any momentum. The Buick felt particularly empty now. Just the sounds of slush spattering the bottom of the floorboards. He reached over and flipped on the radio. "Brother Wease" was putting in another plug for his tattoo shop, talking about the next concert that he'd be hosting at the Dinosaur Barbecue. Wease was sounding pretty good. The cancer was in remission, his voice was, well, not strong, but damn near back to normal. His signature sound had lost little from his operation and treatment a few years back. Though they'd been through much different experiences, hearing the Wease back on the radio was just the touch of normalcy that Jamie needed. People hit unexpected bumps in the road, dealt with them, and moved on. That's what Wease had done, and that's what *he* was doing now. Hopefully.

If nothing else, he was back in school, and he had a new girl in his life. This relationship felt different from anything in the past. It was physical and intense, but there was something different going on. For all their erotic adventures and misadventures over the last month or so, there was more at work here. Intimacy was part of it, but not entirely; after all, he hadn't told her anything about the operation yet. He knew she had some inkling that something was wrong. Or at least... unusual. Hell, he'd caught her looking at his pills and the scars on more than a few occasions. She just had to Google the names on his pill containers to get an idea of what he might be dealing with. Since she hadn't brought it up, and since she showed no signs of backing away from him, if Kelli *had* looked up any of the medications, she must not have found enough to totally scare her away. Not yet anyway. So why hadn't he told her everything?

Was he afraid something was wrong?

Always.

Nothing specific. Just normal concerns. Superstition. He reached over and knocked on the dashboard's fake wood paneling.

God forbid anything was wrong. Aside from the headache that first week, and a growing sense of fatigue, perhaps from a bit too much late night fucking, and a few too many early morning runs, he was feeling good. This morning they'd exchanged their Christmas presents. They hadn't opened them yet, but he'd wanted to. Christmas Eve they'd call each other and open their gifts at the same time. He'd found an antique locket at a shop downtown several weeks ago, and had put together a couple of photos of the two of them that he'd doctored in Photoshop. If you looked at the photos quickly, you might not see that anything had been done, just a couple of sepia toned prints of two young lovers, which was essentially what they were, but he'd added some extra touches, hints of color that would stand out to the studied eye. Maybe it was cheesy. He hoped not. The main gift was the locket, which was really cool - an old-time, engraved set of interlocking silver shells, with a firm clasp, just the right amount of tarnish in the details, and a beautiful matching chain. It had set him back a couple hundred dollars, and it looked it. Maybe it was overkill, but then again, Kelli seemed to be in this for the long haul, so he'd gone for it. Not that he'd have passed it up either way.

It might be good to go for a run today if the weather cleared. It had been a couple of days since he'd had some good exercise. If the snow slowed at all, he could jog the path behind the house and make his way to the Pittsford golf course. A run would feel great right now. That is, if the weather shifted. As always, the last thing he wanted to do was to fall and hit his head. Maybe one day that would stop being a constant fear for him, but it was still too soon.

He was deep in his mind, going over the path he'd take to the course. He'd done it a million times before, could see every root, every turn off and muddy slope along the way, as if he were running the course then and there, could anticipate the sensation of his feet pounding down on the snowy ground. He was too relaxed behind the wheel, was letting second nature set in as he made the turnoff onto the side street from the main drag and up into his own neighborhood. The Buick seemed to be taking the turn just fine, its nose jutting out into the road, wheels following the line, then, at the last minute, the back end spun around just a bit too fast, and the car started to go into a spin, whirling around on the icy white pavement, and spinning out into the line of oncoming traffic. Jamie spun the wheel instinctively in the opposite direction, even as a guttural scream rose up from his belly. His eyes bulged at the sight of an oncoming truck, its horn sounding with the baritone burping of an ocean liner. Jamie pulled one hand from the wheel, his arm jerking up to shield his eyes. This was it.

*Honnnnnnnk! Honnnnnnnk!*

The truck let off two long bursts of air through the horn. The car seemed to slow down, a little extra sway going into the twirling motion. Then the sides of the tires hit the curb, slamming the car to a stop as the truck arced around the Buick and roared down the road. Jamie kept his eyes clamped shut. A burst of hot blood exploded in his forehead. He sucked in a deep breath of air and opened his yes.

He looked at his hands.

No blood. No broken glass.

He'd been distracted. Taken the turn too fast.

The road was empty again. The truck's tail lights disappearing in the whiteness beyond.

"Jesus Christ," Jamie muttered to himself. Jesus Christ.

A feeling of oozing cool flowed out from his forehead and radiated through his face. He reached over, put the car back into gear, and pulled a U-turn in the middle of the road. He pointed toward Pittsford and started on his way home again.

* * *

The house was dark when he arrived. He walked up the front steps, his knees weak, feet leaden. He could feel his face sagging.

"Mom?" he shouted.

No answer. She was probably out skiing.

He needed to take a short nap. Recharge from the shock of that near miss. His body had gone into panic mode; now it was crashing.

He stumbled across the living room, pulling off his damp clothing as he staggered to the couch and collapsed in a heap.

He saw a purple haze, then the crimson curtain of his eye lids, then nothing.

He slept.

At some point he heard the creaking of the front door. Lynn was home, walking through the house. She sang and hummed to herself as she went about her routine. Then, she must have seen him sleeping and grew quiet, slipping into the kitchen and closing the door behind her.

He heard the wind outside. Felt drafts of cold air whistling in under the front door, curling their way through the house, and sailing past him as they swirled into the fireplace and up the chimney.

Still he slept.

Finally, he woke with a start. Sitting bolt upright and

gasping for air.

He looked around the room in confusion, wiped a mist of cold sweat from his forehead, and stared at the fireplace.

A fire was burning now.

How long had he been sleeping?

It was dark outside.

He walked over to the front door and turned on the light. The snow was still coming down. This storm was a monster.

A monster.

Jesus. He still couldn't wake up. He shook his head, rubbed at the edges of his eyes. All for naught. The mental cobwebs held their ground.

He headed for the kitchen and the sounds of Bob Dylan.

Lynn was standing at the counter, paying bills.

"Ohh, mama, can this really be the end?" she sang. "To be stuck inside of Mobile with the Memphis blues again." She danced to the music as Bob picked up with the next verse. Then she spotted Jamie from the corner of her eye and jumped in surprise. "You're up!"

"Yeah, I'm up. How long was I asleep?"

"A long time. Long enough for Kelli to call for you, say she'd made it down to the city okay."

"Oh my God," he muttered.

"Everything all right?" Lynn watched him closely as she pulled the lid from a covered dish. Steam swirled up around her as she spooned leftovers out into a bowl.

Jamie sat down at the table. "Yeah, I was just

exhausted. The schedule I've been keeping must have finally caught up with me."

"You're probably right." Lynn set the bowl down in front of her son. "Have something to eat and see if you feel better."

Jamie ate quietly, staring at the flickering flames in the fireplace.

"You have anything you want to do while you're home? Any holiday requests?" Lynn asked him.

"Hmm?" Jamie responded absently.

"Boy, you're still in dreamland, aren't you?" she replied.

"Oh," Jamie started. "I dunno, just watch the usual movies, hang out. I assume we're seeing the family too."

"Yeah, we'll head over to your cousin's place on Christmas for dinner and the regular routine."

The regular routine largely involved snubbing and critical glances. Jamie had grown used to it over the years.

"That should be fun."

"Yeah," Lynn rolled her eyes. "A regular laugh fest. Let's make the most of things in the meantime shall we? You up for a movie tonight?"

"Absolutely."

"You need to call Kelli first?"

"Nah, I'm sure she's tied up with family stuff her first night home. I'll catch her in the morning."

Lynn nodded.

Jamie sat and ate quietly. The thoughts in his head slowly clearing, like he was coming out of a trance. His mind was foggy, and his body was tired. It wasn't an entirely unpleasant sensation. That's what worried him.

~

Jamie awoke in the hallway with icy cold air blowing around his ankles. The house was pitch black, and it took him a moment to get his bearings. Then, in the moonlight, he realized he was standing in the middle of the upstairs corridor, halfway between his bedroom at one end, and the second floor landing at the other. He could just see the outline of the curved staircase that led downstairs, and he knew the other flight of stairs lay hidden in the shadows to the right, leading up to his father's abandoned third-floor office.

His eyes adjusted to the darkness as he looked around. He couldn't remember getting up and walking out here, but how else could it have happened? Had he been sleepwalking? He'd never done it before, but there was no other explanation. The hair on his arms and legs stood on end. He shivered and rubbed his hands over his arms. His body was shaking, and he tensed up suddenly in panic.

*No!*

He willed himself to stop.

"It's just the cold," he muttered under his breath.

A gust of wind whistled at the end of the hall, and an icy draft of air swirled around him. Jamie looked behind him and saw the curtains on the window near his room billowing freely with each gust. Snowflakes had swirled inside, collecting on the red carpeting. The window was pushed all the way open. Jamie rushed over and slammed it closed. He looked down at the snowy yard. What time was it? Deep in the dead of night, that was for sure. There wasn't a glimmer of warmth in the sky. He stared out into the darkness, then pulled the curtains tight.

The hairs on the back of his neck bristled.

His imagination was trying to get the better of him.

"Calm down," he muttered to himself.

The upstairs hallways had always scared the hell out of him when he was a kid. If he was downstairs with his folks and they told him to go to bed early, or he wanted to get up and grab a book or a game, he'd always done it quickly, not wanting to be alone. He'd brace himself for the worst, step off the stairs on the second floor landing, glance up the second set of steps to the third floor, then take off running for his room, where he'd search frantically for the desired item before heading back down the hall, his socked feet peeling out underfoot as he scrambled to gain footing and flee. Even now, more than a decade later, he felt his legs tensing up, ready to run from the ghosts and goblins that waited for him in the shadows.

Course, that's when he noticed something else, down the hallway, at the point where the stairs to the third floor poked out from their little stairwell. It was dim, but it was there. A light was shining down from upstairs. Someone had been up on the third floor.

Jamie's mouth pulled tight. "Fuck."

He hesitated, then ducked into his room, grabbing a hooded sweatshirt from the corner of his bed and pulling it over his head.

"Goddammit. You're a grownup. Act like one for Chrissake."

He marched out into the hallway and down to the second floor landing. No lights glimmered up from the first floor. He turned toward to the third floor stairs. Hesitated. Then ducked his head around the side of the stairwell. As a kid, this was when he'd always expected someone to come lunging out at him. When he did it now, all he saw was a crooked, narrow set of steps that led up to a small corridor at the top with two doors on either side. The light was coming from the room on the left. His father's office.

"Ohh goody."

*Childhood demons, on the next Dr. Phil.*

Jamie stepped up onto the first stair. It groaned under his weight. So did the next. If someone was up there, they'd know he was coming.

"Mom-?" Jamie whispered, his voice a blown out speaker. He cleared his throat. "Mom? You up there?"

Nothing. No response.

"Christ."

Go for it.

He headed up the stairs.

The wood creaked and popped wildly. The doorway to Jeff's office approached in topsy-turvy POV spasms. Then he was at the top of the stairs, two steps from the next landing. Still no noise from inside.

He took the remaining stairs in a confident stride.

One. Two.

Doorway.

Turn.

Then, when he got around the corner, there was nothing. The light was on. The chair at the desk was pushed back, but no one was sitting in it. Here again, the windows were all pushed open. Jamie wondered if he'd been up here too. He walked into the room, glancing behind the door as he entered. No spooks or goblins or burglars were standing with their backs pressed against the wall, waiting to spring on him. He rounded the corner of the desk and felt a crinkling of paper underfoot. Dozens upon dozens of manuscript pages were spread out across the floor. Jamie paused and looked over the yellowed sheets. The font was thin and blocky. The columns of text frequently narrowed into line after line of dialogue. The stuff Jeff Pepper was famous for. He shivered, and quickly closed the windows, flipping the latches securely into place. Then his attention shifted back to the papers.

It wasn't *Dub Taylor*. He wasn't sure which one this was. Maybe it was something different, another collection of essays and stories from the files. Was his mother sorting out his father's papers, helping to organize another collection of his unfinished work? She hadn't mentioned it. He couldn't imagine her going through any of that again. Jamie crouched down and gathered up the papers, sorting them quickly according to the numbers on the top right corners, then he sat down in the chair.

The first few pages read like a diatribe against, well, life, and work, and just some vague *something*. A pile of ranting, raving language, the subject of which was unclear exactly. There was dialogue. There were a few mentions of hands flittering over breasts, talk of tongues in the corners of mouths. Other stuff, good bits, but no real explanation of whether the hands and the appendages they were grabbing belonged to the same people. Were these acts of absentminded self-appreciation, full-out attempts at seduction, or were they something better? Knowing Jeff Pepper, it was any of the above. On the third page he saw the word "professor" written out a few times. On the fourth he saw the give-away, "Dub."

So, this was the original manuscript for the infamous sequel. *Dub*. The one that had all but paid for this house, and probably his college, and most certainly the operation. Well, Lynn had paid for all of those things too, but *Dub Taylor* had always sort of been - not the foundation - but sort of the oven for whoever was bringing home the bread in the Pepper household.

The sequel to Dub Taylor, *Dub,* had snagged one of the biggest advances in publishing history, an advance that would have made even Stephen King rest his chin on the tip of his index finger and narrow his eyes at the absurdity of the whole damn thing -- absurdity, and luck. Whether the book had been any good was beside the point. *Dub Taylor* was a touchstone by the time of Jeff's death. Jamie could remember the hype machine blustering into town when the sequel started coming together posthumously. There were meetings between Lynn and Jeff's editors. Meetings between Lynn and the marketing people. There were news crews. Interviewers. Big ones. Barbara Walters had come, smelling of baby powder and sharp perfume, and had wandered through the house, bossing her crew around, taking a moment to sweet talk Jamie as he sat on the stairs. Charlie Rose had been there, rumpled shirt, mussed hair and all. Jamie had liked him much better than Mrs. Walters. He had that soothing voice, and he never yelled at his crew, or really, at anyone. There had been books everywhere, the feeling of hot lights. Today he realized what a circus it had been.

People talk about Salinger and his mysterious ways, and yeah, Salinger has his mystique, but there's also the mystique of the alternative celebrity writers and journalists, the ones who have covered the *big* stories, met the big names, and slowly seeped into the collective consciousness of the audience. Lynn had certainly done that with her stories from the seventies and eighties. Everyone knew Annie Leibovitz, and everyone knew Lynn Pepper. They were like the founding earth mothers of the magazine now. Jeff Pepper's fame went without saying. But for the big kahuna of one medium to marry the boy genius of another, well, that was like an arranged marriage of literary royalty. For those same two people to be madly, and publicly wild about each other, that was taking it to a whole new level. Then, for one of them to flip his shit after a literal crack-up, well, that was the stuff of legend and publishing magic.

As expected, *Dub* was huge. Out-of-control huge. Everyone bought the damn thing. Everyone had it on the shelf next to their high school and college bible, *Dub Taylor*. Course, not everybody made it all the way *through* the sequel. There was the curiosity factor, the nostalgia factor. Some reviewers, the minority, claimed that this

book was as good, if not *better* than the original, but for
the most part, the book panned out like a heavily revised
bookend. It sat on the shelf, next to its brother, or rather,
its younger half, and it completed the collection. Course,
for academics, and true fans, this was something to be
divied up and savored, decanted, studied against the light,
and absorbed in slow, savory, luxurious sips. Jeff felt his
mother had not so much enjoyed the book, as she had
thought of its preparation as the closest she would get to
closure. He'd seen her a few times during its completion,
sitting by the fire downstairs, reading the pages, then
staring off into space. They'd never found his father's
body, but a year after his disappearance, his memory had
washed up in the shape of this book, and it seemed for
everyone, including Lynn, that that was what they needed
to move on.

Did the book have the answers?

No one seemed to think so, or no one of note had
yet found them.

So how did the manuscript end up spread out on the
floor tonight? Were the published pages and the original
proofs the same, or were they altered somehow? Was it
crazy to assume there were no other versions of the book?

Well, yes, a bit. Jeff wasn't known for approaching
things from multiple angles. He wrote what he wrote,
and that was that. What came out first was the way he
saw things: very rarely did it change. So the first draft of
a book or paper might have one or two brief differences
from the final work, a turn of phrase, an exchange of
dialogue, but not ten or twenty-page alternative passages.

None of that business. With Jeff Pepper, what you saw was what you got, and that was it.

Jamie stopped flipping through the pages and tapped them on the desktop to even the edges. He set them down again, then reached across the desktop for an old hardback copy of *Dub Taylor*, which he placed on top of the manuscript to hold it in place.

Answers. Hmm.

*He*, Jamie, must have been up here then, looking through all this stuff. What a freaky feeling to have been sleepwalking. He didn't like the idea of it. Good thing he hadn't fallen down the stairs and broken anything. Or worse!

A shiver rippled through him again. He hurried to the door, flipped off the lights, and hustled down the stairs. He stopped at the bottom of the landing, suddenly aware of a feeling radiating out at him from the darkness. That sense of being watched. His breath caught in his chest as he waited for his eyes to adjust to the blackness around him. Then, before anything became entirely clear, Jamie ran through the darkness to his room. His imagination was getting the better of him.

~

"You were up last night."

Jamie sat at the table silently, lacing up his running shoes.

"Everything all right?" Lynn continued.

"Yeah, fine. Hope I didn't wake you."

"Me? I fell right to sleep. Just heard you banging

around down the hall a bit, then I was back out like a light."

Jamie pulled on a set of fingerless gloves and stood up to stretch.

"Think I'm still trying to wind down from the start of the quarter," he said. "I keep thinking about the projects I have waiting for me when I get back to school."

"That's gotta be exciting." Lynn smiled.

"Oh yeah," Jamie said with a sigh. "So far so good." God he hoped so.

Lynn sat down with a cup of coffee and started flipping through the paper absentmindedly.

"I'm going for a run."

"Be careful out there," Lynn replied as she looked over the crossword puzzle.

She'd slipped into the zone, so Jamie headed for the door. He swung his arms from side to side, pulled them back behind his head, feeling the blood seeping into his muscles. He stepped out onto the front porch and continued stretching.

He tried to push last night out of his mind. It was a fluke of fatigue. He just needed a run to make up for the exercise he'd been missing lately. He leaned against the railing with one hand, reaching down with the other to pull his foot back behind him, feeling the long muscle fibers in his hamstring pull and stretch under the skin, then he switched sides. He was feeling good. He walked down the front steps, pulling his knit cap down over his ears as he stepped off the last riser and took a series of quick steps down the driveway, starting out in a slow jog, then moving a bit faster. He headed out the driveway and down the long path to the main road as he broke out into a full-out run.

"Whoo!" he let out, excited.

*It felt great to move!*

The snow crunched and slipped underfoot. He ran to just the edge of the road, then turned off on a path that meandered into the woods to his right. He maintained his pace, but watched the ground carefully, ever wary of that dreaded fall.

The blood was pumping now as he raced through the trees. Branches skittered and swooped past him as he bobbed and weaved down the hillside. Then he burst out into the snow-covered open stretches of the golf course. Aside from one or two sets of cross country ski tracks, most likely Lynn's, the place was untouched. The icy powder came up over the tops of his sneakers. He could feel moisture seeping into his socks and the bottoms of his sweat pants, but he was going so fast that he hardly even noticed.

How many times had he run this same course? When was the last time he'd been through here? Probably back in September. That was the first time they'd started having a bit more confidence that the implant was going to work out. About the middle of the month, Dr. Price had given him the okay to go out for a run, and a day or so later, Lynn had reluctantly given him her nod of approval. He'd felt a little shaky on that first jaunt off the beaten path in over two years, but it was at about the same point on the course, on the fairway to whatever hole this was, that he'd started feeling good again, started opening up his stride and pumping his arms to work up some speed, just the way he was doing now.

He thought about last night. And he thought about Kelli. And he ran a little faster. Nothing was going wrong. There was nothing to worry about. He was just tired and confused. People do strange stuff when they're short on sleep and high on stress. Housewives end up at the grocery store in their nightgowns and rollers, wandering the aisles with their shopping lists and recipes. Truckers wander off course, following another vehicle for a couple hundred miles, suddenly snapping to in the middle of nowhere, or worse yet, Texas, trying to remember how they'd managed to maneuver stoplights and intersections for the last few hours, while in their minds they'd been snuggling up to a nice, warm, downy pillow. That's probably what he had done, woken up in the night, boiling hot, opened some windows, wandered down the hall, and absentmindedly thought, "Maybe I'll poke around upstairs."

Yeah, that was it. That was it.

Bull. Shit.

Why upstairs? He hadn't been up there in years. Why *that* book? Why the manuscript and not the final published edition?

He had a flash of Professor Ryan asking about his father.

"He was a good guy."

Had they known each other? The comment suggested that they had.

But who cared?

It was nothing.

But the fact was, he'd been thinking about his father again recently. More importantly, he was thinking about his father as *he* had known him, around the time Jeff Pepper had started sailing off the deep end. That was the period when Jeff had written *Dub,* and whether he'd realized it or not, Jamie had been scanning through that book in his mind recently. His father had had more than his share of emotional confusion. Maybe Jamie was feeling some of the same things.

He'd seen an interview with Michael J. Fox a few years back, where the actor had spoken in detail about an operation he'd undergone to try and control the errant signals from his own Parkinson's. They had essentially bolted a framework to the outside of his head, then bolted the other side of that framework to an operating table in order to prevent unwanted movement. The surgery was invasive, opening up the brain and gently exploring the nooks and crannies inside, figuring which areas did what, smoking out the sources of the communication breakdown. At one point, the surgeon gently prodded an area of tissue as he asked Fox to speak, and the actor described how he'd felt his mouth draw up as he struggled to form words.

"Heeeeey. Yerrrr messing witttth myyy braaaain."

Jamie knew how he felt. They'd been messing with his brain too.

His father's mind was a different matter. It wasn't a case of an actual, physical problem, so much as it was one of mental confusion. Jeff Pepper was never much for looking on the bright side, which made him an especially bad candidate for the sort of serious car accident he'd been through. A good knock to the head, a fair share of physical and emotional trauma, that was a recipe for trouble, and it often sent victims into a mental tailspin, one from which it could take years to recover. Though he'd often veered from the mainstream and gone his own way, in the case of Jeff's recovery from the accident, he had, unfortunately, followed an all too-familiar course. The shift was evident in everything he did, and in everything he wrote. *Dub* had a clear and sudden shift in mood, one that predictably occured at the point Jeff picked up writing again after months of therapy and rehabilitation. Jamie had read the book before, but it was everything from that shift onward that he seemed to be puzzling over. Was there any point in reading the book through again? Probably not. He was just obsessing. What could be worth dredging up?

Jamie was still running all out, his arms pumping at his sides. His throat grew rough with the cold as he climbed up and over the crest of the hill, opened up his stride, and plunged headlong into the woods on the other side. The trail twisted its way through the trees and back toward the house. The snow was melting and forming puddles along the path. Jamie took a turn a bit too sharply, his shoe sliding in the mud as his body lunged forward. He caught himself before he hit the ground, shivering with relief as he continued on. He broke free of the woods and emerged on the gravel lane leading up to the house. He walked the rest of the distance as a cool-down, rotating his arms, pulling them behind his head, and stretching his body from the run.

He wasn't going to look at the manuscript anymore. There was no point.

He walked up the front steps and pushed open the door. A rush of heat enveloped him as he stepped inside, already pulling off his damp shirt. Three hundred and twenty-five crunches, then a shower, then some sketching. If, that is, his fingers would cooperate.

No point in reading any more pages.

He pulled off his shoes and walked into the living room. Crunches. He lay on his back by the couch, feeling the carpet against his bare skin. One, two...

No point.

No point in going up there.

Forty-eight, forty-nine, fifty-

He should focus on his own work.

Switch sides.

He'd call Kelli later, find out how her vacation was going.

Ninety-eight, ninety-nine, one hundred. Switch sides.

He should talk to his mother, tell her what's bothering him.

He jumped to his feet and headed up the stairs to the second floor landing.

Time for a shower and then he'd relax. It was holiday break.

There's no point in going up to that office. Nothing

to be found. Only the old papers and books of a ghost. No hidden secrets. No revelations. Just yellowed paper and dust.

Take a shower. Get on with your life.

He would in a bit.

Just one more time, just to see what he could find.

Jamie turned and headed up the staircase to the third floor.

\* \* \*

"We'll drive down to see family tomorrow morning. What about you?"

"Just going over to my Aunt and Uncle's place for dinner," Kelli replied. "Same thing as every year."

"Same here, same here."

There was a crackle of hesitation.

Jamie was sitting on his bed. The house was quiet and dark. It was around seven o'clock, but it felt much later. Lynne was probably in her office, working. Neither one of them had eaten dinner, despite it being Christmas Eve. The way things worked in the Pepper house, the way they had always worked, was not to plan meals ahead, but to suddenly realize, with the churning of a stomach or the growling rumble of hunger, that it was well past mealtime. In a couple of hours they'd both wind up in the kitchen, scavenging the cabinets for food. For now, they were huddled in their own sections of the house, Lynn absorbed in her work, Jamie on the phone, talking in the warm comfort of his room.

"I miss you," Kelli said.

"I miss you too."

"Wanna open them?"

"Absolutely," Jamie replied. "You first."

He could hear Kelli breathing into the handset, then the sounds of tearing paper on the other end. The paper was off. She was opening the box now. Lifting the tissue.

He heard her breath catch.

"Oh Jamie. It's beautiful."

"You like it?" he asked.

"I *love it.*"

He sat silently, imagining her fingers as they picked up the locket, fingered the latches and etchings, then gently pressed the latch and felt it spring open in her hands. He knew she was doing this, and he knew the moment she folded the halves open and saw the pictures inside.

"Ohh…" her voice said softly through the receiver.

Jamie's breath caught in his chest.

"I love it," she whispered.

Jamie let out a sigh of relief.

"Open yours," Kelli said.

Jamie picked up the package from where it sat between his crossed legs. It was small and square. No bigger than a CD case and about two inches high.

"What is it?" Jamie asked.

"Open it."

The paper was a shimmering deep red, gothic but romantic. Jamie ran his fingers over it's surface, slipped a nail under the folded edge, and pulled it away. The distinctive Tiffany-blue peeked out from the box underneath.

"Wow," he whispered. *"Ka-ching."*

He lifted the lid to find a small silver flask, engraved with his initials. A pattern of skulls and hands surrounded the letters. Jamie took the flask from the box. It was heavy.

"You filled it."

"Yep."

"What's inside?" Jamie asked.

"You'll see."

Jamie unscrewed the cap and held the opening to his nose, breathing in the warm fumes. He raised it to his mouth and took a long drink. The liquid rippled over his tongue, spreading down the back of his throat, where it blossomed into warm vapor. Jamie's eye popped open as his jaw dropped instinctively to exhale. He shook his head in startled appreciation.

"Phew. What is that?

"That's a secret," Kelli laughed. "I'll tell you when I see you. Try not to drink it all before I get there."

Jamie again lifted the flask to his nose, drawing in another warm breath. He cocked his head at an angle as he took a whiff. Then his eyes moved to the doorway, and a shiver ran up his spine. He saw something, ever so briefly.

"Jamie?" Kelli asked.

His jaw dropped.

"Jamie-"

"Yeah?" he asked sharply.

"Is everything okay?"

*Is* everything ok? He thought. He wasn't sure.

"Jamie?"

He turned back to the phone. "Sorry," he answered. "I thought I saw something."

"What?" she asked again.

"Some sort of déjà vu."

*Or a ghost...*

That's what he'd seen. Just for a second. A flash. The corner of a face, and a winking eye, but a familiar one.

Jeff.

He had distinctly seen his father peaking around the corner at him.

"I don't follow," Kelli said.

Jamie stood and walked to the door. He peered around the corner and down the hall.

"Is this thing filled with absinthe?" he asked.

"I'm not telling," Kelli replied.

The hall was empty.

"Think I must be getting hungry," he continued as he turned and walked back to his bed. He slumped on his back, staring up at the ceiling.

"Do you like your present?"

He stared into space, looked up at the ceiling, just as he had so many months earlier as his body had shaken uncontrollably.

"I love it," he said softly. "Thank you."

\* \* \*

Christmas came and went. Red wine, family, and food. For the first time in years, Jamie celebrated the holidays in full health. Yet, he spent each hour thinking about Kelli. He needed to be with her again. On his last night at home, he felt a tingling sensation in the back of his head, at the base of his skull. That night, he dreamt he was his father. The dark clouds swirled in his head as he stood over the cold, black water, stepped off into oblivion, and sank to the bottom alone.

# CHAPTER TEN

By December twenty-eighth, Jamie was ready to go back to the dorms. Kelli wouldn't be back for another day, but he liked the idea of having time to settle in and relax, entirely alone. He'd be away from the house. Away from his father's papers, which he'd had to forcibly stop himself from rifling through again. He could go to the dorms, hunker down in the empty space, and give himself some time to wander the caverns of his mind.

Was it bad that he looked forward to being alone? A bit too Jeff Pepper-like perhaps? Maybe so, but for all the similarities to his father that he liked to believe he possessed, dark, brooding unhappiness wasn't one of them. Even at the lowest point, when he'd been bedridden and shaking like a drug withdrawal patient, Jamie had never lost his determined, hard-nosed streak of optimism, something that Jeff had *never* had. He was too young to think he'd hit the end, he was too… different. The time in the dorms would be good for him. No distractions. No fucking around. Not yet anyways. He'd go for some runs, he'd focus on his artwork, and he'd have some time to hear himself think.

What he hadn't stopped to ponder was whether

Attebery

the campus would even be *accessible* during the holiday break. When Lynn pulled up to the main drive, Jamie suddenly realized that *no one* was planning to be around any time soon. The roads that looped around the RIT campus were completely unplowed. Nothing but long stretches of deep, thick snow stretched from the main road to the brick buildings off in the distance. It was just as they were pulling up to the edge of campus that a new storm began moving in. It started with a couple of flakes, which swirled down out of the gray in a Charlie Brown Christmas-manner, loop-di-looping lackadaisically in the air around Jamie's head. Then the flakes started coming down faster, picking up speed as they grew in number.

Lynn looked up at the sky, then gave him a skeptical look. "You sure about this?"

Jamie nodded. "Yeah."

"You think you can get in?!"

He looked towards the buildings again. "Not a problem. I've got keys."

Lynn sighed. "Okay. If you change your mind about this, call me."

"I will."

He got out of the car, walked around to the trunk, and pulled out his travel bag, which he slung over his shoulder. Lynn rolled down the driver's side window.

"Happy New Year."

"Happy New Year!"

Then a pause.

"Be careful."

"I will."

Lynn put the car in gear and drove away, leaving Jamie at the end of the unplowed road. He stood for a moment, utterly still, staring out across the fields of snow. Ice crystals crackled on the ground and in the air around him. There was no wind. No air practically. Just the falling flakes, and him, alone in the biting cold. He started walking, watching the buildings' red brick faces rise up ahead of him. There were three main dorm towers on the campus, each with a dozen or so floors of rooms. Then there were the dorms for the NTID students, the National Technical Institute for the Deaf. Their building looked like the residential towers, only slightly taller, decked out with a complex series of strobe lights in each room, lights that functioned as both door "bells" and part of the building's fire alarm system. Unfortunately, the NTID lights mostly served as an endless source of amusement for the more malevolent characters on campus, as well as the members of the Greek community at the University of Rochester across town, who found it riotously entertaining to make their way to the NTID building, set off the fire alarms, and watch the building light up like a Christmas tree as everyone inside went ape-shit. Having been woken just once by a false alarm in the middle of the night, Jamie could only imagine how aggravating nightly evacuations must be. Still, watching the systematic display of strobe lights flash-bulbing through the building was strangely hypnotic; he couldn't deny that. His eyes scanned the windows of the NTID tower. Everything looked dark. For that matter, everything in the other buildings looked dark too. Were there people hiding in the other parts of the campus? Probably. Sort of creepy, but exciting to think about.

The going was slow, and exhausting. The snow was several feet high now, and it creeped down the tops of his boots as he trudged toward the buildings. His jeans quickly became soaked through as the snow clung to his pant legs and dissolved from his body heat.

Was this really such a great idea?

He climbed up the hillside along the side of the road, cutting through the residential parking lots as he headed for the building. The snow was coming down faster now, the sound of the wind adding its own gothic touch. Jamie looked up at the buildings overhead; their sharps angles towered over him now. Snow on the rooftop roared over the edge of the building, swooping down towards him and shooting off across the fields. Jamie pulled down his ski cap and lowered his head now as he made his way down the steps to the outside of the door. He reached into his jacket and pulled out the keys Fritz has slipped into his hand a week earlier.

"Don't let anyone know about these," he'd said.

Had anyone else on campus finagled the same deal? Probably. At this moment, in each of these massive buildings, there were probably a dozen couples huddled up in their rooms, fucking the hours away in the cozy, private warmth of the empty dormitories.

Jamie turned the key in the icy lock. The frozen metals of the bolt and the door frame let out a hollow click. He shuffled into the foyer. The heat was on. Thank God. Jamie unzipped his coat as the warm air swirled around him. It was surprisingly hot inside. The school must keep the heat cranked when no one's around to prevent a frozen pipe or a burst sprinkler line. Half the ceiling lights were off, every other panel, casting the halls in a striped pattern that receded down the corridor and into blackness at the end. *Was* there anybody else in the building? Again, kind of creepy to ponder. He headed upstairs to his dorm room, where he pushed the door open and reached inside to flip on the light. Everything looked the same. What was he expecting, that Kelli might surprise him by coming back early and spreading out naked in his bed?

Maybe.

He shut the door behind him, instinctively flipping the lock with his thumb as he threw his jacket and backpack on the bed, pulled off the ski cap, and scratched at the scars on his head with a gloved hand; they were itchy and clammy from the weather. He kneaded the skin, enjoying the pressure on the thick scar tissue.

Unpacking was a cinch. He slipped a few clean shirts and pants into the dresser drawers, tossed his rolled up socks into a bucket in the corner, and set out his bottles of pills, one by one, along the back edge of the dresser top.

Jamie let out a long sigh.

How best to kill the better part of the next day?

He walked over, fell backwards onto the bed, and lay staring up at the ceiling. His eyes grew heavy, the lids swelling - sleep and fatigue pushing together over his eyes.

He shifted his body on the bed. Arms and legs oozed into the mattress. Head floated. The light flickered. Then he was asleep, a deep sleep, the sleep of a drunk man, collapsed in a snowbank as the storms swept in and buried him from view. Jamie pulled the blankets up around him, drew his knees up to his chest, and drifted out of the world as the wind whistled outside his window, and the snow fell. Faster. And faster.

～

"It looks like I'm snowed in here."

Jamie lay on his bed, his socked feet resting on the rounded metal edge of the radiator.

"I am too," Kelli's voice came through the phone receiver. "This morning's train north was delayed indefinitely."

"Think you can get out of there tomorrow?" Jamie asked.

"I hope so."

"Me too."

"What have you been doing with yourself there? Or don't I want to know? You going crazy?"

"No Jack Torrance symptoms yet. Getting a little itchy to exercise though. Kinda creepy in the building with no one here."

"I can imagine! What are you doing for food?"

"The vending machines are all working. Been eating some Ramen I brought from home and getting snacks from the vending machines in C wing."

"It must be kind of cool though, right?" Kelli asked. "I always wanted to get snowed in at school when I was a kid."

"At school?!"

"Yeah, you know, when everyone was younger and nice to each other. Not middle school or anything."

"I suppose. High school would have been fun, assuming all the hot girls were there and their boyfriends were trapped outside."

Jamie raised his legs up toward the ceiling, twisting his back. He groaned.

*"Yeah,"* Kelli said. "I really don't want to know what you're up to right now."

"What? I'm just stretching. My body's getting stiff."

Kelli laughed again, softly.

The air rumbled as a flurry of snow pummeled the window. The building's brick walls seemed to tense up around him, like a canvas sail fighting to stay in place.

"It's *really* blowing out there." Jamie hesitated. " I really hope you're here by New Year's or this is gonna suck."

"It already does."

Jamie stood and paced the room. He stretched his arms as he peered out the window at a wall of white. The fields were smothered in snow. Earlier in the day, a couple of plows had been coming around each hour, trying their best to get a foothold in the ever-increasing accumulations on the loops and roadways around the campus. Now they'd both stopped rolling past. Probably snowed out.

*This was a crazy storm.*

Jamie leaned his head against the glass, looking down at the sidewalks leading up to the tower.

"No footprints."

"What was that, babe?" Kelli asked.

"Sorry, I was looking for footprints around campus. Nothing."

"Hoping to find a hot chicky hiding out there with you?"

"Hardly. Just hoping *my* hot chicky can make it up here on the train tomorrow."

"I'll try my best."

Jamie's feet were restless. He arched up on his toes, then rolled back on his heels and squatted, feeling the muscles in his legs stretching and pulling. He sighed again.

"Stop that."

"I'm stretching. I need to get some exercise. Didn't think I'd be stuck here, unable to get outside and run."

"Then run inside. There's no one there, might as well take advantage of it. Get the energy out of your system."

"That's actually not a bad idea," Jamie answered.

"Take care of yourself, baby. Don't go crazy on me."

"I won't," Jamie answered. "Don't worry about that. Don't even joke."

*"Don't go crazy on me."*

Why did that sentence keep flashing in his mind now? Of course he wouldn't go crazy. Why would she even say that? Well, all right, family history, the whole snowed in thing, his health. Maybe sanity *was* something to worry about.

Or maybe she was just joking. That was it, he knew, but the words kept surfacing in his thoughts as his arms and legs pumped up and down. Sweat streamed down his face, soaking through the front of his shirt and running down his abdomen. He could feel the wet fabric of his running clothes clinging to his skin, stretching and pulling, spattering sweat in a flurry of perspiration.

Don't go crazy. *Don't go crazy.*

He was ripping through the building now. He'd started on the first floor, sort of jogging down the long, darkened corridor at first, letting his feet and legs adjust to the carpeted concrete surface. Then he'd picked up speed, moving a bit faster. A bit smoother. The building was mostly warm, with just the slightest shiver of cold in the air - just enough to remind him that it was a couple dozen degrees below zero outside. He breathed in a chestful of air, then let it out in a steady wheeze, feeling his lungs come into sync with his movements.

A little faster.

He burst out in the front corridor, twisting on one leg and darting up the stairs to the second floor. Twisting again and racing down the next murky hallway. He'd done this through five floors of the building before working his way back down in reverse. Twice. Back down the fourth floor hallway, to the stairs, down another level, his knees coming up high, feet pattering over each step, then out on the third floor and away in a full stride. Halfway down the third floor hallway he stopped and started walking.

He had to take a leak.

This floor, like all the rest, was silent. No sounds of

TV's eaking out from the dorm rooms. No music. No couples. Only the sound of the wind outside, roaring over and through the empty campus.

*"Take care of yourself, baby."*

Was he getting lonely?

*"Don't go crazy on me."*

He brought his hands to his hips, feeling the flare of his hip bones shifting under the surface his sweaty skin. He kneaded the tissue with his finger tips. His fingers slipped under the band of his running shorts, creeping towards the front of his lower abdomen, where the muscles tightened and flexed softly. He stopped in the hallways outside the bathroom door. His hands started to creep farther down than they ought to. Not that it mattered. The building was empty. If he wanted to pull off his shorts and run through the building like a wild banshee, he could. If he wanted to pull out the business and jerk off in the corridor, he could do that too. But it was neither of those things that was bothering him, or occurring to him, it was just the simple fact that he was alone, and had been, totally, not speaking or looking at another person in the flesh for almost two days. It was a strange feeling, the type of atmosphere in which widowers sit alone on the couch day after day, week after week, scratching at themselves, making a slow, endless loop through the staticy channels on an old TV set. It was the same atmosphere in which older women became fixated on their lawn boys, wandering out of the house in nightgowns and curlers, maybe some little fuzzy slippers, and nothing else, making honest-to-God attempts

at seducing men twenty or thirty years their juniors.
Craziness. Loneliness. The utter silence. The realization
that nothing you do can, or will, be held against you.
Cause hell, no one will be there to see it or care!

Now that was a scary thought!

Shut up Jamie. Just take a leak and get back to your
run.

He pushed the door open and stepped into the
darkness, his heart crackling with cold as he turned in
a blind half circle, feeling for the switch. He found it,
flipped it, and watched green swirls of light appear at
the ends of each fluorescent tube overhead as something
sizzled inside them, then, *hoooowhum*, the room filled
with a sickly yellow light. He blinked and looked around
the tiled bathroom. Aside from some different scratch
marks on the counter, and most likely, some subtle
variations on ejaculating dick illustrations in the stalls,
this bathroom was nearly identical to the one on the third
floor. Jamie walked over to the urinals, pulling down the
elastic band of his running shorts and adjusting himself
for business as he stepped forward. He stared at the brick
wall in front of him. Nothing written in the mortar
between the painted concrete blocks; that was always
another favorite place for guys to write shit like "For a
good time call…" or "Too much Dick and Bush." This
bathroom on the other hand was remarkably graffiti-free.
He let out a long sigh as he finished up, and was just
tucking the goods away when he glanced to his left and
saw a man, dressed entirely in black, standing off to the
side staring at him.

Jamie's heart burped ice water as he jumped. *Fuck.*
He looked away, then back again. Nothing. But he knew
what he'd seen, the same thing he'd seen in his dream
a month ago, right around the time he got so sick. The
same guy. Same look. Dressed entirely in black, no
clear face, no clear shape, like the edges were fuzzy, or
continually shifting.

In the dream the figure had come after him, reaching
out with something, not just his hands, something was
in them, something sharp, threatening, meant to hurt,
even kill. This time the guy was gone as quickly as he had
appeared.

*It was something in his mind. It had to be.*

Jamie crossed over to the bathroom sink, his eyes
glancing to the side as he moved. He watched the
reflection of the toilet stalls in the mirror as he rinsed his
hands under hot water, then he turned off the taps and
stepped backwards, still watching the mirror. He crouched
to the floor, looked under each stall door. Nothing.

Of course not.

*He was standing on top of one of the toilets.*

Stop it.

*Waiting for you to push the door open, just the tiniest
bit.*

No. There was no one there. He was completely
alone, and his mind was playing tricks on him.

*Then open the door. Prove it.*

No.

Jamie stood quickly and rushed for the door.
Turning the light off as he left, leaving the bastard

standing in the dark.

The bastard who wasn't there. The one who didn't exist.

He rushed out the door and dove for the floor as the man in black lunged at him from across the hall.

*Christ! He was real!*

Jamie felt wind from the sweeping arms that came towards him. He tucked his shoulder in and fell to the side, smashing into the corridor wall, even as he began to run. His body straightened as he took off like a shot, the sound of the imaginary starter's pistol in his head. His legs were numb, unfeeling. He ran as fast as his body would let him. Even as he moved, his mind continued telling him that no one was there.

*NO ONE was there.*

One look back would confirm that, but he just went faster, tearing around the corner and rushing up the next flight of stairs. Down the corridor and up the stairs to the fourth floor, then the fifth, arms and legs a blur of motion as he rushed down hallway after hallway. His lungs burned now. It felt good. It felt fucking great. Cabin fever breaking. Whatever.

No one was there. He was still alone in the building.

Run God dammit it. *Run!*

Down the length of the fifth floor. Taking the stairs in one fell swoop. The fourth. Then the third. He opened up his stride, cold air rushing over his face. He was feeling good now. Dorm room doors sailed past on either side of him. He stared ahead at the center of the bleary tunnel around him, anything and everything topsing and turving off to the sides. For a moment, for the first time in months, he was perfectly in sync, mind, body, everything. Then he rounded the corner, glanced at the ground with a blink, and when he looked back up, a figure was standing in the middle of the hallway, a figure who turned to him at the last moment wearing an expression not of threat, but of utter panic.

*Fritz.*

Jamie twisted his body to the side, barely deflecting the blow, just enough to prevent the crunching and popping and splintering of bones had he hit Fritz head on. Even now, the impact sent the two of them flying, the initial collision and grunts of pain dropping to silence as Fritz staggered back over his own duffel bag, and fell to the corridor floor. Jamie angled off the side wall, arms and legs splayed wildly. He soared over Fritz, and touched down in a cloud of flailing limbs as he skidded across the floor, and come to an abrupt stop as the top of his head rammed into the front of his own door.

\* \* \*

"Phew, it's okay," Fritz said with a sigh, as he took a small crystal bottle from his duffel bag and pulled a cork from the top.

*Thoop!*

"What is it?" Jamie asked.

"Smell," Fritz commanded, as he held the bottle under Jamie's nose.

Jamie took a whiff, his eyebrows pulling together.

"Tequila?"

"Not just any tequila, my friend. Top shelf Patron. The best. The stuff the *owners* of tequila distilleries drink. The stuff the owners only keep for special occasions."

"What's it called?" Jamie replied.

"That is, well, I can't remember the *exact* name." Fritz handed him the bottle. "I just know this stuff is two hundred bucks a pop, comes in numbered, hand-blown crystal bottles, and my father will never know it's missing."

"Your father?" Jamie asked incredulously. "He's not gonna miss a two hundred dollar bottle of tequila?"

"Not when he has a half dozen of them."

Jamie looked at Fritz questioningly.

"Half his clients buy him this stuff each Christmas. He usually keeps a couple bottles for himself and re-gifts the rest. But even with years of practice, it takes a while to polish one of these things off. He's getting behind, so I grabbed one before I left."

"And he's not gonna notice?"

Fritz shook his head.

"So what are you gonna do with it?"

"Drink it," Fritz replied.

"All of it?" Jamie asked.

Fritz looked at him for a beat, incredulous, then he changed the topic.

"Where's Kelli?"

"Delayed. She won't be in until tomorrow."

"Good. Then you'll be drinking it with me tonight. No reason you need to keep your faculties functioning tonight. No lady friend. No fucking. But this," he held the bottle aloft, "this is the next best thing."

Jamie looked down into the empty shot glass. A glimmer of crystal-clear tequila reflected up into his eyes. *This shit was good.*

He looked up, everything around him was moving in a thick haze. He was sitting in the open doorway of Fritz's dorm room, his back pressed against the frame. Fritz was sitting on the floor, leaning against the side of his bed. A TV across the room was playing some sort of porn movie; two women on screen sat on either side of a shirtless businessman, fighting over him. Curiously, their fighting included a great deal of nipple pinching and lingering French kisses, both with the man and with each other. How had this video even been put on? Jamie's head lolled over to the half empty Patron bottle. Oh yeah, around the fifth or sixth shot, Fritz had confided in him and brought out his porn collection, which was quite... comprehensive. Jamie hadn't gotten a precise tally on the number of films in his RA's collection, but the fact that he kept them in a foot locker and in several shoe boxes showed that the guy had a true passion, if not a downright problem. At some point a disc had been put in the DVD player, the 'play' button was pushed, and after a few moments of uncomfortable joint viewing, the movie was quickly forgotten. The sounds of pornstars and bad music faded into the background, a flickering backdrop for a drunken evening.

"You want another?" Fritz asked him.

Jamie turned his head gingerly, fearing any momentum might twist his head loose from his spine. His first words came out in a mumble. "I buhbuhbuh." He stopped himself, opening his mouth wide, enunciating carefully. "I'm- all- right," he replied.

Fritz looked at him with a lopsided grin. "We're gonna be so hurting in the morning."

Jamie nodded his head, a bit too effusively, *"Yeah we are."*

Fritz shrugged his shoulders. "Eh, fuck it."

"Fuck. It," Jamie agreed.

Then they sat quietly.

Fritz looked up at him suddenly. "Is it working?"

"The tequila?"

"No, no, no," Fritz replied. He reached out a drunken hand, waving his index finger in the general direction of Jamie's head. "You know, that *thing*, the fifty year battery thingy-"

"Oh. Yeah. Well, it seems to be-"

Fritz looked at him blankly, his expression detached. Jamie lolled his head to the side peacefully.

*Yeah. Everything was great, except for, you know, hallucinating and running from creepy figments of my imagination from time to time.*

He glanced up at Fritz who was still looking at him expectantly.

"What?" Jamie asked.

"That's it, nothing more than 'it seems to be?'"

"I'm afraid of jinxing it."

Fritz nodded. "I hear ya." He motioned towards the

TV. "Probably the same as when I try to go cold turkey on this stuff. Can't even let myself even think about it, or trouble starts up again."

"Yeah, pretty much the same thing," Jamie agreed with a smirk. "Let's just say it's working, all systems are go, and leave it at that.

"Leave it at that!" he repeated emphatically.

Fritz opened his mouth as if to speak again. Jamie watched as he bobbed his head up and down.

"Yes?"

"I gotta piss," Fritz exclaimed as he struggled to his feet and marched for the door. Jamie ducked out of the way as Fritz disappeared into the bathroom across the hall, leaving the door open and shouting from inside.

"Weird being here with no one around!"

"Yeah," Jamie called back.

"Makes me wish I had keys to the residents' rooms, so I could go inside, see what the girls have hidden in their drawers."

"Yeah," Jamie closed his eyes. "That would be a *great* idea. No trouble could *possibly* come from that!"

The toilet in the bathroom flushed. Jamie heard Fritz washing his hands in the sink.

Fritz stumbled into view.

"All I wanna know is what kind of stuff chicks have. They gotta have porn, right, man?"

"I dunno-"

Fritz drew an inebriated hand to his forehead, wiping the sweat from his brow. "They gotta!" He took another haphazard series of steps across the hall. Jamie again dove out of the way as Fritz hopped, skipped, and awkwardly jumped over him and flopped face down on his bed.

"You tired, Fritz?"

There was no answer.

"Fritz?" Jamie said again, but all he heard was heavy breathing, and the frantic moaning coming from the TV. Jamie got up and pressed STOP. He glanced at the older boy who lay with his head to the side, belly down, back rising and falling with each breath, then he left the room, pulling the door shut behind him. Jamie glanced around the empty hallway and hustled to his room. He locked the door behind him and lay down on his back in the bed, staring up into the darkness.

~

He woke with a start. Felt the tiniest quiver in his heart as he realized he was not alone. He looked into the darkness, waiting for his eyes to start sending back information. There was the outline of the room, the desk, the dresser. A faint glow of moonlight sent a dim stream of light toward the door. His eyes sifted more shapes from the blackness, layer upon layer of space coming toward him. There was his chair. The corner of the bed. And there, standing over him, was Kelli. Nude. Hands at her head, pulling her hair back behind her ears. The movement brought her chest into view, the pale white shapes of her breasts rising with each breath. He felt her fingertips on his foot as she slipped one hand under the covers, slicing up into the warm pocket of air beneath the bedding. She slid into the bed and lay on top of him.

"When did you get here?" he asked.

He felt the weight of her breasts sliding over his chest.

"An hour ago," she answered, her lips pressed against the corner of his ear. "I caught the late train out of New York."

He felt her legs straddle his thigh. Her pubic hair tickled the top of his leg. She was warm.

"Why didn't you call me?"

She set her arms on each side of his chest, lifting herself up to look down at him. Jamie's fingers ran up the sides of her ribcage and gently cupped her breasts.

"I wanted to surprise you," she whispered.

She relaxed her arms, bringing her chest down against his. Her legs moved up the bed, bringing the two of them face to face. Jamie looked up into her eyes as his lips parted ever so slightly.

"Did you miss me?" she asked as she leaned in to kiss him.

He didn't say a word, just pulled her closer against him. He ran his fingers down her spine, held his hands against the small of her back, and rolled her to the side, where they kissed and held each other until they slowly drifted off to sleep.

Outside, trees moved in frozen gusts of wind, their branches bristling under the weight of the snow, the bite of the cold. Inside, they held each other close, feeling the pulse of their hearts, the heat of their skin, and the comfort of not being alone. Not now anyway. Not in the middle of this storm.

The weather cleared overnight. Jamie woke to the glare of the sun reflecting in through the windows. Make that the *blinding* glare. His body was stiff, out of practice with sharing a bed. The soles of his feet were sore. Must have been kicking the foot of the bed in his sleep. The rest of his body was tired, but invigorated. Having a gorgeous girl in your bed tends to do that to you. Kelli was still asleep. The covers of the bed were pulled away from her body, leaving her breasts out in the chilled morning air. Her nipples were hard, even under the growing warmth of the sun. The curls of her hair framed her face in a shimmer of haze.

Jamie slipped out of bed to stretch his back and massage his muscles. He placed his hands on the bare skin of his lower back, arching his spine and feeling the bones crack into place one by one like dominoes. He stretched his legs, kneading his calves and thighs, which burned as though he'd been out running a marathon. He was just leaning over, bringing his chest down towards his feet, when he heard a voice behind him.

"Whew, check that guy out."

He turned to see Kelli watching him.

"Good morning."

"Get over here," she replied.

He walked over to the edge of the bed, where Kelli reached her arms out towards him, placing them on his hips, then gently running her fingers down the fabric of his boxers, and tugging on the lower edge until his pubic hair started peeking out from the top. She looped a fingertip under the cloth, tugging gently as she rolled back onto the bed and slid the covers farther down towards her.

Jamie slipped silently into bed beside her. A week might be enough time to fall out of practice sharing a bed, but in other areas, they had no problem. They made love for the better part of the morning, stopping only to rest and recharge and to slip off down the hall for water. They passed Fritz's door, which remained closed, the grumble of snores rumbling out into the hallway.

When they'd worn themselves out, they lay in bed talking, their hands always on one another's bodies. Kelli ran her fingers through the hair on Jamie's chest, her head pressed against his shoulder.

"You couldn't sleep last night?" she asked.

"What do you mean?"

"You were up for a while. I thought you had insomnia."

Jamie cocked his head to the side. "Oh," he hesitated. "I forgot about that."

"Did you get up and read or something?"

*Something.*

He brought one hand up and massaged his shoulder. "Just thinking I guess."

"Everything all right?"

Jamie gazed down at her. "Everything's fine."

Kelli lowered her head again, her hand slipped down to his stomach. The weight on his body grew heavier as she fell back to sleep.

The rest of the day was a haze. They got up in starts

and stops, making it to the middle of the room, then, either collapsing in a pile of sloth on the bed, or finding other, repeated distractions. In the afternoon, they finally staggered out into the corridor and down the hall to the girls bathroom, where they slipped into a steamy shower, breathed in the thick, moist air, and felt the heat relaxing their tired muscles. As they were returning to Jamie's room, they passed Fritz, risen at last, but half dead, lying spread eagle on the common area couch. He was watching *The Today Show* and massaging his temples with his fingers. Kelli and Jamie eyed him warily. His eyes opened and darted in their direction.

"When did you get here?" he asked Kelli.

"Last night."

"Huh," Fritz drawled. "I don't remember that."

"It was late."

"How ya feeling?" Jamie asked.

"How I'm feeling doesn't matter. We've got errands to run. We need hooch and bubbly."

"Maybe you need to rest," Kelli answered.

"Maybe you're right. You guys need to track down some bubbly and some hooch. It's New Year's, we gotta have the proper supplies to watch the ball drop." He turned to Kelli. "Or to watch the ball drop, again."

She curled her lip in disgust. "Whatever that means."

Fritz smirked, his head lolling back against the couch.

"He's still drunk," Jamie interjected. "His clever wit is drowning under a thick layer of Patron." He turned to Fritz. "Leave the supplies to us. We'll catch a bus later and see what we can rustle up."

"Okay," Fritz slurred as he teetered toward oblivion, "but don't wait too long, it's a jungle out there."

It was indeed a jungle out there. Jamie and Kelli caught a mid-afternoon bus to the strip mall off Jefferson, where they went first to Discount Liquor for cocktail supplies and champagne, then next door to Wegman's to stock up on party food. Planning a last minute New Year's spread that could be prepared entirely in a dorm microwave proved easier than expected. Fighting the crowds was another matter. By the time they made it back to campus, the light in the sky was growing pink.

Fritz was just staggering out of the bathroom as they wandered out of the stairwell, bags in hand. Neither was surprised by his expression of pure, hungover misery. He wasn't so much fresh from the shower, as he was sporting the drowned rat look, eyes sunken, wet hair clinging to his forehead. Jamie thought the better of a few "hair of the dog" one-liners.

"Jesus man, you look like shit."

"Thanks," Fritz muttered.

"Are you really gonna be wanting to celebrate tonight?" Kelli asked.

Fritz looked up suddenly, stumbling back against the brick corridor wall. "What are you talking about? It's New Year's!"

"Still," Kelli began.

Fritz took a wary step forward, wobbled in place, then pushed himself free of the wall. He stood in the middle of the corridor, wavering in place like an inflatable figure on a used car lot.

Jamie shot Kelli a look from the corner on his eye. She smiled.

"At least get a little more sleep, man," Jamie added.

"Oh-h yeah," Fritz mumbled as he staggered back to his room. "Oh-hh yeah."

Funny thing about New Year's, about college life in general: no one *wants* to be alone on certain occasions. For even the most entrenched loners on the planet, there are simply times when solitude *sucks;* New Year's Eve is one of those times. No wonder then that as the night wore on, as Fritz's condition improved, and the volume of his voice grew louder with each round of champagne, that the people in the buildings around them, the mole people, the software engineers, and one freaky-ass nympho couple, slowly emerged from their rooms and ambled down to Gibson G, lured by the promise of booze and hedonism. By nine o'clock, two Japanese girls, neither of whom spoke a word of English, started passing around bottles of Saki and doing stripteases on the common room coffee table. That was about the time Fritz's hangover seemed to instantly resolve itself. In another part of the room, two software engineering types, both guys, sat on a couch, laptops at the ready, as they debated the merits of various operating systems. Then there were the sketchballs, the freakshows, the guys who shaved in the dorm bathroom without shaving cream, the girls who stayed in their rooms and clung to the corridor walls whenever they ventured to the bathroom or headed out to class, even those folks, the guys *and* the girls, they showed up in droves. An assortment of singles slowly grew attracted to one another throughout the evening, eventually pairing off in preparation for midnight kisses, and snuck away for the final and first hook-ups of the outgoing and incoming calendar years. Jamie and Kelli laughed and whispered to each other. Fritz did his best to get in tight with the striptease girls and make his porn star fantasies come true. At midnight, the crowd paused to watch the ball drop on the television, then they went back to their respective conversations or positions. Outside, the snow was again falling. Inside, they were enjoying the last good time of the year

At some point, Kelli took Jamie by the hand and led him away. Maybe *that* was the last good time of the year, or the first of the next. Either way, it would be their final moment of peace for a long time to come.

# CHAPTER ELEVEN
## COMPLICATIONS

Classes resumed with a bang. No sleepy winter warm-up period. They were three weeks into the quarter when they left, so they jumped right back into the thick of things. January and February were always a long, grey stretch of nothing but the same. Classes and work and the weekend, repeat. Course, in routines it's the little things that stand out, a change in mood, a bend in the monotony. It seemed to Jamie he was growing more irritable. Kelli didn't say anything, but she also felt the shift. His actions were harsher, his response to almost everything just a bit quicker, a little sharper. What Kelli didn't know, what Jamie kept to himself, was that little by little, he was feeling subtle shifts in his mind, little things, like a flash of an image, or a sudden daydream. Occasionally, he would totally disconnect from where he was, what he was thinking, and find himself in the middle of a moment, real or imagined, entirely removed from the present.

That was happening to him a lot actually. It worried him, but since he couldn't find a pattern for when it was occurring, he continued going about his routine. He went to his classes. He ran. He did his work. And he hung out with Kelli. Most importantly, he did his best to ignore what was happening.

Media and the Mind was the only time he truly allowed himself to analyze how he was doing and what he was seeing. That wasn't necessarily a good thing.

"Well my little media masters," Ryan began as he walked in the door. " I trust you all had happy, healthy, homestyle holidays. I did. Ate some tasty meals. Drank the nog. Watched *It's A Wonderful Life*. Didn't stop to process any of it. Any of you do the same?"

One or two people raised their hands. The rest of the room stayed quiet.

"Wow, everyone's just ready and rarin' to go I see."

A couple of scattered, sleepy laughs.

Ryan looked around the room. Hmm, who to talk with, who to engage? Kelli and Jeff Pepper's kid were seated next to each other in the front row. That had to be her work - no way he'd have picked that spot. Guys in wool caps were not front row sitters, so sitting in an uncharacteristic location meant one of two things: Either Pepper was interested in her, or they were fucking. Judging by the detachment in the kid's gaze relative to their physical proximity, it had to be the latter. To mess or not to mess? The girl was cute. Hell, she'd crossed his mind on more than one occasion during the break. What was it, her hair? Her body? No, he loved her for her mind. Of course, that had to be it. He locked his eyes on Kelli and walked over to her. Jamie looked up.

"Anyone learn anything new over the holidays?" Professor Ryan turned towards Kelli. He held her gaze for a moment, tilting his head ever so slightly to the side. "Ms. Petronio? Any new experiences over the break?" He drew out his words carefully.

What the hell was this? Jamie wondered. He glanced at Kelli, who looked down at the desktop and brushed a curl of hair back behind her ear.

"Uhh," she ran her fingers over the surface of the table. "What kind of experiences? Media experiences."

"Whatever. Movies. Maybe you went ice skating. Maybe you skied. Decorated a tree. Made love."

Jamie's brow furrowed.

"Whatever you did, you must have had something to compare it to. Past experiences. Maybe, at the bare minimum, you saw someone doing it in a movie once. That had to have some influence on how you went about it, how you did it, if you enjoyed it. So, did you do any of those things? Did you enjoy them?"

Kelli's face was getting flush. "What are you talking about? Did I make love?"

"Well, that was *one* of the things I mentioned. You kids, always latching onto the sex things." Ryan turned and started for the white board in the front of the room. " I also mentioned decorating a tree and ice skating. The picture-perfect Hallmark Christmas passtimes. Did you happen to do either one of those things this weekend? Maybe we'll stick to the less risqué." The class laughed.

"We can save the sex talk for another day."

*"What the fuck?"* Jamie muttered under his breath.

"So, Ms. Petronio…" He glanced at Jamie. "Did you happen to… decorate a tree over the past weekend?"

Kelli nodded her head, the corner of her mouth pulling up into a hooked smile.          "Yes I did."

Ryan turned and walked back towards her. "And how did it measure up?"

"Not bad. Not too bad."

"Just like in the movies?"

"Close enough I think."

Ryan walked over and sat on the corner of the table. "Close enough? See, now that is an interesting statement, isn't it? Close enough. Sort of implies that there's some sort of measuring stick to judge from. Don't you think?"

The room was quiet, but one or two students nodded their heads. Ryan noted them silently. Most importantly, he watched Jamie Pepper's expression. The kid did not like someone fucking with his girl. Ryan's own mouth curled in a little smile. It had been a while since he'd had a little student fling. This one might have some real dramatic possibility. He looked at Kelli again, holding her gaze.

Jamie's eyes were on the professor. He looked at Kelli, studying her face and eyes for some sort of discomfort, but either she didn't pick up on the guy's totally inappropriate string of comments, or she was enjoying it. His forehead was starting to pull in towards the bridge of his nose. His ears were getting hot. He stared at the guy, bore his eyes *through* this asshole. He could feel his own heart racing, hear the pulse in his ears.

Then something in his head burst. The tiniest little pop, followed by the feeling of warm, thick liquid trickling down and around the coils of his brain. His hands went limp on the table, nothing but pins and needles.

When he looked up at Professor Ryan, the guy's expression had changed. His eyebrows were now arched inward, his expression angry. Jamie turned from Kelli and focused on the professor, who was walking towards him.

"You know," Ryan was saying, "how would you like to know what really happened to your father?"

Jamie lifted his head, returning the man's gaze. "What do you mean?"

"What do you think I mean?" Ryan replied angrily. "You've gotta think there's more to the story. Don't you? I worked with the man-"

"And what does that mean?" Jamie asked.

"I know some things-"

"Go fuck yerself-"

"I *know* some things!"

"Go fuck yerself!" Jamie yelled again.

Jamie turned to Kelli, who sat in her seat, staring into space. Playing with a lock of her hair. Didn't she *hear* what was going on? Then Ryan was in his face again.

"What's a suicide?" he asked. "And what's murder?"

Jamie was quiet.

"I said, what's a suicide and what mur-"

"Would you just shut the fuck up for a minute? I'm trying to think."

Jamie closed his eyes. Then another voice came to

him through the darkness. Another voice. Calm, and collecting, and controlling.

"You're trying to think, are you?"

Jamie nodded his head. "Yes."

"Trying to think."

It was Dr. Price's voice.

Was he awake or dreaming? Jamie opened his eyes and looked around the classroom. Ryan was no longer standing in front of Jamie's desk. Was nowhere *near* him. The man stood at the front of the classroom in his tweed jacket, chatting with a student, nodding his head and smiling as he spoke. Then Jamie turned to the side, and then he was in another room. Back in Dr. Price's exam room. The good doctor was sitting on his rollaway stool, leaning in close, his hot breath burping out in hot gasps, flecks of spit hitting Jamie in the face. He heard his own voice coming up from below him.

"I'm just trying to think. I'm trying to keep my mind straight."

Price reached for an instrument on the exam table. He'd used this thing a thousand times before. Described it as a tuning fork for Jamie's head. Get the whole thing in working order. Keep the signals from getting tangled up again.

"My mind," he heard himself say.

"Your mind?" Price echoed. "Your mind is not the problem. Your mind is not the issue. Your mind is not the fucking thing I'm trying to fix. Your body is the problem, and now it's fixed. Your mind is your own fucking problem. Your mind can do whatever it goddamn pleases."

But what about the other thing? About living his *life?*
*Fine.*

Now he was hearing Price's voice inside his head.
*You wanna live your life? Go ahead. Do your best.*

Jamie leaned forward as Price brought the device to
his head, started reading it's gauges as it got close to the
surface of his skin. Lights flickered and some readouts
pinged. It was all very *Star Trek. A*ll very—

Jamie sat up suddenly.

He looked around.

He was sitting in a darkened room, in front of a
large computer monitor. There was a knock at the door.

Now he remembered. He was in one of the
computer labs on the third floor of the photo building.
He'd been in here working on his assignment for *M&P.*
What time was it? He must have been in here for hours.
He looked at the clock in the corner of the monitor.

6:45

That had to be P.M.

The knocking started on the door again. He heard
Victor's voice. The cage guy. He was shouting at him.

"Time's up buddy. Clear your stuff out, this room is
booked."

Jamie looked at the screen. Empty. What had he
been doing all this time? How long had he been here? He
couldn't begin to guess, had only the vaguest recollection
of even entering the building, coming in here in the first
place.

"Just a  minute," he shouted toward the door as he started getting his things together.

He'd gone to class. He remembered that. He'd seen Kelli, if only briefly. They'd talked about getting together for dinner. What time exactly? He had no idea. Then there was the other thing, the thing with Price. How much of *that* was real? He wasn't certain about that part either. He'd gone to see him this week. Price had adjusted the implant to try to level things off a bit, deal with the complaints Jamie was having. The headaches. A general sense of… something.

Had Price really leaned in that way? Said those things? It seemed like it might have-

*"Let's go!"* Victor shouted again.

Jamie jumped to his feet, grabbed his backpack, and threw the door open. Victor jumped out of the way, then led another student inside as Jamie walked down the hall.

He returned the room key to photo cage and headed down to the main floor. The lobby was cold. Melted snow and tracked-in slush covered the brick entryway. Through the darkened windows, Jamie could see snow falling. He pulled on his gloves, zipped up his coat, and tucked his chin down. His breath warmed his stomach and chest. A gust of wind shook the double doors.

Jamie braced himself, then walked out into the darkness.

The cold air sliced into his face. He took in a long breath, feeling the chill move in through his nose and down through his chest. His mind felt clear again, but his head was still heavy. Mealy. It had been one of those

days. One of those days. He could barely remember it.
Getting ready. Snippets of classes. Victor yelling at him.
*Victor*. That asshole. He'd been hoping to get more done
on his photo project, but he was still far behind. He'd skip
a regular dinner tonight, get a noodle cup at The Corner
Store in the tunnels, then see how long he could work
back in the dorms before he collapsed.

Will was sitting in the lounge, watching TV. He shot
Jamie a look as he watched him put his cup of noodles in
the microwave.

"How's it going, man?" Jamie asked him.

"Fine."

An awkward pause.

Jamie slipped his hands in his pockets and turned to
the TV, nodding his head as he watched. He could still
feel Will's eyes on him and glanced back at the guy, who
immediately turned to the screen.

The microwave crackled and hummed in the
background.

"You have a good vacation?"

Will raised the remote and turned up the volume.

The microwave beeped.

Jamie removed his food and headed for the door.

"Good talk. Good talk."

He walked down the hall, where various *Dave
Matthews Band* numbers murmured out from under the
doors. Jamie closed his own door behind him and sat
down at his desk, propping a book open as he pulled the
paper lid from his noodles and breathed in the steam. He

twirled the noodles onto his fork, slurped them down, and glanced over at the answering machine. The light was blinking.

He punched the button.

"Hi, Jamie," his mother's voice came through the static. "I was just calling to see how you were doing."

Jamie took another bite of noodles.

"Listen," Lynn continued. "I was just going over the insurance statement, and I saw that you'd been in to see Dr. Price *again*." She paused, trying to hide the tension in her voice. "When I called to check, his assistant said something about another visit earlier this week. Is there anything I should know about?"

No, Jamie thought to himself.

"If there's anything happening, we need to get it taken care of."

*Nothing is happening!*

"Anyway, I know I promised not to worry, but… give me a call when you have a chance."

Nothing was happening! Nothing. Except, maybe he was losing his mind.

So, he *had* seen Dr. Price. He knew that he had. Those flashes were real - Price leaning in front of him, shouting in his face. *"Your mind is not the issue. That is NOT the issue!"* That had happened.

Then again, maybe it hadn't. What about the rest of the day? Media and the Mind, Ryan fucking with him, messing with Kelli *in front of him.* What else had or *hadn't* happened today? He hadn't run. His mind was swimming. Too much time at the computer. Too much time with the lights out, mental and otherwise. His body was aching. He walked over to the dresser and uncapped his meds, shaking a pill from each canister into the palm of his hand. He leaned his head back and tossed them in his mouth, walked down the hall and took a drink from the water fountain.

"There he is!"

Jamie turned around, wiping water from his mouth with the sleeve of his shirt. Fritz was coming down the hall.

"Jamie, what's happening?"

"Not too much, man."

"Any plans for Saturday night?"

"I don't know," Jamie hesitated. "Probably."

"Kelli, right? Man, ya gotta spread yourself around a little, don't shoot your wad on just one girl!"

Jamie's lip curled. "You have a way with words, Fritz."

"Come on, you know I'll not serious, not entirely, but all the girls have been wondering what happened to that dude in the winter cap."

"Fuck you."

"I'm joking with ya, man. I just want you to come out. If you want, you can bring your girl. I wouldn't, but you can, or let me bring her, you fly solo."

"What's the occasion for this party?"

"Celebrating everyone getting back from break. Get things started right. We're gonna have a dozen kegs, which you won't even have to help deliver! Food. Music. A DJ. *Girls*. It's a tradition, we do it every year."

Jamie looked at him. His head was starting to ache. "All right, I'll think about it, how's that?"

"One step from going, but I'll take it." Fritz answered.

"Jamie!" Kelli's voice came from down the hall.

Jamie and Fritz watched her approaching. She looked angry.

"You're a popular guy tonight," Fritz muttered. "You're also in trouble apparently. Might be going to that party with me after all."

Jamie walked down the hall to meet her.

"Hey, sorry I missed dinner tonight-"

"Missed dinner? Fuck dinner. I thought you'd at least call first to apologize for this afternoon," Kelli shouted.

Jamie stopped short. "What about this afternoon?"

"The whole storming-out-of class-without-a-word thing!"

"What?" Jamie hesitated.

"What *what?!*" Kelli said, barely keeping her voice in check. "More like what the *fuck?*"

"I didn't do that."

"Yeah," Kelli said. "You did."

Jamie brought a hand to his head, closed his eyes and sucked in a breath of air. "Can we go to my room?"

Kelli's expression softened. "Are you all right?"

"Just feeling a little funny."

"Funny how?"

Jamie couldn't answer, he just turned and started for his dorm. Kelli walked beside him, reaching for the lights as they closed the door behind them.

"Could you keep those off? " Jamie asked as he shielded his eyes.

"Sure," Kelli answered, curiousity in her voice.

She held his arm as he lowered himself down on the bed, then lay on his back, eyes closed.

Kelli watched him closely. She raised her fingers to his face, tickling his lips with her fingers tips. Her other hand smoothed his forehead. The skin was warm and wet. She slipped her fingers under the edge of his cap, sliding it off. The hair underneath had grown longer, but she could still feel the scars under her fingers.

She listened to his breathing.

"Is there anything else I did today?" Jamie asked.

"I don't know, Jamie."

"Anything else I did that I don't remember?"

She didn't say anything. She had been planning to ask him about Victor. Ask about what her friends had told her earlier. How Jamie had gotten into a shouting match with the guy, used every four letter word in the book until he got his way, until he got a photo lab to work in. But this wasn't the time. Something was wrong with him. Something was changing, and she didn't know if he even realized it was happening.

"Everything is fine," she said softly.

Jamie's breathing grew deeper now. His body was relaxing. His hands lay at his sides, palms up, the fingertips curling inward in loose fists.

Kelli ran her fingers over the ridges of hard flesh under his short, sweaty hair. She'd have to ask him about the scars soon. She just wasn't sure if she wanted to know the truth about them.

Saturday night was nearly perfect, marred only by two incidents, one at the start of the night, the other discovered much, much later. Kelli gave the go-ahead for the party. Actually, she'd told Jamie to do his own thing that night. She had class assignments to work on and was thinking of dropping in on some friends she hadn't seen recently. The unspoken undertone was that she needed to be on her own for a bit, if only for a night. Stretch the legs, see if she still functioned as an individual. Things seemed all right between them, barring a few incidents of detached, anxious behavior on Jamie's part.

Gibson G was atwitter from the outset. Arlin and Vanessa were off to see her family. One rumor was that there had been, or still was, a pregnancy scare between them, and whatever the situation, she'd decided it was time for her parents to meet the guy she'd been "seeing" for the past two years. They were meeting them at *Ciao* on Jefferson, a place Vanessa felt warranted Arlin's donning a shirt and tie.

"I don't get it man," Arlin shouted to Jamie over the shower stall.

Jamie was taking a shower as Arlin stood in front of the mirror, wrestling with his tie.

"What about meeting a chick's parents requires me to wear this?"

"She's just nervous. She wants you to look nice." Jamie called back.

"It's like I'm hiding behind this little strip of

fabric, not letting her folks see what I'm really like or something."

Jamie tilted his head up into the hot water spray. It felt great streaming down his face. He wiped his fingers over his eyes.

"What *are* you really like?" Jamie asked.

"Well, you know, I'm not a tie guy. I'm just… the guy their daughter likes to screw around with."

"Yeah," Jamie replied, "I wouldn't advise sharing that insight tonight."

"I'm not an idiot, man!"

"How's that tie coming?"

"Not good man. Not good." Exasperation was seeping into Arlin's voice. "Does Fritz know how to do this?"

"Nah, but he's got a few ties hanging on his doorknob that I rigged up for him."

"Fuck this," Arlin shouted back. "I'm taking one of Fritz's."

The bathroom door slammed as Jamie turned the hot water higher and closed his eyes. No incidents lately. Mind seemed good. Body was having no problems. He'd gone for a major run that morning. Really pushed himself. No symptoms had surfaced afterward. If anything, the cold air and movement had made him feel better, and that was the whole point, right? He'd come back, caught up on some work, and relaxed for the afternoon. He'd talked to Kelli on the phone earlier, but hadn't seen her that day. He got the feeling she was a little nervous about him going to the party with Fritz, but neither one of them thought there was anything to worry about. Maybe if their sex life was quieter, or they weren't so crazy about each other, then the trepidation would have been called for, but hey, that's relationships. No matter how secure you seem, there's always that leprechaun of worry on the shoulder, dripping discombobulating poison in your ear. He was gonna stop by her place before they left. Time for a quickie maybe? Jamie smirked. Wishful thinking. He shut the water off, stood in the middle of the steamy shower stall, and felt the water dripping down his body. When a chill caught his skin, sending up a brigade of goose bumps, he grabbed his towel and dried off.

The rest of the floor was going about the customary Saturday night routine. Doug was in the lounge, lifting one of the couches onto cinder blocks and sliding the other one in front to make the poor man's stadium theater seating. Another Saturday, another '*Star Wars*' marathon. By now they could turn off the sound and let Doug say every line for every character himself. *Every. Character.*

The first of the evening's unexpected twists occurred as Jamie rounded the corner to his room, only to see Will standing with his back leaning against the corridor wall. A brown bag paper bag sat at his feet, a DVD was tucked under his arm. His expression told Jamie he wasn't there to discuss the cinema of Billy Wilder. Jamie stopped in the hall, only a towel wrapped around his waist.

"What can I do for you, Will?" Jamie asked.

"Can we talk?" Will responded.

"Sure, if you don't mind me changing."

Will shook his head as Jamie walked past him and opened the door. He walked inside, tossed his dirty clothes on the bed, and started going through his dresser drawers.

"What is it Will?"

Will stood at the door. Jamie pulled the hat from his head, ducking towards the bed so Will wouldn't see the scars as he quickly dried his hair. He reached over to the dresser, grabbed another cap from the top, and pulled it on as he turned back to Will, who still hadn't said a word.

"*Well?*" Jamie asked again.

"You and Kelli, you guys are pretty much, seeing each other, right?"

Jamie felt the corner of his mouth pull to the side. It was an angry, cocky smile.

"You might say that, yeah." He dropped his towel and watched Will's eyes quickly dart down and up to the far upper corner of the room. "You like her, right? I know that."

Will closed his eyes for a moment. Jamie pulled on his boxers and a T-shirt.

"You're wondering if we're serious or not?"

Will nodded his head. "Yeah."

"Do you want me to 'end the courtship' if this isn't forever?"

Will hesitated. "I don't- I guess I just wanted to know for sure where things stood with you guys, and with…us."

"I hope by 'us,' you mean you and Kelli." Jamie watched for the kid's nod. "You know there's nothing there, don't you? You can't watch movies and drink beer with a girl every couple of months and call that a relationship.

Then, Jamie wasn't sure what happened. He remembered Will opening his mouth to speak, could see the expression on the kid's face as Jamie rushed at him, but aside from the sound of the bag with the beer bottles hitting the floor, everything was a blur. One minute he was standing at the dresser, picking out a pair of pants, the next he had shoved Will against the back of the door, his left forearm to Will's throat, his right hand clasped to the guy's chin, as he barked a garble of angry threats in a hushed voice. His right hand pulsated, smacking the back of Will's head against the door. His forearm pressed into his throat just a bit too hard. He felt something pop under the pressure he was applying. Then, he was standing in the middle of the room, the pounding pressure in his temples fading away. His arms trembled as the adrenaline seeped out of his muscles. Will clasped his hands to his neck, sucked in several gasps of air, then grabbed his things and ran out of the room. Jamie felt his heart in his throat, started to rush after him, then stopped and let him go.

He finished getting dressed, put on some cologne, and met up with Fritz to head over to the party.

\* \* \*

Kelli was shanghaied *immediately*. She'd gone months without seeing Will or enduring the endless evenings devoid of chemistry but filled with old movies. She

actually missed it now, the movies *and* Will. She still had
no romantic inclinations for him, but she did like having
him as a friend. God, she was going all *Sweet Valley High*.
No point examining every emotional whisper in her head.
She was hanging out with Will tonight. No sooner did
she tell Jamie to go to that party with Fritz, than an e-mail
popped up in her inbox. This time Will had a fresh print
of *The Apartment* that gave him "goose bumps." Good
lord. But she could use the distraction.

Christie and Joe were at it again, while blaring
music the likes of which she had never heard. Christie
must have grown tired of wearing her headphones while
riding her man into the sunset; now she wanted to share
the experience with the floor, or at least with as wide a
swath of the building as she could manage. Disturbingly,
the noises coming from her roommate's bedroom had
changed over the last few months. Louder squeals, some
softer moans, and longer, deeper grumbles of pleasure.
Either Christie and Mr. Schlong were exercising their
vocal ululations, or they'd made the leap to the next level
of cringe-inducing lovemaking.

As if on cue, a yodeling voice cut through the
adjoing wall, a warbling, undulating cat cry of female
orgasm. That was not Christie.

Jesus, they were swinging. Gross.

Kelli turned on the TV and cranked the volume.
Where the hell was Will? Maybe they could go over to
Gibson G and watch the movie over there. If they stayed
here, Jack Lemmon and Shirley Maclaine would have one
hell of a time falling for each other over the racket next

door, that was for sure.

Kelli glanced at her watch. He was thirty minutes late. Not like Will to be late for one of their movies nights, or anything they did together, actually. If anything, she figured he got there early and waited in the hall til he was right on time. She opened the door and glanced out into the hallway. Nothing.

The voices in the next room were getting louder. Kelli grabbed her jacket and headed for the tunnels. Either Will had forgotten, or he was mad at her for something, again. Christ.

\* \* \*

The usual gang was there. Jamie recognized Chris "Big Red" right away. Joe and Matt aka "Ron Jeremy" and "Slick Willy" took a moment or two to place; the lack of jerseys made the names more elusive.

Joe was drunk already. He walked over to Jamie, a plastic cup of beer tilting back and forth in his hand.

"So, ya pledgin' next quarter?" he slurred.

Jamie pulled his hands from his pockets, ready to deflect Joe's drink if it came tumbling toward him. "I'm not planning on it at the moment," he replied.

"Ah, come on, ya gots to, man. Ya gots to."

Jamie nodded his head. "We'll see, dude. Maybe."

"Maybe's good enough for me," Joe exclaimed, a shit-faced smile bursting to his face. Then he turned, proudly exclaiming to no one in particular, "Maybe!" He spun around again. *"Maybe!"*

Jamie pulled a cup from a stack on the counter and

helped himself to a beer. Fritz wandered into the crowd as Jamie made his way to the corner of the room and looked around.

The party's opening lull dissipated by eleven. By then, the crowd had swelled considerably, and music and alcohol would work out the rest. The bedroom doors down the hallway were all open. Either none of the brothers were entertaining female guests at the moment, or they were, and they weren't being shy about it. Probably too early for that yet. However, *that* would certainly be happening tonight. Just scanning the apartment, Jamie saw one or two couples well on their way to steaming up the room. A closer study of the crowd, and Jamie picked out a familiar face.

Erica.

Jesus.

She was all over some jock on the couch, dryhumping his leg and straddling him as she kissed his neck and nibbled on his ear. If she could hold down her booze for a bit, that guy was guaranteed a blowjob in the bathroom, at a minimum.

Fritz was on the far side of the room, talking with one of the brothers and bobbing his head to the music. Jamie nodded to him and raised one hand. Fritz nodded back, then turned to watch a couple of blond chicks heading for the back bedroom. With only the slighted hesitation, be began bopping and "whiteman-shuffling" his way through the crowd and heading down the hallway after them. Either one of the guy's porn fantasies was about to come true, or he was at least about to see *something* interesting.

Then, Jamie saw someone he would never have expected at any sort of frat function. Actually, the person tapped him on the shoulder, and when he turned around, he was suddenly face to face with Victor. Photo cage Victor.

"Pepper, right?"

Jamie nodded his head. "Yeah, what's up, man?"

Victor ignored the question as he opened the fridge and slid a twelve pack of Labatt Blue onto the shelf. "Want one?"

Jamie raised his cup. "No thanks."

Victor pulled a bottle from the box and popped the top, taking a long swig as he leaned against the countertop. "So, are you pledging or something?"

Jamie shook his head, "I'm just here with a friend. You?"

"Same." He took another drink. "Just here to drink and scope out the easy pussy."

Jamie faked a smile. Something about this guy. What was it? This was not the frat type. Course, neither was he, but Victor, Victor was something else. He was more of the too cool for *anything* type. Easy pussy indeed. God, the bedroom decorum of this guy, that would be something nightmarish to see. That would be-

"You liking the program?" Victor asked him.

"You mean the photo program?" Jamie nodded. "So far."

It would certainly be easier if assholes like Victor would let him do his work without banging on lab doors

and hassling him about sign-in times. Jamie hadn't had to deal with the guy much after that initial tour of the facilities, but his one or two interactions with him had still been grating. In fact, he ranted about Victor regularly with the folks in the photo cage line. They universally dubbed him an asshole, but more than one of them had added that he was talented. "He's got a great eye, you've gotta give him that" was the phrase that had come from more than one of their mouths. Jamie had yet to see the guy's work. He really didn't want to. It was one thing to hate a guy, it was another thing to hate a guy but envy his talents. That was a complication he didn't need, especially if Victor's photos struck him as greater than his own; he was, after all, a painter first; photography was his consolation prize.

They didn't have much to say to one another, and it was clear that Victor was as disinterested in searching for common ground as Jamie was. They just stood in the kitchen a few minutes longer, watching the tide of partiers swirling past them. Then someone Victor knew came into the kitchen and reached for the tap. Vic started talking to the guy, then followed him back to a larger group of guests, mostly women, who were standing on the far side of the room. Jamie leaned against the fridge and chugged his beer. He floated over to the tap just as Fritz walked by with a bottle of Patron Silver.

"Any luck back there?" Jamie nodded towards the back hall.

Fritz just smiled.

"Shall we kick this up a notch, my friend?"

Jamie eyed the bottle warily. "I don't know. Shall we?"

Fritz set two shot glasses on the counter with a flourish, pulled the cork from the tequila bottle, and quickly filled each glass to the rim. Fritz raised one of the glasses to his lips, motioning for Jamie to do the same.

"You liking tequila yet?" he asked.

Jamie shook his head. "Not a bit."

Fritz smirked and tossed his head back.

Jamie followed suit. The tequila splashed up and around the roof of his mouth, washed over his tongue and slid back into his throat. A peppery haze swelled up through his nose. His throat tingled pleasantly. Maybe he *was* starting to like tequila.

Fritz watched the expression on his face melt from wary to surprised. "And another," he said as he took Jamie's glass and topped it off.

They grabbed the glasses and threw back another round.

"Ooh yeah," Fritz wheezed appreciatively.

"One more," Jamie gasped as he wiped his mouth with his shirt sleeve.

Fritz didn't waver. The glasses were filled one last time, then the bottle was slammed to the counter, the cork replaced with a thump.

"To good times," Jamie toasted.

"To insanity," Fritz countered.

The glass was heavy in Jamie's hand now. He raised it to the light, watching the spirits and the crystal shimmer. The light through the liquid seemed splintered, hotter somehow. He brought the glass to his lips and poured one more savory helping down his gullet. It burned so good. The heat oozed down his throat and blossomed in his belly, the waves of alcohol rising up through his nostrils. The music was pumping now. Everyone around him was dancing. At some point Fritz, undoubtedly feeling his own Patron-induced sense of flight, wandered into the crowd, where Jamie saw him grinding up against a number of gorgeous, albeit interchangeable sorority sisters. Jamie wasn't one for dancing, but under the influence of the music, and the crowd, and the liquor, he found himself out in the middle of the room, moving him body to the music. He closed his eyes, savoring the feeling of motion, *controlled* motion. It was one thing to shake and rattle when you didn't want to, when something in your head was misfiring, driving you insane, but it was something else to let the music take control, to relax and just *go* where the mood took you.

Jamie opened his eyes and the room was moving. Not just the people, or the crowd, but the *room*. He turned his head and a girl's smile caught his eye, then hung in the air before him, even as he looked around, taking in the rest of the scene. Outlines of faces, figures and shapes, all shifting around him in a swirling, drunken blur. The tequila had raced through his bloodstream. His mouth tasted of silver. A silver spoon.

He laughed. He didn't know why.

*Had Jamie Pepper been born with the taste of a silver spoon in his mouth?*

Christ he was drunk.

He looked to the side again, that girl was there. All blond streaks and skin-tight clothing. When you thought of sorority girls, you thought of her. She floated through the crowd. Jamie laughed again. All part of the experience, right? All part of the experience. She came in closer, raising her hands up to his arms, slipping her fingers down to his waist. She was dancing now, moving forward and backward, her legs spread apart, just on either side of his left leg. Jamie was dancing. He was really drunk. He smiled and she leaned forward. He could smell her shampoo. She was wearing perfume. White Musk. Christ almighty, this was too much.

"What's your name?" she shouted over the noise.

"Jamie!" he thought he shouted back.

Another smile.

Her fingers moved below his waist to the tops of his jeans, where they hung on the fabric. Then they slipped under the edge of his t-shirt, tickling his skin. Jamie felt stirrings, blood flowing to all the right places. Or all the wrong ones. She came in closer and stared him in the eyes. He watched the lines of skin at the corners of her mouth. Her lips fell open slightly, a pink flash of tongue behind white teeth. He glanced from the mouth to the eyes, nervous. She smiled at him again.

*Jesus.*

It seemed like she was saying something, but he couldn't hear what. He closed his eyes and circled her waist with his arms. Her body was taut and warm under his hands, under her shirt. He felt just the slightest movement of skin over ribs, supple perfection. He opened his eyes again, his head lolling back in a slow, heavy roll. The girl's smile faded, replaced by a seductive, determined stare as she pressed herself against him, kissed the side of his neck, and looked up at him. Jamie leaned forward and kissed her. She opened her mouth and kissed him back. The room was still turning as he closed his eyes.

At dawn, something in his head popped. He felt hot liquid, hot syrup, running down his head. Down the *inside* of his head. He opened his eyes, suddenly expecting to see the girl beside him. The girl! Christ! Instead he felt the dull pain of sticks and leaves. Hard, compacted earth and tree roots. Where the fuck was he? Though still early, the light was blinding. He stared up above him, through tree branches, and up to the dark, overcast sky. He was outside. His back ached. His body was stiff. He moved slowly, deliberately, hearing the sounds of crunching, frozen leaves around him. He brought a hand to his head. Christ. Where *was* he? What had happened? Where was the girl? What about the party?

There were flashes. Images. But nothing he could pin down. Had they had sex? Who knew? Oh God. Kelli… What else? From the moment on the dance floor, when he'd kissed the girl, to now, *what had happened?* It must have been hours since he'd been at the frat house. Since Fritz had poured the shots. Since he'd talked to that guy, that asshole Victor.

*Victor.*

There were other flashes now. Flickers of the woods. Moonlight. A chase through the trees. First hiding, waiting for someone, then a chase. Then? Nothing. No faces. No words. Nothing to hold onto.

Jamie fell back to the ground. His hands and body were sore. He'd missed at least one of his medication times, assuming this was only the next day. He had to get back to the dorms, back to campus if that were the case. He struggled to his feet. His head throbbed, the pain growing sharper, even as he dug his thumb and index finger into his temples and rubbed deeply. He turned around. Must have wandered away from an access road and into the woods. Jamie felt his way through the trees, eventually coming out in a clearing, where he could just make out the tall brick outlines of the dorm towers. How he'd made it this far was beyond him.

A ray of sunlight broke through the clouds overhead, blinding him. In the burst of light, he saw more flashes of the chase, again felt the rush of pursuit. It couldn't be real, but then again, he *was* in the middle of nowhere, with no idea how he'd gotten there. That wasn't imagined. That was real. Walking through this field was real. A face again popped up his mind. Victor. Something with Victor. Every time he blinked another image flickered across his eyelids.

He stopped, closed his eyes, and focused on the darkness. He squeezed his lids together. Stop thinking about this.

You're *making* yourself see these things now.
*Stop it!*
He opened his eyes and continued on.

\* \* \*

This was certainly the most disturbing crime scene John Gridley had handled in the fifteen years since he'd left the force to take the campus safety gig at the Institute. Way back when, he'd spent the majority of his time showing up to crime scenes to direct the first response and make sure the blood puddles got mopped up properly. Name a time of year and he could name a horrific public incident he'd dealt with downtown. He'd seen drive-bys at Easter egg hunts. A strangling in the Fifteenth Ward over corn beef and cabbage. The last year he'd been on the force he'd seen a stabbing in line to see Santa at the mall. Two days later he'd shown up at the *same mall* to deal with the stabbing of Santa *himself!* That was the last straw for him. When little kids waited in line to request Red Rider air rifles, and instead saw the man in the red suit get slashed to death, one had to ask if the city was losing its battle to reclaim downtown for the suburban shopping crowd.

The next morning he'd poured a cup of coffee, taken his cholesterol medication, and opened the paper to the want ads. The interview was a snap, the job was a match, and that had been that. Aside from the odd sexual assault, and the occasional frat house altercation, it was mostly an administrative job: Submitting paperwork to insurance companies for car break-ins and collisions in the parking lots. Doing quarterly safety presentations for University Chairs. Once or twice a year he'd deal with a suicide from one of the residential towers. Those were always disturbing. The sheer waste brought about by some kid's foolish belief that a C in programming, or a stumble in mechanical engineering, could so thoroughly disgrace their family that a face-plant onto the sidewalk a dozen stories down was the only remedy. Still, just as frat guys had been banging sorority sisters since time eternal, uptight bookworms had been offing themselves on college campuses since well before he'd been born, and they'd continue to do so long after he'd retired to spend his days watching football on his big screen TV.

The point was that he no longer dealt with events that scared the shit out of him. No longer came face to face with the blood and guts of violent crimes. At times he even asked himself if he'd gone soft too soon. If he lacked the stomach, or the courage, to really pursue the career he had chosen. Maybe he'd end up back downtown someday, take a position in the investigations unit, work on the murder and assault cases that sat molding in file cabinets year after year. One glimpse at this crime scene, however, told him he'd *never* go back

They got a call around nine that morning and sent a car to the outer campus loop. A young woman had been taking her morning run on one of the nature trails, when an undulating scream and a claw of bloody fingers had reached out for her from the bushes to the side of the path. The girl had grabbed her cell phone, high-tailed it for the main road, and dialed campus safety. The first officer on the scene called for an ambulance and asked that Gridley to come out there himself. Which he had done. They were just hauling the kid out on a stretcher when he got there. From the smell of him, the guy was still flying high on vodka fumes, but he was starting to sober up enough to feel the pain setting in. And there was pain. There'd be more soon enough, but by the time the medics got to him, he was hurting plenty.

From the look of him, he was some sort of artsy type. Definitely a student. Definitely not the typical crime victim. Possibly annoying. He had long black hair, a spattering of piercings, and what looked like eye makeup. At least, what looked like makeup on *one* eye. It wasn't clear if he'd worn it on both. The left eye was blue, with long lashes, and a thin ring of black liner around the edge. But the other eye. The other eye was a pulpy, bloody mess. His face and neck were covered in cuts and scratches. Chunks of the kid's hair has been ripped from his head. From the way he held his side, he'd taken a hell of a beating in his midsection, might even have a stab wound or two, but it was the eye that was the thing. Primarily, it was the *absence* of the eye, the sight of the torn, shredded tissue that hung from the bloody, clumping eye socket - that was what turned the stomach, what gave Gridley and his men that little tinge of panic in their guts. In the midst of whatever attack had taken place, someone had take a knife or a piece of glass, and slashed this poor kid down the front of his face, splitting his forehead, tearing his cheek open, and rupturing his eye in the process. The face would take a lot of plastic surgery to patch up. In Gridley's unprofessional opinion, the eye was a goner. Just looking at the kid as the medics worked to get him stable, Gridley thought he could make out portions of the kid's eye itself; the iris, the white stuff, which lay shiveled and destroyed on the kid's cheek, a popped balloon. He was still alive, in shock, but breathing. The medics tried to speak to him as they struggled to get the gurney up the hillside and into the back of the ambulance.

"We'll have you to the hospital in no time kid," one of the men was saying. He and his partner grunted as they worked their way up the embankment. The ground was still slick with icy grass and weeds, and their feet kept slipping before catching hold.

They made it to the top and the other guy leaned down. "Can you tell us your name?"

The boy looked up, confused. He tried to lift one hand to his face as the first medic held him still.

"Try not to move son. Try not to move."

The kid's mouth was a straight, serious line. His eye rolled from one medic to the next. A third EMT opened the doors to the ambulance as the two men lifted the gurney and rolled it inside.

"Lets get going."

"You taking him to Strong?" Gridley asked.

"Yeah," one of them shouted.

Gridley looked up one last time as one of the men took the victim's wallet from his baggy jeans. He flipped through the cards, then pulled out a student ID and tossed it to Gridley. "You may want to call this kid's parents."

Gridley nodded.

The doors closed, the lights blinked on, and the ambulance drove away, turning onto Perkins Road, then switching on its siren as it took a left onto John Street.

Gridley looked down at the student ID, where a picture of the kid in better days looked back at him. The name in the bottom right corner read: Victor Smallwood.

* * *

"Where were you Jamie?" Kelli asked him again.

He looked around, exhausted.

"I told you, I fell asleep at the party," he mumbled.

"Why didn't you come back with Fritz? He was here this morning, he was back last night."

Jamie shook his head. "I don't know."

He needed his meds.

"Did something happen?" Kelli continued. "You look like hell."

"I feel like it," he replied.

She had cornered him at the door as he came up the back stairway. She'd been sleeping on the couch in the small lounge around the corner from his room. Must have been there all night.

"Hold on a minute," he held up his finger in a pausing motion and unlocked the door to his room. Kelli glared at him as he ducked around the corner, shook some pills from his dresser, and tried to swallow them dry. They caught in his throat, nearly causing him to gag. He walked back into the hall and took a drink from the fountain.

"Jamie," Kelli started. "Will told me what happened last night."

Jamie stopped, his back to her.

"What was that about?"

He was quiet. "I don't know."

"Where were you last night?" she asked.

He turned around and looked at her. "I don't know. I had a, I had a thing, a blackout or something."

She was looking at him differently now, staring with a tinge of skepticism that melted into concern.

He looked like shit. His clothes were caked with mud, mud and... it couldn't be. Not that.

Jamie was still looking at her, his mouth open, wanting to speak.

"All right," Kelli said finally. "I believe you."

She walked over and put his arms around him. They held each other tight.

"Do you need to see your doctor again?" she asked.

"Yeah, I think I might."

# CHAPTER TWELVE

She didn't ask anymore about the incident with Will. Hell, Will had already told her everything, in detail. Rattled off the story like a little kid tattling on his older brother. 'Jimmy knocked down my block tower. Jimmy smashed my fire engine with a rock.' To Will's credit, he didn't come running to her room right away. When he didn't show up at her dorm with *The Apartment,* and as her swinging, key-party roommate and her companions were getting into high gear, Kelli had grabbed her coat and rushed over to Gibson G to see what was happening.

Jamie and Fritz had left for the party by the time she arrived. Some of the other residents were out for the night. Doug and a few of the Film/Video geeks, including Gabe, were sitting in the lounge watching *Return of the Jedi.* Gabe glanced up as she stepped into the lounge. Kelli gave him a questioning look and he shrugged his shoulders, motioning to the door just to the left of the public area, where light from a reading lamp shone out from a crack in the door. Will lay on the bed, his back to the entrance, his face to the wall. A book was on the mattress in front of him, face-down. He was brooding, his eyes burning a hole through the cinder block wall.

Kelli stepped into the room, glancing out into the lounge, where the better part of the *Star Wars* crew had turned to watch her. She closed the door with a click, leaving Jaba and the other freaks outside.

She stood for a moment, not saying a word.

Will didn't look at her.

"What's the matter, Will?" she asked finally.

"What do you mean?" he said to the wall.

"What happened to our movie night?"

"What's the point? You didn't really want to watch it with me."

She hadn't. That was true. But now she didn't know what to think.

"I was looking forward to it. We haven't watched a movie in ages now."

"Yeah?" Will huffed. "You missed it?"

"Will, what is wrong with you?"

Nothing.

She knew what was wrong. He wanted to be with her, had wanted that for years now, but she was never interested, and now she was with someone else. Someone who hadn't even needed to pursue her, who she'd gone after with the same intensity that he felt for her. Now Will was pissed at her, was letting out the anger over being rejected.

"Jamie told me to leave you alone," he said finally.

"He what?"

"He told me to stop bugging you. Choked me, actually, then said the other stuff."

"He *choked* you?"

Will rolled over, one hand to his throat. Kelli stepped closer to have a better look at him in the light. There were a series of bruises under the tips of his fingers, which were massaging the skin on his neck. Kelli breathed in deeply, then took Will's forearm and lifted his hand out of the way. A bruise was forming around his neck, a bruise in the indistinct, but recognizable shape of a hand.

"Were you two fighting?" she asked flatly.

"No. I went to talk to him about… you guys, and he just came at me. I don't even remember him saying anything."

Kelli was quiet. Embarrassed and angry. She looked at Will. Stared him in the eyes. He looked back for as long as he could hold her gaze, then he cast his eyes down to the surface of his bed.

Kelli let out a sigh and looked up, "You still want to watch the movie?"

He had. And they did. They stayed up talking afterwards. Movie stuff. School. They didn't discuss the two of them; that was all said in the silences. Kelli started to nod off around two in the morning, and Will seemed barely conscious himself, so she'd hauled herself up, wandered down the corridor, and lay down on the small couch around the corner from Jamie's room. She fell asleep immediately.

Around four o'clock she awoke to the sounds of Fritz fumbling drunkenly with the lock on his door. She looked up and mumbled to him.

"Where's Jamie?"

Fritz looked over at her and shrugged his shoulders.

"I don't know."

"He wasn't with you?"

"He was," Fritz slurred, "but he wandered off at some point. He'll probably be back soon."

Kelli had nodded, then fallen back asleep.

She woke three hours later as the sun was just beginning to rise. The hallway was silent. Anyone who'd been listening to music or pulling a Saturday study session was now fast asleep. She heard the sounds of the building, the rumbling of the steam heat, but little else. She got up and walked down the hall a short ways. No light under Jamie's door. She tried the doorknob. Still locked. Maybe he'd come in without seeing her and passed out. Locked the door behind him. She tapped on the wood with her knuckles. Once. And then again, louder.

Nothing.

When Jamie did show up, an hour later, he'd come in quietly, trying not to wake her. His steps were heavy and uneven, landing harder, then softer, exhaustion clearly making it difficult for him to gauge the momentum of his movements. She'd opened her eyes and watched him as he disappeared around the corner, then came back, peering around at her, sizing her up uneasily. He had just slipped around the corner again when she called out after him and struggled to her feet.

That was hours ago now. She'd left Jamie in his room to sleep. Bob and Carol and Ted and Alice, or whoever the orgy members in her suite were, had to be either sleeping or gone by now, but she had work to do. Some sound dubbing for her 16 millimeter sync class. They'd been working on one of her classmates' productions the week before, and she had two reels of audio to transfer to mag stock before the next class screening. This seemed like as good a time as any to get over to campus, transfer the tapes, and get out of there before the slack pack came in and started fighting over the same equipment.

She arrived at the photo building by ten and grabbed the reel-to-reel tapes from her locker on the third floor. It didn't click immediately, but as she headed for the fourth floor stairwell, she realized the third-floor photo cage wasn't open. It was always bustling by this time. A couple of photo students were slouched on the floor, looking exhausted and impatient, but there was no buzz of activity. Kelli made eye contact with a kid in a torn, chemical-stained Fuji T-shirt, who gave her a defeated look and shrugged his shoulders. She turned and walked up the stairs to the fourth floor.

Two of her least favorite people were working at the film cage counter: Scooter and Brick. Scooter was a gossipy, arrogant piece of shit, who liked to wear T-shirts with bizarre phrases on them, stuff that made no sense to her. Today's slogan said, "I eat farmed fish. Got a problem?" She had no clue what that meant. She doubted whether he did either. It was just some inexplicable, random bit of meaninglessness with which to cover his skeletal frame. Brick, on the other hand was built like an inflatable house, big as a bus and bulbous as a blow-up carnival playpen. He wore a bright yellow shirt with a picture of Uma Thurman in *Kill Bill*. She didn't know if Brick was his real name. Probably not, just another cutesy film guy nom de plume or something, like McG. Of the two of them, Brick was still the more likable. Whereas Scooter was cocky and bizarre, he still got his share of play, owing to the fact that he was, well, cocky and bizarre, and one of the only attractive guys in the film program. The ratio at the school was certainly not in favor of the male student population, but when the majority of the men in competition for female affections were either software engineers, trashy looking art majors, or flat-out slobs, like Brick, a guy like Scooter, with a cocky attitude, but a curiously enticing manner about him, somehow did pretty well for himself. For a period of time the previous year, Kelli had regularly seen the guy sporting a shirt emblazoned with the term "Panty Peeler," which set off two highly conflicting reactions in her gut. On the surface she was utterly disgusted by the guy. He was a creep, an asshole through and through, but, well, he did have a certain sexual element to him. He had a good body and a smirk that did the trick, but she was proud to say she was one of the few females in the program who had not yet given in to his charms. Brick on the other hand, he could be a real prick too, but he did try to be likeable from time to time, at least to the ladies, a fact Kelli found at once endearing, and even more infuriating, as it betrayed how he acted in order to stay tight with the rest of the film program ignoramuses.

The cage counter clowns were talking with the AV technician who managed the film and photo cages. None of them seemed to notice her; they were all too wrapped up in a conversation about some sort of a fight the night before. She strained her ears to hear what they were saying, catching snippets of sentences, but unable to piece anything together. Finally, slightly annoyed, but mostly curious, she spoke up.

"Excuse me, but would you mind telling me what you're talking about over there?"

Scooter shot her an irritated sidelong glance.

Kelli smiled back at him. "I'm not being a bitch, I'm just honestly curious."

Brick looked up, then walked over to the counter. "Mike, our manager, was just telling us about something that happened to one of the photo cage guys last night."

"What?"

The manager came over now. "This probably shouldn't be getting out--"

Kelli waited expectantly. Mike glanced at Brick as Scooter wandered over from the back. Finally, Mike shrugged his shoulders and walked away.

"Do you know Victor?" Brick asked.

"I know *of* him,"Kelli replied.

"He got attacked last night, somewhere back in the swamp,"

"Really? Who did it? Was it bad?"

"They don't know who," Brick said, "and yeah, it was bad. One of Mike's buddies works in the campus safety office and took the first call. He got beat up pretty good, cuts and slashes on his face-"

"The guy lost his fucking *eye*," Scooter interrupted.

Kelli grimaced. "Shit."

"Yeah. That's sort of the gossip here. Guy's supposed to be an amazing photographer, an asshole, but an amazing photographer."

Kelli just nodded her head.

"It's kinda scary though," Brick continued. "I know we're out here in Henrietta, this isn't some Iowa corn town, but you don't think about something like this happening here, you know?"

A sliver of ice slid through her lower skull. Her spine went cold.

"Did anyone see this happen?"

Scooter shook his head. "It was late."

A voice was whispering in the back of her head now. Soft and breathy. She couldn't hear the words.

Brick pointed his index finger at her. "You need something?"

"Oh, yeah, could I check out the patch bay and a nagra machine."

Brick turned to get the key.

"You got it."

\* \* \*

Kelli was in the sound room pretty late, later than she needed to be. She was stalling, delaying the moment she'd go back to her dorm room, or back to see Jamie. She knew she'd be going back to Gibson G. They hadn't had a fight. She was just alarmed by the total sense of confusion he'd been giving off. He'd looked like shit, seemed completely foggy. It had scared her. There was something about him that she'd have to find out eventually. The scars on his head. The medication. But she just wasn't ready to ask, or to know.

Fortunately, when she *did* return to the academic side, after first stopping at her dorm to shower and change, she found that she'd finally slipped out of the mental obstacle course she'd been maneuvering all day, and had almost forgotten the events of the previous night, as well as the photo cage conversation that had so disturbed her. She walked into Jamie's dorm room, and was pleasantly surprised to see him sitting at his desk, freshly showered, his short hair slicked back, studying. He turned and smiled at her, even as his hand reached for his cap. She walked up behind him, resting one hand on his shoulder, and kissed the top of his head. She felt the knotty scars under the thin layer of hair. Jamie hesitated before pulling the cap on and turning to her.

"You wanna go to dinner? I'm starving."

The news of Victor's attack was the primary topic of conversation at Gracie's. Snippets of each table's conversation, combined with the late evening release of Monday morning's campus paper, fed the ongoing murmurs about the previous night's events. Kelli watched Jamie closely as these wisps of discussion swirled around them. He seemed interested, but guarded.

"You know him, don't you?" Kelli said.

Jamie was lifting a spoonful of fruit cocktail to his mouth, grimacing as fluorescent light glistened off the edge of a cling peach. "Yeah, I know him. Can't stand the guy actually, but that's terrible news."

Kelli wanted to ask him more, but the sinking in her

stomach said to hold off. She didn't want to know. That would change everything. One flash of Jamie's old smile -- that's all she needed to wipe the slate clean. Tabula rasa, as her old Latin teacher would say.

They finished their meals, walked back through the snow, and slipped into Jamie's room, where they lay in the shadows, moonlight shining in through the curtains, snowflakes hovering in the air, and fell asleep. That would have ended all of Kelli's thoughts of Victor, and Jamie's missing night, and the feeling of dread that had taken up residence in her stomach that day, had she not awoken in the middle of the night, 1 a.m. to be precise, and reached out her hand to find a cold, empty bundle of sheets on Jamie's side of the bed. She hadn't heard him get up, but he had clearly been gone for a while.

She got out of bed and pulled on a sweatshirt. The room was cold. She opened the door to the hall. The floor was quiet. Somewhere at the end of the corridor, she could hear Conan O'Brien doing his monologue. A few doors were propped open down the length of the hall – one was Fritz's. Kelli walked down the hall and stopped in the entryway, leaning against the doorframe, watching Fritz as he sat at his desk, hunched over a text-book. Feeling eyes on him, he looked up with a start. Then he leaned back in his chair and looked at her.

Kelli hesitated for a moment, then opened her mouth.

"Fritz, what do you know about the scars on Jamie's head?"

* * *

The moon floated above him as he raced though the night, under the clouds and over the branches, it didn't lose an inch. He couldn't shake it. He was desperate to get out of its glow, but it was always there. It wanted him dead. Wanted him to be caught. He had to get out sight now. The man was following him, the man in black, with the wicked smile and the burning eyes, he was after him again, *really* after him.

He didn't know how he'd gotten here. Or where he even was. He was on the edge of a wooded area, on a trail that stretched out in either direction as far as he could see. He heard the man behind him, his pursuer's feet cutting through the tall grass with a sweeping, thrashing sound. He was getting closer.

Jamie clenched his jaw and ran on. His legs were burning. His arms were rubber. He glanced at the ground, his feet a blur - back up to the trail, which was heading for a tunnel of trees. The last place he wanted to be, but he had no choice. He opened up his stride and pushed it with everything he had. Tears streamed from his eyes. His breath burned in his throat. Then he was in the shadows, running blind. The branches caught at his clothing like fingers, like claws. He thought the man was catching him, pulling him back. He twisted his upper body, pinwheeled his arms. Dipped and dodged.

Then the tunnel opened up. Moonlight beckoned a dozen yards away. He closed his eyes and willed his legs to move faster. Still the footsteps clammered behind him. He didn't stop. If he hesitated, even for a moment, that would be it.

He opened his eyes. He was in the clear now, broken free of the woods, and running on a path, somewhere on the academic side of campus. The sharp brick buildings loomed overhead, their shadows creeping across the snowy lawn, crisscrossing and pooling in the pale blue light. Jamie slowed his pace, felt his body relaxing. Then he heard footsteps again. Echoing around the plaza. They were coming from the passageway between the photo building and the college of fine arts. Then they were coming from the right, the courtyard with the infinity loop sculpture. He ran straight ahead, ducking into the shadows under the liberal arts building and coming to a stop. Jamie pressed his back against the curved brick wall.

The footsteps stopped.

Jamie held his breath.

Then he heard a new sound. A sort of scratching, dragging noise, like an old man in slippers. Small, barely lifted footsteps that dragged along the brick walkway. This was someone else. Someone different walking up behind him now. Even before he saw him, he knew who it would be. Who it was. And he couldn't bring himself to look. Didn't want to see. He stood in the darkness, eyes clenched shut. His finger scratched nervously at the brick and mortar under his hands. The footsteps came closer. Closer. He could hear the man breathing now. Wheezing. Wet and bubbly. Then the movement stopped. The breathing slowed. Whoever was there, he was watching him. Jamie felt eyes on him now. His eyelids fluttered. He balled his hands into fists, and opened his eyes.

There he was.

Jeff Pepper. Standing before him. Older, frailer, but looking remarkably the same as the last time Jamie had seen him. The last time he had seen him *alive*, he didn't count the recent incident at the house. Jeff stood there watching him, his eyes peaceful, patient. Jamie watched as his father nodded his head gently, paused, then turned and walked away, across the courtyard, towards the library. It was starting to snow, the flurries filling the air with white static. Jamie wanted to say something to the man as he walked away, even as the better part of his mind told him that Jeff Pepper *was not there*. He knew that for a fact now, all in an instant of perfect, clear understanding. This was a hallucination. Yes, he was standing here now, out in the cold, that was real, but the figure of his father that was leaving him now, that was something else - the product of a damaged mind. The implant. If he had suspected anything earlier, then what he felt now was nothing short of pure certainty. Something had gone wrong. The implant, the medication, something in his brain had shifted. He wasn't well. This wasn't right. His body was working, but his mind, his mind was turning in on itself, folding back to the past, stripping away reason and logic, replacing it with instinct, fantasy, and anger.

Jamie watched the silhouette floating through the snow, fading with each passing step, swallowed up by the white. Gone.

He walked out from the building's overhang, following the path his father had just taken. He turned in the middle of the courtyard and headed back to the dorms. Above the soft glow of the snow, the sky was growing lighter with the break of day.

\* \* \*

Kelli was in the waiting room next to Lynn.  Hard to believe they'd met just two weeks earlier under such different circumstances. Christmas seemed a lifetime ago now. Back then she'd just been a girl who was nervous to meet her boyfriend's mother. She didn't know the truth about the scars, about Jamie's condition, or the implant. She didn't lie to herself; she didn't *want* to know. A part of her had just hoped his hair would grow in and cover the evidence, the unspoken secrets would never come to the surface. The corner of her mouth curled slightly. Maybe that was the story with all relationships, it certainly had been with all of hers.

Lynn sat in the chair next to her, going over several pages of longhand writing in a notebook. She hadn't said much on the ride in. Had said even less once they arrived at Jamie's doctor's office and settled into the waiting room. Jamie and Lynn's mannerism at the reception counter told her they were veterans of the process. They'd clearly been jumping though the medical system's hoops for a while now. Paperwork was filled out promptly. Questions answered succinctly. Then they'd sat quietly until Jamie was called into the examination room. They didn't discuss the night before. There was no mention of Victor, or the party, or where he'd been until the moment she'd seen him again. She'd gone through her day, and she

supposed he had gone through his. Then he'd shown up
at their class, come in the door just at the top of the hour,
and sat at a table across the aisle from her, where he sat
and watched her. Looking from Kelli to Professor Ryan,
then slowly back to Kelli. She caught his eyes a couple of
times, alarmed at the angry glint she detected there. What
had he been thinking? Was it just her, or was he getting
paranoid? At the end of class they'd walked out into the
hallway and fallen wordlessly into step together. Jamie
reached down as they walked, took hold of her hand, and
held it tightly.

"Let's make a call," he said softly. "Something's gone
wrong."

Now he was in the doctor's office and she was here.
She didn't know what was happening, what was being
said, but when he came out, things would either be better,
the same, or, much as she hated to think it, much, much
worse.

* * *

"Tell me again why you're here." Price had taken off
his glasses and was facing the window, looking out onto
the parking lot as he twisted the ear pieces angrily. This
was getting to be a problem.

Jamie sat in the chair across from him, watching the
man's shoulders tense up. "I told you, something's wrong.
I'm not acting normally, not thinking normally-"

Price had had enough. This kid, making him well,
none of that had *ever* been the goal of the program.
His body, the ability to control his muscles, keep his

frame and faculties in check, *that* was the goal, had been all along. Who gave a fuck if there was another artist out there on the streets, wasting a good mind and a sound body for the pursuit of some bullshit paintings. Photographs. Films. Whatever the fuck it was. He could give two shits about any of that. Science was for one thing. The body for another. The mind was a different matter altogether; for some it was important, for him maybe, but not for this kid. And certainly not for what he was hoping to achieve. What he *had* achieved.

"We spoke about this last time," Price interjected. "What are you hoping to hear?"

Jamie stopped short. His mouth hung open, unsure what to say next. Price turned and stared at the boy. His eyes narrowed as he slipped his glasses back up the bridge of his nose. He was after one thing, the ability to stop tremors in neurologically disabled individuals, the people that might otherwise serve little purpose to society. Artists weren't necessary, were never necessary, except perhaps for the amusement of a more worthwhile class of people. As he saw it, and as the funding agencies for his research saw it, a body handicapped from a misfiring brain was the *real* waste in the big picture, the true shame. How many people out there would have been classified 4F in the draft thirty, sixty years ago? How many of them could have stormed at the forefront, taken the first wave of fire? Thousands. Millions even. Now they could and *would*. Take people that would otherwise be nothing more than farts in the wind, rework their minds, send them out to fight. If their instincts turned violent, if their

their base instincts won out, so much the better. A blood-thirsty soldier, unafraid of self-injury, undiscerning in his attacks, that was just a bonus in the big picture. Hell, the pentagon spent millions of dollars each year trying to bring out just such instincts in their soldiers. Now perhaps, his research, this program would give them extra manpower and bring all those underlying instincts to the surface. This kid. He was just the first in hundreds to follow. He'd served his purpose. Done the most that could be expected of him. Time to cut him loose and move on.

Price stood silently. His brow furrowed over his glasses, his mouth tightened in a thin line across his face. Then, his face relaxed, as though the cords that drew back his features were suddenly cut. His face fell free and slack, and his lips worked in place softly until the words began to float out.

"I've told you before, your mind is not the issue."

Jamie looked at him blankly.

Price continued, "And, I'm afraid our work together has come to an end."

With that, Price pressed a button on his phone, stood up straight, and left the room by a side door. A moment later the receptionist opened the main door and waited patiently until Jamie rose from his seat and walked out of the room.

# CHAPTER THIRTEEN
# UNDER THE SENTINEL

It was snowing as the three of them walked out to
the parking lot. The temperature had plunged, and their
breath seemed to billow out of their lungs, freeze in the
air before them, and tumble to the ground in icy clouds.
The snow itself was small, and sandy, and hard against
their faces. A thin layer of white was already gathering on
the roof of Lynn's car, which Jamie brushed away with a
scraper as Lynn turned the ignition to warm the engine.

Kelli didn't say anything. She knew better than to
break the silence. Jamie had come out of Price's office
with a grave expression on his face. His mouth set. His
eyes cast downward. Lynn glanced from her son to Kelli,
and the two of them made eye contact. The news could
not have been good. They wouldn't press him on it. If he
had something to tell them, he would raise the issue in
his own time. Still, the ride back to campus was painfully
quiet. As they pulled out onto Mt. Hope, Lynne reached
over and flipped on the radio where the DJs were talking
excitedly about the weather. Lynn turned up the volume.
This was Rochester, for the radio guys to get excited about

*anything* weather related meant that it had to be big.

"-coming in from the lakes," it began in midsentence, "and hitting this second storm front dead on. Which you long-time residents know can only be bad. It's gonna get ugly."

"Just how much snow should we be expecting, Randy?" A co-host chimed in.

"I don't think the question is how much, it's how long. This could last for the next few days. Like I said, just as bad as the snow will be the *cold*. Get a hold of yourselves fellas, cause if you don't watch it, they're gonna freeze right off ya this-"

Lynn clucked her tongue on the roof of her mouth and clicked the radio off in disgust.

"Stupid," she muttered softly.

Kelli was sitting in the passenger seat. Jamie was in the back behind her. She folded down the sun visor and glanced back at him in the mirror. His expression was blank. He'd checked-out on them. Kelli turned and looked out at the road as another volley of snow hit the windshield with the tinkling sounds of broken glass. What would they do when they got back to campus? Would he tell her what had happened? Would they just split up and go back to their rooms? That's what he might try to do, but she wouldn't let him. She told herself that. She'd grab his hand and tell him to stay put. To tell her what the *fuck* he'd found out. Instead, when they pulled into the loop that circled in front of the NTID tower next to Gibson hall, Lynn and Jamie exchanged some mumbled goodbyes before Lynn gave Kelli a half smile and a nod, then drove away.

The two of them stood alone on the curb by the driveway. Kelli turned and looked at him. He stared back.

"I'm going out for a run," he said finally.

Kelli nodded her head. "Okay."

\* \* \*

Thirty minutes later, Jamie was waiting in the shadows at the entrance to the administrative building, waiting for *him* to come outside. He knew his schedule by now, had been watching the man's routine after class. He'd caught him on off days following an almost identical routine. Jamie knew when he went to his office, when he went to his classes, when he grabbed lunch, where he parked his car on campus. The funny thing was that he didn't remember making a conscious effort to pick up such details, to follow the man like he was some sort of mark. It just happened. He seemed to find himself walking by certain places at certain times of day, somehow finding himself in the same locations again and again.

Tonight it has seemed particularly important for him to be here at the end of the day. Even as his mother's car had been turning into the drive for the residential side, he'd been glancing at his watch, thinking to himself that he had to get here in time. He couldn't miss the guy today.

He didn't know why.

He was afraid to know why.

That nervous, swimming feeling welled up in his stomach. The sensation you get before asking someone out, or making a big play in a game. The feeling of going out on stage, not knowing what you're going to do next.

What was he going to say? What was he going to *do*?

The wind was blowing harder now, shooting thin slivers of ice through his clothing and into his arms and legs, pinning him against the wall. Jamie pulled the hat down on his head, lifted the hood of his sweatshirt, and tightened the strings. He slipped on his gloves and stepped back into the corner.

There he was. Dressed in his usual professorial coat and pants, his shoulders hunched under a heavy topcoat. Professor Karl Ryan, Media and the Mind aficionado, finished with another day of classes, no doubt headed home to a pretentious glass of port and more cerebral ponderings of the ways of the media world. Jamie felt clouds of anger billowing up behind his eyes. His stomach hardened. He clenched his hands into fists.

Ryan made his way across the academic quad, trudging through the snow-smothered breezeway along the side of the photo building, and heading down to the parking lot across from the campus. Jamie waited until he was a good ten yards ahead before he slipped out of the shadows and began following behind him. The snow was coming in harder than ever now and he doubted that anyone could see the two of them from the buildings up the hill. Hell, Ryan could probably have turned around and stared directly in his direction with no clue that he was being followed. Then again, you always knew if someone was watching you, right? The hair on the back of your neck, the prickling chill on your skin. That was one of the ancient survival instincts, still buried in your body, no matter how many generations had gone by.

Ryan was walking slowly on the icy sidewalks and Jamie had to slow his pace to avoid catching up to him. A great number of students were heading off campus early today, no doubt trying to avoid the icy highways. Ryan stood at the crosswalk, waiting for one of the cars to let him go. Jamie ran down the driveway and headed around to another sidewalk, took another crosswalk to the parking lot. He'd circle around, come in from the side as soon as Ryan got into the more secluded portion of the lot. That's when he'd move in and…

*What? Do what? What was he even here for?*

Jamie flexed his hands stiffly. Ryan was walking through the lot now. Jamie followed along from the other side. He tightened his coat around him as another gust of wind came barreling across the flat open space. He could just make out Ryan's shape. A little farther and the two of them would be out of sight from the road when the professor got to his car. Jamie started to hurry now. His feet shuffled on the icy concrete, slipping and sliding beneath him. His heart stuttered once or twice as he almost went down, but he regained control.

Then Ryan was at the door of his car, pulling at the door handle, and Jamie was running. Racing across the lot. Launching himself at the man. Going at his face with his hands. Clawing at his eyes and reaching for something in his own coat which he pulled out and slashed at Ryan's face. He snuck a glimpse off to the side as he drove the weapon in his hand deep into Ryan's stomach. No one could see them from here. No one was around to see who had done it, to tell the police what had happened.

\* \* \*

Gridley arrived as the ambulance was pulling away. It had probably been twenty minutes from the moment the call came in to the moment the guy was taken away. The EMTs said his name was Ryan. He was a professor at the college. Looked like a real tweed coat kinda guy - tweed coat with leather patches and a good soaking of blood that is. His own blood.

A student who'd been trying to get off campus before the storm went apeshit when she saw him. Said she'd been fumbling with her keys when she looked over and saw a car with its door open and two legs sprawled out into the parking lot. She went over to check on the guy, and had gotten more than an eyeful. Multiple puncture wounds to the abdomen, blood all over the fucking place. Gridley glanced around the car to see if they'd missed anything. The snow had been kicked away underneath the driver's side door. Blood jumped out at Gridley's eyes from the bright white backdrop. The inside of the car smelled like new leather, but the seat and the floor were both soaked with congealed, frozen blood. The seat back was slashed in a ragged downward angle, no blood in the cut, probably a missed slash to the face. The medics said there were plenty signs of struggle, the good professor had tried to defend himself and had gotten a few good gashes to his face and hands for the trouble. He bled a whole hell of a lot. Nice car. 'cept for the blood. Shame, there was no chance the guy would ever get his money out of the thing now, assuming that he even pulled through. He wasn't in good shape when they took him away. Lungs were collapsing on him, body doubled over in pain. He couldn't even get the words out to tell them who he was. Had to get that info from his wallet. The wallet had still been there. Good sign this wasn't a robbery. This was either real personal, or a totally random attack.

"Frank," Gridley turned to the officer behind him. "Send the guys out, get word to our folks and the Henrietta police department. Whoever did this is gonna have blood all over himself."

Frank nodded and walked over to the patrol car.

Gridley glanced around the inside of the car again, then crouched down on his knees and felt around under the seat with gloved hands. A minute later he held up a small, bloody serrated knife.

"Hey, Frank," Gridley called again as he got back on his feet. "That look like one of the knives from Gracie's?"

Frank walked over, his eyes on Gridley's hands as they rotated the cheap handle and blade.

"I think you're right," Frank said.

"So, either the professor's been stealing knives from the cafeteria and one got turned against him, or we're definitely dealing with someone else from campus."

Frank nodded his head, "Way this guy's acting, we'll know for sure soon enough."

\* \* \*

He woke from the nightmare in fits of shaking.

Yet, it all felt too real. The moments coming out of the darkness were too cold. Too convincing. He wasn't sleeping. Wasn't in his bed. He was really tearing through campus, running down the passageways between the buildings. Ducking into the shadows to plunge his hands into snow drifts and desperately scrub at the blood that covered his hands. What had he done? He'd attacked Professor Ryan. Tried to kill him. Even succeeded maybe. *Why?* Christ. He didn't know, but he was fucked. Utterly fucked. So he kept running. Running into the blackness.

When he came out of it, he was again in the shadows of the administrative building.

Why?

He was freezing, his body shaking uncontrollably. It brought back bitter memories. He had to get warm again. Get out of sight! Stop the trembling. His clothes were soaked through with blood. His coat, his shirt. The knife had ripped up his hands in the struggle. He wiped them on his pant leg, leaving long, finger-shaped smears of blood, both his own and the Professor's.

The quad was clear. No students. No one. He ran through the slush, feeling it clinging to his jeans, freezing the fabric solid. The snow was whipping around him. Blinding him, slashing at his face. The face. He ran to the side of the library, staggered along the south wall, then found what he didn't even know he was looking for. The door to the tunnels. His fingers were numb from the cold; they struggled with the handle before he finally got a grip and forced it open. The stairway beneath disappeared in the tunnel's shadows. He stepped inside, pulled the door closed behind him, and melted into the darkness.

\* \* \*

Kelli knew something was wrong again when he hadn't returned by dark. Why had she ever let him wander off? Why hadn't she stopped him? Confronted him? She didn't know. She was afraid of him maybe. Afraid *for him* at least. The snow was coming down hard now, sweeping in sideways and roaring over the sidewalks and fields. From the Gibson G lounge she could just make out the dim glow of the overhead lights in parking lot K across the way. She looked at the clock on the wall, then glanced at the TV to confirm it.

Where in the hell was he?

Just running?

*Impossible.*

People were coming back from classes now. Talking about the weather, shaking the snow from their clothing, shivering and moaning in the heat.

The sun was gone by four thirty, and the lights around campus were blinking on along the footpaths and down the length of the quarter mile as Kelli and Fritz headed out to search for Jamie. There was no strategy. They headed for the academic side and were just passing the Student Life Center when they heard sirens, and looked up to see an ambulance tearing down the road. Two police cars were following behind it with their lights on, one of them followed the ambulance as it turned and headed off campus, while the other took a right toward the front entrance and up to the Student

Alumni Union, coming to a stop under the gaze of the massive Sentinel sculpture which towered over the brick sections of the Quarter Mile below. The Sentinel was an enormous metal sculpture, reminiscent of a knight clad in jousting armor and holding a lance, it stood taller than even the administrative building, and had quickly become a campus icon shortly after its construction. It seemed right at home within the college's 1960s slash 70s design scheme, but was still frightening enough to lend the quad a modern gothic twist. Fritz and Kelli watched an officer get out of the car and walk beneath the Sentinel, his hand on his pistol. They exchanged glances and headed for the SAU.

Just as they were approaching the building, a fresh gust of air roared out around them, tearing a volley of ice shards loose from the sculpture overhead, sending them tumbling through the air, where they narrowly missed the two of them, and ripped into the side of the brick Union building in an explosion of debris. Fritz turned and pulled Kelli closer, shielding her against the shrapnel

"We've gotta find another way through here!" he shouted. "Those things could *kill* someone."

They pressed their backs against the wall and watched the campus safety officer run across the slick sidewalk and into the building. Then they turned away from the opening of the covered pathway, found a door down into the tunnels, and ran for cover.

* * *

Classes were canceled for the night. Campus was

closing down thanks to the storm. It was only the second time in the last twenty years that RIT had called off a day of classes. Maybe the guy was still on campus. Maybe he wasn't. But if he was, he probably wasn't out in the elements anymore. Not with the way things were currently shaping up outside. Gridley fought against the wind as he pushed the door open, and was nearly knocked off his feet as another gust slammed it shut behind him. He walked through the atrium of the SAU. The place was empty. Not a soul around. Nothing but the sounds of wind and ice on the windows above. He scanned the front area, then headed down the side hall, past the cafeteria, past the student government offices, and out into the foyer by the Campus Connections bookstore. The store's security gates had been pulled down now. The interior was dark. He peered inside, then started down the stairs to the tunnels.

Gridley was just nearing the bottom of the stairs, coming out into the dank, strangely hot passageways that ran below the academic side, when the lights started to flicker. All the campus powerlines were underground. Most everything on the property was self-sustainable. If the lights were going, then this storm was *really* a doozy. He looked up at the fluorescent tubes overhead. They flickered back on and held for a moment. He lifted a hand to his sweaty brow, wiped away the perspiration, and continued on. He could *hear* the wind clawing through the ground overhead.

The tunnel was coming to an end. He slowed as he approached the corner where the corridor merged with the long stretch of hallway running from the library, past the bookstore, and around to the hockey stadium, then glanced back in the direction of the library. Silence. He turned back towards the pool and started walking. Still no one around.

He was just about to turn around and head back, when he caught sight of a bloody handprint on the tunnel wall. The fingers of the print stretched downward, leaving four bloody red trails behind them.

*Fuck.*

Then a flicker, and the lights went out.

* * *

Jamie knew the figure was not his father. Not this time. He was beginning to realize that his own mind wasn't entirely reliable. The person behind him was either a stranger, or a fabrication from his twisted, contorted mind. The man in black. It had to be. The moment he felt the man's presence he'd run through the tunnels, frantically. He was after him. He'd no doubt been after his father. Come back for the son. Christ, no! He was going mad! Thinking insane, illogical, impossible thoughts. Then again, the man *was* after him. He ran down a side tunnel, glancing over his shoulder then down at his feet. He came to the end of the tunnel, reached out for a handhold, then spun around the corner of the wall, where he crouched down, drew a new knife from his pocket, and waited.

A moment later, the lights went off.

The man meant business now. Meant to kill him.

Get him in the darkness where no one, not even Jamie, would ever see what happened.

And so he waited, sweaty and shaking, his body trembling with agitation, fear, and something else, something he didn't dare think about. He was symptomatic again. He knew it. He held the knife handle in his quivering hands, waited for the moment he knew was coming. A footstep echoed on the concrete floor around the corner. Without thinking, with hesitation, he leapt to his feet, whirled around the corner, and drove the knife blade home. It sank into the man's chest with a sickening, *thoonk*, and he immediately felt slick, hot liquid gushing out onto his hands. He pulled the knife out and drove it home again.

The man in black, the man in the shadows, let out two shocked yelps, then doubled over and fell to the floor. Jamie turned and ran into the darkness.

\* \* \*

"Wait here," Fritz whispered.

"Where am I gonna go?" Kelli hissed back.

They were in the tunnel. Had been crouched there since the moment the lights failed.

"I'm gonna try to find a light to get us out of here"

"All right." She responded.

She reached her hand out into the black, feeling through the air, tapping Fritz's chest with her fingertips.

"Be careful," she said.

He grunted and headed into the darkness, feeling his way along the painted brick walls and metal locker doors. He was still in the hallways beneath the basketball courts. The tunnel to the hockey rink was somewhere to the right. He felt a steady flow of icy air moving down the hallway toward him. No sounds from the rink.

He turned left and felt his way along in the darkness. Then all hell broke loose in the distance. The sounds of a fight, followed by frantic footsteps running off down the hall. No! Running toward him! Shit! Whoever it was was shrieking now. Howling! Howling with the most terrifying, monstrous sound that Fritz had ever heard. Gooseflesh rippled up his arms and legs. Fritz raised his hands in self-defense, then, and only then, did he realize what was happening. Jamie came lunging out of the darkness, reaching for him with bloody, outstretched hands. Fritz dove to the side, leaving Jamie to ricochet off the wall and skitter across the floor of the tunnel. Only this wasn't Jamie. The wailing, frantic angry sounds coming from this creature's mouth, no, that wasn't Jamie anymore. Without waiting to see if he was all right, Fritz pulled himself up and raced away, even as he heard Jamie scrambling to his feet again and coming right back after him. Fritz ran flat out now, arms and legs pumping wildly.

He had to get upstairs. He had to get outside. But he couldn't see shit. Still he sprinted full out. The end of the tunnel, the stairs to the SAU, they'd be coming up any minute now. *Any second.* Just as he approached the tunnel, his foot hit something on the floor, something that groaned on impact, and sent Fritz flying head over heels, landing on his shoulder and sliding across the paved floor. Something in his arm socket crunched sickeningly.

He pull himself to his feet and continued running, even as he heard the other person in the darkness scrambling up and pulling himself to the side. Fritz lunged up the stairs, smashing into the closed stairway door in the darkness. Something in his face crunched.

"Get out of here!" He shouted, wailing in panic. *Get out of here!*

He pushed the door open, but he sensed Jamie lunging out after him. Fritz's right foot set down on the first outside step, just as a hand grabbed his other ankle, stopping him short and sweeping his face down to the concrete steps.

*Wham!*

His face and jaw struck the steps with a concussion inducing smash. The upper row of Fritz's teeth exploded in his mouth. Blood and chips sprayed down the back of his throat, and before his eyes. He drew up into a ball and pulled himself against the wall, waiting for the attack, but none came. Instead, he heard Jamie hit the ground himself now. Heard his feet slipping and shifting on the brick walkway. Heard his breathing. The sounds of a confused animal. Nothing more. An angry, violent, dangerous animal - rabid and unaware. Fritz pulled himself against the wall now, gasping for air and sucking in mouthfuls of pain. He fought to form words through the mess of shredded skin, shattered teeth, and gushing blood that poured forth from his lips, burbled through his clasped fingers. His eyes shot open wide—

"Jamie! Jamie no!" he screamed.

Jamie spun suddenly, his foot arcing around in a

sharply angled kick that shattered Fritz's cheekbone and sent him sprawling.

Fritz watched as Jamie stepped calmy over him and took off into the night. The wind roared again and the lights flickered back on, just as his world went dark.

\* \* \*

The power held, and Kelli took off down the corridor. Near the end, she hit a slick spot on the floor, damn near going down as her feet slid out beneath her. She turned back as she ran, stumbling to the side at the sight of a bloody puddle. Smeared handprints swirled out from the red. Boot tracks moved away from the pool; a dragging trail pointed in the direction she was moving.

She went faster now, turning down the side corridor, afraid of what she'd find. She had to get the fuck out of this place. She took the tunnel steps three at a time, coming out in the Campus Connections foyer, and threw the double doors open with all her  weight, only to stop short, turning on her heel, as she leapt over another pool at the bottom of the stairs.

*"Oh Jesus. Oh Jesus, oh Jesus, oh Jesus!"*

She rounded the corner, her feet barely touching the ground.

What had happened? What had *happened?!!*

She burst out into the snowy courtyard and stopped in the walkway, where she could only watch in horror at what was playing out before her.

A figure was running down the walkway towards the Sentinel statue. It was Jamie.  Another man was slumped against the wall of the SAU building, a figure in a uniform, who held something in his hand, and screamed after him. He was telling Jamie to *stop,* threatening to fire. Fritz was staggering down the middle of the walkway, one hand held to his face, his arms and hands soaked with blood. He was screaming something too. Something drowned out by a blast of wind. The clock stopped - time stood still. Kelli slid to a stop as a flash of hot light glinted from the edge of the officer's gun. At the same moment, a burst of red exploded from Jamie's thigh, and he went down in the snow at the base of the sculpture. Fritz stopped short as the man in the uniform collapsed against the building and slumped to the ground.

Jamie was spread out in the snow, his upper body crumpled against his knees. One hand held his thigh. From a distance, Kelli saw the sudden shift in his body. His movements grew slower. Smoother. She raced towards him again. Past Fritz. Past the officer, who lay in a motionless heap.

She would get to Jamie and help him now. He was going to be okay. It was serious, but he would be okay. Even now, he was climbing to his feet. He was standing up and turning toward her. His face was calm. He saw her coming.

Kelli's ears filled with thunder, needles of ice stung her face, and the wind, the wind came blowing through the courtyard around her.

The buildings threw echoes everywhere. The Sentinel started to rumble and quake. She looked up slowly at the sounds of fireworks crackling and fizzling above her.

Only these weren't fireworks. These weren't hot explosion of sparks and fire, but rather the cold, brittle eruptions of ice shearing free from the uppermost portions of the statue's metal frame. The wind caught the first lethal wave of shards, throwing them against the buildings, but even as they exploded in an icy hail, another gust was ripping away an even bigger sheath of ice.

She looked at Jamie. He looked back at her. And time slowed again. The air grew silent; a vacuum rising around them. Then, a single blade of ice, thick as a metal rod, long as a yard stick, blasted down through the air, driving itself through the top of Jamie's head and out through the bottom of his mouth.

Jamie's eyes locked on her in shock as Kelli's mouth fell open.

There was no spray of blood. No blood at all. Crimson ice formed at both ends of the bloody shard.

Jamie stood for a moment, slumped to the side, and fell on his back.

Kelli ran to him as he began to shake and convulse in her arms. She looked into his eyes. They were totally calm. Smiling back at her.

He held her gaze as his eyes rolled back, and his head tilted up toward the sky. The two of them watched the snow swirling down on them from the darkness overhead.

# WAITING

There have been plenty of million-to-one shots. The bullet that hits a cop in the eye, flies clean through his head, but otherwise leaves him fit as a fiddle and ready for Krispy Kremes. There's the miner blasting TNT into a bank of rocks, who accidentally sends a metal rod up through his jaw and out through the top of his skull - forgets who's President, but goes on with his normal life. And then there's the guy who sustains a massive head injury, who by all logic should be dead, but somehow survives and wishes that he hadn't. That was Jamie.

Dr. Price always said the implant couldn't be fixed if it failed, and boy, had it failed, leaving behind a trail of broken bodies and tortured souls, all fighting for survival.

The fleeting benefits had come at a heavy price.

What good was a mind without a body? Well, what good was a body without a sound mind?

Jamie had plenty of time to ponder that now.

The ice.

That shard of ice.

An archer couldn't have made a better shot.

Down through the top of his skull, dead center in the middle of the good doctor's nightmarish device, and back out through the bottom of his jaw. In an instant, Jamie was back at square one. As he lay in the snow, his body spasming, the medics at the scene had treated him like any other mortally wounded patient, but he knew differently. This wasn't new. This wasn't the end. He was back where he'd started.

They stabilized him. Treated the injury. Operated on his brain, and checked him into critical care. That's where he was now. His head wrapped in bandages. His skull braced against the frame of his bed to keep it still. To let it recover. Just in case.

The shaking was gone, but who knew if it would return? It didn't look good. The implant was gone. His brain had been skewered. There would be many more operations to come, but no more implants. Not likely.

No more miracle cures.

Now it was a waiting game. They'd wait and see if the symptoms returned. Maybe it had been *better* than a million to one shot. Maybe it had knocked out the regions of Jamie's brain that put him through such hell, but he doubted it. He stared up into space, his thoughts all but drowning him now. Then he felt small, warm fingers slipping around his hand, wrapping together with his own. He looked up at Kelli. She smiled down at him. His eyes were calm again. He was back with her, back in his own world. She squeezed his hand and nestled up to him. They lay back together, waiting to see what would happen.

# ACKNOWLEDGMENTS

Thank you to Jason Croatto for the snazzy new cover art and interior layout!

Thanks to my editor Louise Ladd, who inspired me to found Cryptic Bindings in the first place and start getting some "creepy little books" out into the marketplace instead of spending years mulling over the many ways to attempt to storm the castle. Louise did her best to point out the weaknesses in this book, while providing enough encouragement to keep me going. Where, because of deadlines, laziness, or flat out stubbornness, I have failed to iron out the "cheats" in this book, I can't only hope that I cheated in style.

Thanks to my friends and former coworkers, Suzanne Coopersmith and Sharyl Burson, who both made their way through the early drafts, and continue talking to me, despite everything they've had to endure.

Thanks to my mother Elizabeth Attebery, who has always supported by writing, and really, every creative venture I've ever undertaken, even when they involved the questionable use of steak knives, cardboard boxes, monster masks, and the use of her station wagon.

I can't forget the help of my editorial assistants, Bueller and Mimi and their sisters Winter and Mocha, who have all provided welcome entertainment and amusement as I've poured over the text of this book over many, many years.

Thanks also to Cathie Attebery and Robin Jensen, who gave me a place to live when I was trying to figure out what in the hell to do with my life. Cathie's motto "everything happens for a reason" just might be right!

And of course, thanks my wife Stephanie, who has put up with me for 13 years now, and didn't throw me out on the street when horrible jobs, silly excuses, and plenty of frustration undoubtedly made me an absolute monster to live with. She's also fairly patient when it comes to the way I obsess about, well, everything.

Mike Attebery earned a Bachelor of Fine Arts Degree from the School of Film and Animation at the Rochester Institute of Technology. When he isn't writing or editing books and screenplays, Mike spends his days worrying about... everything, and kicking and knocking on stuff to see what it's made out of. He lives in Seattle, Washington with his wife and daughter, and their two ferrets, Winter and Mocha. He is currently at work on his fifth novel.

www.mikeattebery.com